THE SILK'S

Volume 5 of The Silk Tales

A NOVEL BY

JOHN M. BURTON QC

This book is sold subject to the condition that it shall not, by way of trade or otherwise, be lent, resold, hired out, or otherwise circulated without the author's prior consent in any form (including digital form) other than this in which it is published and without a similar condition being imposed on the subsequent purchaser.

TEXT COPYRIGHT © JOHN M BURTON, 2017

ALL RIGHTS RESERVED

John M. Burton has asserted his right under the Copyright, Designs and Patents Act, 1988 to be identified as the author of this work.

This novel is a work of fiction. Names and characters are the product of the author's imagination and any resemblance to actual persons, living or dead, is entirely coincidental.

First Edition 2017.

FOR MY DAUGHTER SOPHIA, WHOSE EARLY JOURNEY THROUGH LIFE WAS FILLED WITH THE SAME DIFFICULTIES AND SETBACKS THAT LITTLE ROSE EXPERIENCES IN THIS NOVEL

Books by John M. Burton

The Silk Brief, Volume 1 of The Silk Tales

The Silk Head, Volume 2 of The Silk Tales

The Silk Returns, Volume 3 of the Silk Tales

The Silk Ribbon, Volume 4 of the Silk Tales

The Silk's Child, Volume 5 of the Silk Tales

Parricide, Volume 1 of The Murder Trials of Cicero

The Myth of Sparta, Volume 1 of The Chronicles of Sparta

The Return of the Spartans, Volume 2 of The Chronicles of Sparta

The Trial of Admiral Byng, Pour Encourager Les Autres, Volume 1 of the Historical Trials Series

Treachery, The Princes in The Tower.

TABLE OF CONTENTS

CHAPTER 1
THE NEW ADDITION 10
CHAPTER 2
THE EMERGENCY CALL 18
CHAPTER 3
THE RELATIVES' REACTIONS 25
CHAPTER 4
THE ARRESTS AND INTERVIEWS 31
CHAPTER 5
THE SCAN 39
CHAPTER 6
NEW INSTRUCTIONS 44
CHAPTER 7
THE SPIRITUAL VISITOR 50
CHAPTER 8
BRISTOL 57
CHAPTER 9
THE OLD PUPIL MASTER 65
CHAPTER 10
PLANNING FOR THE FUTURE 73
CHAPTER 11
THE DEFENCE EXPERT 79
CHAPTER 12
THE CLIENT 85

CHAPTER 13
DEVASTATING NEWS 88
CHAPTER 14
THE NEW ARRIVAL 96
CHAPTER 15
THE FIRST FEW WEEKS 103
CHAPTER 16
FURTHER EVIDENCE 113
CHAPTER 17
THE TRIAL 118
CHAPTER 18
THE 999 CALL 130
CHAPTER 19
THE PARAMEDIC 136
CHAPTER 20
THE POLICE OFFICER 147
CHAPTER 21
THE HEALTH VISITOR 156
CHAPTER 22
CHALLENGING THE ACCOUNT 169
CHAPTER 23
THE HOSPITAL DOCTOR 181
CHAPTER 24
DISTURBING NEWS 195
CHAPTER 25
THE PATHOLOGIST 201

CHAPTER 26
AN INTERRUPTION IN THE EVIDENCE 208
CHAPTER 27
THE NEONATOLOGIST 218
CHAPTER 28
CHALLENGING THE EXPERT 232
CHAPTER 29
INTERESTING INFORMATION 246
CHAPTER 30
A FURTHER OPPORTUNITY 251
CHAPTER 31
THE PUB WITNESS 259
CHAPTER 32
BOB'S MOTHER 273
CHAPTER 33
UNRAVELLING FAMILY ISSUES 281
CHAPTER 34
MORE TRAGEDY 291
CHAPTER 35
THE OFFICER IN THE CASE 295
CHAPTER 36
A MOTHER'S EVIDENCE 300
CHAPTER 37
RACHEL CONTINUES 318
CHAPTER 38
A DIFFICULT TIME 322

CHAPTER 39
THE DEFENCE EXPERT 334
CHAPTER 40
THE WEIGHT OF THE SOUL 342
CHAPTER 41
FURTHER PROBLEMS 348
CHAPTER 42
THE NEIGHBOUR 352
CHAPTER 43
THE PROSECUTION FINAL SPEECH 359
CHAPTER 44
THE DEFENCE FINAL SPEECH 369
CHAPTER 45
THE JURY DELIBERATIONS 387
CHAPTER 46
A NEW ARRIVAL? 395
CHAPTER 47
HOMECOMING 402

CHAPTER 1

THE NEW ADDITION

The view from the window was breath taking. Looking over the wide expanse of the lawn towards the lake and the cupid style fountain in the distance, David Brant was momentarily in a dream, ignoring all the stresses of life at the Criminal Bar.

Wendy and he were spending a long valentine's weekend in an old Manor House which had long ago been converted into an expensive five star-hotel. They had arrived on Friday night, 12th February 2016 and now it was Sunday morning, St Valentine's day. He had planned a sumptuous eight course meal for the evening. The weather had remained perfect and both had enjoyed a perfect stay in a beautiful setting with wonderful food and fine wines.

At least David had enjoyed the fine wines. Wendy had told him, to his obvious surprise, that she was happy with sparkling water this weekend and was taking a break from alcohol. She had even refused a glass of champagne, normally her favourite tipple.

As he watched a pair of magpies terrorising the hotel's cat on the lawn outside, he was interrupted by Wendy emerging from the bathroom carrying a pen like device. He noticed the look of concern on her face and gave her what he hoped was a reassuring grin. In response, she spoke quietly to him, "It's positive!"

Well at least that sounded good he thought and then asked naively, "What's positive?"

She raised her hands and showed him the device she was holding. Momentarily he gazed at the large diamond engagement ring she was wearing on the ring finger of her left hand. It had cost him his entire receipts from a three-week long murder case, but it had been worth it. His gaze moved slowly across to the blue device she was displaying. It had a small LED display in its centre which was facing him. David could just make out the figures and letters '2-3 weeks'.

The grin froze on his face as he suddenly realised what this meant, as Wendy added an unnecessary confirmation, "I'm pregnant."

The news struck him like a full blow in the face from a southpaw boxer. He tried desperately not to react, but his powers of advocacy had completely left him as all he could grunt in reply was, "P Pregnant?"

Wendy moved closer to him proudly displaying the device that had suddenly changed their life. She beamed at him as she planted a large kiss on his cheek and added the word, "Daddy".

11

Again, he showed a distinct lack of oratory as he responded, "B... But how?"

Wendy gave him a distinct look of disappointment as she answered, "I think you know how."

He recovered quickly but still could only manage, "Of course, sorry, it's just a bit of a surprise."

She touched his right arm with her left hand as she told him, "I had wondered when I missed my last period, normally, I'm like clockwork. I was wondering if I was pregnant, which is why I've stopped drinking alcohol."

He nodded and could not think of anything else to say in reply.

She pressed him, "Aren't you happy, after all we are getting married in July?"

He attempted a smile but only managed a sickly grin and a poor joke, "I know, but I'm still slightly traditional, I tend to think the marriage should come first and the baby second."

She frowned at him, "How boring and conventional you are David, you really have to move with the times."

He managed a full smile whilst inwardly fighting shock, "Of course I'm happy, it's great news."

Wendy was not fooled, "Don't overdo it."

He observed her expression for a few seconds. He was beginning to feel they were already married. He never seemed to get anything right in her eyes these days.

"I'm not overdoing it, we talked about having children. I am happy, I just wasn't expecting it to happen so soon. I didn't know you had stopped taking the pill."

She grimaced slightly at what she saw as a possible criticism.

"I only stopped last month. I read somewhere that it can take up to a year to conceive after you stop taking the pill so I decided to stop now. I wasn't expecting to get pregnant so quickly."

He said nothing, there was nothing more he could say. They had talked about having children but he thought that was something in the far distance after they had enjoyed a few years of married life; holidaying, partying and whatever other things married couples got up to these days.

It seemed such a long time ago that he was married to his first wife, Sarah, that he had forgotten what it was like. Now everything had changed in a moment. Suddenly thoughts of dirty nappies, crying babies and sleepless nights filled his mind.

He had to think hard. His practice had become better of late and he was getting more cases, most of which were in London. However, he had not banked on Wendy being forced to give up her career, possibly for years, making him the sole provider for three hungry mouths.

He could see she was eyeing him closely, no doubt accurately reading his thoughts. He quickly added, "It's great news, I am sure the three of us will have a fantastic time together."

She read his thoughts exactly and could not help herself add, "It could be four, I might be having twins. It does run in my family."

She noted his crestfallen face and quickly tried to restore the situation, "Don't worry, I'm sure we will just have one child. That will probably be more than enough for you!"

The rest of the day had been an unusual one for him. He had tried to remain cheerful seeing how happy Wendy was, but he could not help himself think back to earlier in his career when he was married to Sarah and they had their children together. It had been wonderful at first but quite a struggle financially, particularly when Sarah had insisted that the children both had a private education.

It had helped that Sarah was not a criminal barrister, tied mainly to legal aid criminal cases, and that after looking after each child for six months, she had returned to the Bar and had provided a good income from her private matrimonial practice. However, Wendy was a criminal practitioner and although she was currently busy, that would change when she took time off to have the baby.

He realised he had no choice, he would just have to make sure that his practice continued to progress and that he increased his income to guarantee that he could provide for his new child.

As the day progressed he started to put the negative thoughts aside and continued to observe how ecstatic Wendy looked. His thoughts changed, after all, it might not be so bad as all that, being a father again.

The evening meal was a romantic affair and both of them ate well from what was on offer. Wendy had checked the internet to find the latest guides on which foods a pregnant mother should not eat, but she had still been able to eat heartily as alternatives were offered to the seafood and soft cheese courses. She had declined any offer of champagne or wine with the meal.

David had wondered whether he should similarly abstain but she had insisted that he should enjoy himself, adding ominously, that they might not be in a position to enjoy such meals again for quite some time in the future.

David drank a fine claret with the meal, savouring the taste of the fine food, the bouquet of the wine, and the ambience of the restaurant. He held his large wine glass up close to the candles on the table checking the wine's viscosity whilst ruminating to himself on his practice. He had a few cases in his diary, a couple of attempted murders coming up in the next few months, one in the Old Bailey and one in Bristol. Both would be just a few days long and would probably barely pay for the child's nappies for the first year.

He had one good fraud trial listed. That was the case of Tatiana Volkov, the Russian interpreter that he had met last year and who had been charged with six others with a banking fraud. She denied the charges claiming she had been duped by her brother who had disappeared back to Russia. That case should last three months and was listed to start the following January in Southwark Crown Court. As none of the defendants were in custody they had been lucky to get a listing as early as that!

If the case went ahead in January it should finish around April, inevitably, even if Tatiana was acquitted, there would inevitably be some convictions and no one would be paid until they were sentenced a month later. On that basis, he should be paid for that case sometime in or around August or September 2017. There were a great number of witness statements and exhibits in that case so he should be paid handsomely but August or September 2017 was a long time to wait. He needed something significant soon to help pay towards the wedding and honeymoon

16

and hopefully leave a little to help with baby expenses!

He sipped the wine slowly, relishing every drop and wondering at the same time, when his next big case would arrive in chambers and what would it be about?

CHAPTER 2

THE EMERGENCY CALL

Sadie Potts noticed the light flashing on the panel in front of her, it was a busy Friday night in Croydon. It was 10:04pm on 19th February 2016 and she had only been on duty two hours and yet this was the tenth call she had had to answer. She pressed the button on her mouthpiece and answered in her most professional tone, "What service do you require?"

There was a crying sound on the other end of the phone and a female voice, tearfully shouted down the line, "Quickly, oh God, it's my baby, she's cold and she's not breathing!"

So far that night, Sadie had dealt with mostly what she considered to be nuisance calls. One about a suspicious person outside someone's house who turned out to be a policeman, another about someone who saw a strange light in the sky and thought that Croydon might be being invaded by aliens! He was a regular caller, promptly calling at 9pm most nights, which she assumed was when the alcohol kicked in. So far, the most serious call had been from an off licence where a couple of youths had stolen a few cans of lager. However, this was serious, a distraught mother worried about her baby. Sadie put on her calmest voice, "Ok, I understand, try to calm down and take deep br…"

Before she could finish the line the crying voice had turned into a loud slur, "How can I fucking calm down, you fucking bitch, my baby's not breathing!"

Sadie bristled slightly. She had received a lot of abuse in this job and understood from her training and experience that people who dialled emergency services may not be acting rationally, but it still rankled with her when she received such treatment from someone who she was trying to help.

Sadie's training immediately took over from her personal feelings, "I understand madam, can you tell me your name and provide me with your address so I can send an ambulance straight away to assist you."

"My name's, Rachel Wilson, I live at 12 Addiscombe Drive, Croydon. Fucking be quick about it! God she's stone cold."

"The ambulance and the police are on the way."

There was silence at the other end of the phone for a few seconds, then Rachel exclaimed, "Police? Why are you sending the fucking police? I need a doctor, not the fucking police."

"There'll be just there to help," Sadie quickly lied and before Rachel had an opportunity to respond she added, "Is there anyone with your baby at the moment?"

"Yes, she's with me now".

"Is she breathing? Put your ear to her mouth."

There was a pause. "No, she's not, Oh Christ!"

"Lay her on her back, and look inside her mouth to make sure there's nothing in there that might be causing a blockage."

Again, there was a slight pause before Rachel screamed down the phone, "There's nothing there. Fucking hell, when's that ambulance going to be here."

Sadie responded again in her most professional voice, "It'll be there soon, now you need to try mouth to mouth resuscitation. Place one hand on her forehead and the other on her shoulders and gently tilt her head. Now cover her mouth and nose with your mouth and gently breath two puffs of air one second each."

"Oh fuck!"

Sadie waited a few seconds before saying anything else.

"Did you feel the air going in and out."

"No, where's the fucking ambulance?"

"It's on its way. It will be with you soon but you need to try a few things before they arrive. Have you tried any chest compressions?"

"What are those?"

Sadie explained the procedure to adopt, asking Rachel to leave the phone on in case she could assist further. After a minute, Rachel spoke again. "It's no good, I've tried what you said. She's not moving and she's not breathing. She's stone cold and as stiff as a board. Where's that bloody ambulance?"

"It's on the way and should be with you in a few minutes."

Suddenly there was a loud scream from the other end of the phone and Sadie moved her earphones away from her ears for a second. She could hear Rachel cry out, "Bob, Bob, I think our little Annie's dead!"

Sadie tried to talk to her again, "Is there someone else with you?"

"Yes."

"Who is it?"

"It's my boyfriend, Bob, Annie's dad."

Sadie could hear other voices now, "Has the ambulance arrived?"

"Yes, they're finally here!"

Sadie told Rachel she was in safe hands now and gratefully ended the call.

Rachel put her mobile phone down and took a sip from a glass she had.

Andrew Biggs, a paramedic had rushed into the open door to the house from the ambulance that his colleague, Geoffrey Gilroy, had parked outside. Andrew quickly made his way into the house shouting out that he was a paramedic. As he entered the hallway he almost stumbled over some gym weights, which had been carelessly left near the door. He strode over them and made his way to the living room where he immediately noticed the large glass of clear liquid that Rachel was sipping from and saw the half empty bottle of vodka on the table by her side. As he looked at the bottle, Bob reached for it to pour a large glass for himself. Rachel noticed Andrew's expression and looked at him coldly, "What you fucking looking at? You should be helping my baby."

She drank the entire contents of the glass as if to make some point, and then grabbed the bottle from Bob and poured a large amount into her own tumbler and drank deeply from that as well.

Andrew did not respond to her comment but moved over to the settee where he saw the body of a young baby girl. It was immediately obvious to him that the child was dead, but nevertheless, he went through the necessary procedures.

His colleague, Geoffrey, entered the house a few minutes later and went over to Andrew to see if he could assist him at all. Upon sight of the child's stiff body he realised that rigor mortis had set in. He could also see through her loose clothing, that the purple staining of hypostasis was clearly present on the baby's back. That told him that her heart had stopped pumping blood around the body some time ago. There was nothing that could be done for her.

After a few minutes, Andrew ceased all the procedures he had been carrying out and noted the time on his watch, it was 10:20pm. He slowly got up from the settee and turned to the child's parents.

This was part of the job he hated most. Having to tell the relatives of any person that their loved one had passed away was difficult enough, but telling the parents of a young baby that their child had died, was the worst situation he ever came across and it never got easier.

He turned to the parents who were now pouring the remains of the vodka bottle into their glasses, just as a young Asian police officer arrived in the room.

"I'm …", he coughed nervously and tried again, "I'm so sorry, we couldn't save her. We've lost her I'm afraid."

Both parents looked at him with vacant expressions before Bob shouted angrily, "You're sorry you bastard! If you'd got here sooner, she would've still been alive!"

CHAPTER 3

THE RELATIVES' REACTIONS

David had faced many a difficult tribunal in his long career; grumpy magistrates, particularly obtuse Crown Court judges and dismissive and unresponsive Court of Appeal, Lord Justices, but he knew he had the most difficult tribunal to face now. He had to tell his son and daughter that he was to become a father again after a gap of over twenty-six years!

He chose to speak to them face to face, rather than over the phone as he thought it might be easier. His son, Robert, was now aged twenty-six and a doctor working in St Gregory's Hospital in North London. Like many junior doctors, he was working long shifts with few days off, (save for a few strike days that junior doctors had felt obliged to take against the Government.) He had seen little of Robert over the last few years as Robert had been given hospital appointments in the north of the country. Robert had only recently been transferred to St Gregory's, which was quite close to where David lived and so they had been able to meet for a couple of evening meals and catch up.

David's daughter, Katherine, was now aged twenty-eight and still living with her banker boyfriend, Giles, in a house with a mortgage that David was still guaranteeing. David had never been able to stand the insipid Giles and had avoided meeting him as much as possible. That meant in effect, that David had also seen very little of his daughter.

Today, Saturday, 20th February 2016, David had managed to arrange a meeting between the three of them in China Town in London, in a Chinese restaurant they had all visited before, called, 'The Peking Money Tree'. The restaurant supposedly specialised in genuine Chinese Dim Sum, though David had no idea whether that was true or not. Nevertheless, the food was normally excellent whether it was based on Chinese cuisine or on an English version of the same. David had not invited their partners or Wendy as he felt, the fewer people present at this meeting, the better.

He arrived before either of them and ordered a definitely non-genuine Chinese cocktail. Robert arrived shortly afterwards and greeted his father warmly. Katherine arrived fifteen minutes later and also gave him an affectionate hug. So far, so good. They all ordered cocktails and then a selection of dim sum. David had ordered the traditional Har Gow, shrimp dumplings and Pork Shaomi, a type of pork dumpling he found particularly delicious. He had declined Robert's suggestion of ordering Phoenix Claws. He had made the mistake of ordering them in the past and felt quite ill when four dark red-coloured, fried, whole chicken feet, had appeared at his table, all standing upright as if to attention.

At first their conversation centred on general matters. David asked them how they and their partners were, and they asked after Wendy. It was simply a polite enquiry on his part. He was interested in his children but their partners were a different matter. He had not been concerned at learning that Katherine's partner, Giles, was continuing to struggle in his bank and had not had a pay rise or bonus for years. He was more concerned to find out Giles was worried that he might be made redundant as David was still guaranteeing the mortgage.

David was also uninterested to discover that Robert's partner, Lavinia, was constantly moaning at Robert about the hours he worked and the fact they had a very limited social life. What did she expect if she dated a doctor?

They were half through their cups of warm sake, that they had ordered to accompany the dim sum, when Robert put down a half-nibbled Phoenix Claw and commented, "Dad it's great to see you and Katherine after so long, but I can't help thinking there must be a reason you've just asked the two of us to come here other than simply having a social get together with all our partners."

David was tempted to accuse him of having a suspicious mind if it was not for the fact that he was right! He tried to laugh it off, "Excellent diagnosis, Doctor Brant."

Katherine put a piece of Har Gow back on her plate. "What is it dad? Is the wedding off?"

Both had been invited to his wedding with Wendy, planned for July. Robert had agreed to come with his girlfriend Lavinia, but Katherine had declined stating that she and Giles had a holiday booked and simply could not alter the date. David had known it was a lie. Despite the passage of years, Katherine had still not forgiven him for the breakup of his marriage to her mother and this question of hers was, no doubt, wishful thinking on her part.

"No, sorry to disappoint you Katherine!"

She frowned at him, "I didn't mean anything by the comment, Dad. I'm glad you've found someone just like Mum has. I just couldn't think what else it might be." She paused before continuing, "Unless Wendy is pregnant of course."

He smiled at her in reply. She looked at him and her eyes widened as she exclaimed, "Oh my God she is, Wendy's pregnant."

Robert looked equally surprised, "Is that right Dad, are you going to be a father again?"

David raised his cup of sake, "That's right, you are going to get a little brother or sister ... or maybe even one of each!"

Katherine looked horrified but Robert's expression did not change, he just raised his cup of sake and smiled, "Congratulations to you and Wendy." He looked pointedly at Katherine and added, "It's about time that we had another addition to the family."

Katherine, seemingly reluctantly, raised her cup as well and added, "Congratulations, Dad, to you and Wendy..." She paused before she added, "... but do you think it's wise, at your age?"

The meal had continued in that vein, with both asking David a large number of questions, many of which he had not thought about, such as; was he going to provide his new child or children with a private education, were he and Wendy going to buy a house as the flat in the Barbican was going to be too small to have children in, and the particularly concerning one, how was he going to feel going to the child or children's school on parents' evenings when all the other parents would probably be half his age.

The meal finally came to an end and a physically, mentally and emotionally drained, David said goodbye and left. He loved them both dearly, but he was not going to arrange another meal like that in a hurry.

He returned to his flat by tube train and collapsed into his armchair in front on the Television. He put on a comedy film he had seen many times before, simply because it was a background noise that would take his mind off the questioning he had just endured.

After a few minutes his mobile phone rang. He thought it would be Wendy who had gone out to check on certain wedding arrangements today. He could not remember what she had said she was doing so he hoped she did not ask him. He pressed the receive button almost involuntarily before noticing the name on the phone's screen was not Wendy, it was his ex-wife, Sarah.

CHAPTER 4

THE ARRESTS AND INTERVIEWS

Detective Sergeant Caroline Leadbetter pushed the file away from her and lent back in her chair. As far as she was concerned the case was overwhelming.

She looked at the calendar on her desk, it was Friday 4th March, just two weeks had passed since the little six-month old baby, Annie Harwood, had died at her home. Caroline, divorced and the mother of two young children, had been given the case just a couple of days after Annie's death.

She read all the statements starting with the emergency operator. She moved onto the paramedics and the police officer who had arrived at the scene. All suggested that Annie's parents, Rachel and Bob, were drunk and abusive. PC Tanvir Sidhu had arrived at the house and he stated that he witnessed the parents screaming at the paramedics. As he tried to quieten them down, they had turned on him and Rachel had been racially abusive towards him, calling him a 'Paki cunt.' As the situation was an emotional one, he had not challenged her or threatened to arrest her but had simply tried to calm them both down, but Rachel's words and demeanour had upset him and appeared boldly in his witness statement.

Annie had been taken to St. Barnabas Hospital just on the outskirts of Croydon. There she was formally declared deceased, even though she had clearly died much earlier. A post mortem had been carried out a week later by the pathologist, Dr Henry Numan. He had concluded that the cause of death was 'unascertained' but that dehydration was undoubtedly a contributory factor.

Within a few days, Caroline had been able to contact a consultant neonatologist, Robert Peters, who told her that only severe dehydration could be a contributory factor in a baby's death. He had pointed out that in a six-month-old baby that could only result from a severe illness of some type, which did not seem to be the case here, or the parents had failed to adequately feed the baby and possibly worse, ignored the obvious signs of severe dehydration. In his opinion, that at the very least was strong evidence of child neglect and probably more.

Caroline contacted a solicitor in the Crown Prosecution Service who advised her to arrest the mother and father on a more serious charge of 'causing or allowing the death of a child.' That morning she had arrested them both at their home at 7am. Both had been in bed nursing hangovers. They had been brought here to

Croydon Police station where she had separated them and left them in their cells for a few hours to sober up before interviewing them. Hopefully the time apart might also make them wonder what the other was saying and make them both more receptive to questioning. Fortunately, as far as Caroline was concerned, neither had asked for a solicitor so there was a good chance they might actually answer her questions.

At 2pm Caroline entered the interview room where Rachel Wilson was already seated, sipping from a cup of steaming coffee, holding one hand over her eye. Caroline had read Rachel's custody record and noted the details in her mind. Rachel was aged twenty-five, she was thin and poorly dressed and Caroline assumed that the household income went mainly on alcohol, rather than food or clothing. Rachel had no criminal convictions recorded against her and had only appeared in police records because of offences committed against her by her current boyfriend as well as previous ones

She was looking particularly bad at the moment, undoubtedly recovering from a hangover and no doubt wondering why she was in a police station.

Caroline smiled sweetly at her and told her she could have a further drink or a sandwich if she wished. Rachel declined the offer so Caroline explained the procedure that was going to be adopted during the interview. She reminded

33

Rachel of her right to legal advice and to have a solicitor present at the interview if she wanted, but Rachel replied by saying, "I just want to get this over with."

She dabbed a dirty handkerchief to her eyes and added, "You do know it's Mothering Sunday this Sunday. I wanted to spend it with my little Annie!"

Caroline nodded in an understanding way. She had her own plans for Sunday. She had booked a local pizza restaurant to take her children to. For a moment, she felt sorry for Rachel, but she quickly put the thought out of her mind and started her questioning.

At first, she concentrated on obtaining background information: the fact Rachel had lived in Croydon all her life, that she had met Bob two years ago, and that he had moved in with her. Rachel claimed that she had become pregnant because she had forgotten to take the pill. She volunteered the information that neither she nor Bob had wanted the baby and that Annie was her only child and she had no plans to have anymore. "I could never go through this again."

Rachel also stated that she had no contact with her parents. Her father had died some years ago in a factory accident and her mother was an alcoholic who had started a relationship with another alcoholic and gone to live with him. She had taken her four children with her. Rachel was only ten when they moved and aged twelve when her drunken stepfather had started to touch her sexually. This had finally culminated in rape when she was aged fourteen. She had complained to her mother who had hit her and had refused to believe her accusations and it was only when he tried to rape her again that Rachel had told her favourite teacher at school and she was moved from the family home into care. Her step father had been arrested and convicted of rape and attempted rape and sentenced to twelve years' imprisonment. Rachel's mother had never spoken to her again.

Rachel volunteered under gentle pressure that the whole experience had led to her becoming a heavy drinker and a user of cannabis in her teens and this had continued to date. She drank throughout her pregnancy and she knew she drank more than was good for her now, but she couldn't help herself.

Caroline asked her about her boyfriend, Bob. Rachel told her Bob was also a heavy drinker and could get violent when drunk, "He gave me a real whack when I was pregnant and I had to have stitches." Rachel pulled her straggly, poorly dyed, blond hair back to show Caroline the scar above her left eye.

Caroline moved on to ask about baby Annie. "Was she born full term or was she premature?"

"She was premature by ten weeks. She had to stay in the intensive care unit at St. Barnabas.

She was 'tubated', I think that's what it's called? Then she was in special care for twelve weeks until I was allowed to bring her home."

Caroline nodded in apparent sympathy and then asked, "What was it like when she came home?"

"It was awful! She was always a difficult feeder. She always had a cold, she wheezed a lot which I think caused her not to want to eat. She never wanted her bottle. If she did drink It, she would vomit most of it up, and she always had diarrhoea, Bob and I had real problems feeding her."

"How often did Bob feed her?"

"He took his turn helping me with little Annie. He was a good dad ..."

She paused before adding, "... most of the time."

Caroline continued the questioning dealing with the day of Annie's death until the tape of the interview ran out after forty-five minutes. She then told Rachel she had asked her enough questions for now but would probably have a few more later on that day after she had spoken to Bob.

At 3:15pm Caroline entered the same interview room this time accompanied by Bob Harwood.

She adopted the same friendly approach with him but soon discovered he was going to be less forthcoming. He told her in strident terms that he was exercising his right to silence.

She had obtained his antecedents and noted the long list of previous convictions, mainly for alcohol fuelled violence. These included three previous convictions for assaulting police officers in the execution of their duty. She also noticed that he had been sentenced to three months in custody for assaulting Rachel a year ago. As was the norm, he had served half that sentence before being released.

His silence in interview did not surprise her in the circumstance. She was only surprised that with his experience of the system he had not asked for a solicitor. Nevertheless, she questioned him for forty-five minutes until the tape ended receiving the answer "no comment" to virtually every question she asked. The only question he did answer was when Caroline asked, "Did you ever feed Annie or did you leave it all to Rachel?"

He responded, "Why what's she said? Of course, I fed her, I took my turn."

"How often?"

"I'm not answering any more of your bloody questions, no comment."

Caroline smiled and asked, "Do you think you or Rachel may have been responsible for little Annie's death."

He looked daggers at her as he answered, "No comment!"

CHAPTER 5

THE SCAN

It was Friday 8th April, almost eight weeks since Wendy announced she was pregnant and now David and Wendy were waiting holding hands in the private paediatric wing of St. Gregory's Hospital waiting for her first scan. David looked around the room remembering that the last time he was in this hospital was when his colleague Bill Bretheridge QC had a heart attack. He had not heard from Bill for months now and suddenly wondered how he was, feeling guilty that he had not contacted him.

Wendy took her hand away from his and took a magazine from a pile that was on a table next to her whilst David considered the last eight weeks.

They had waited until some time had passed before telling the clerks and members of their chambers about the good news. A few had made the 'at your age' comment to David, including Tim Adams QC, but most had been congratulatory. Even David's ex-wife, Sarah, who had heard the news from their daughter Katherine, had phoned him to congratulate him and wish Wendy well. It was amusing to David that hers had sounded the most genuine of the congratulations he had received to date and certainly more genuine than that of his own children, particularly Katherine!

After getting over the initial shock of discovering that he was going to be a father again, Wendy had further surprised him by insisting on private health care for the early stages of her pregnancy. It was not because she believed that would provide a better service than the National Health Service, but on the basis that they would probably have to wait less time for appointments and a private hospital would be more flexible with dates to fit around Wendy's busy practice. David was not convinced and had baulked at the cost of £250 plus VAT at 20% for each scan, but he was easily overruled by his determined partner and had agreed to pay the bills.

Now he was getting slightly annoyed as St Gregory's hospital was a National Health Hospital and the 'private paediatric wing' appeared to be the only private part of the hospital. What was worse was that their consultant, Mr Rogers, was already half an hour late for the 8:30am appointment. It had not helped David's mood that the receptionist on duty had said, "Oh, Mr Rogers is such a lovely man, it's just a pity he's always late for his morning appointments!"

At 9:10am Mr Rogers walked into the Wing and greeted the seated couples with a cheery, "Hello." Everybody responded in kind except David who gave him a look that tried to communicate how unimpressed he was with the doctor's tardiness when he was paying so much for the appointment. It clearly had no effect as Mr Rogers immediately engaged the attractive receptionist in conversation, commenting on how healthy she was looking and how it was always a joy to see her. She cooed in response, much to David's repugnance, slight annoyance and probable jealousy. She had been very dismissive when he had smiled at her.

Fifteen minutes later, after the receptionist had made Mr Rogers a coffee and he had presumably had time to drink it, Wendy and David were shown into his consulting room. He greeted them warmly with an apology, "I'm so sorry for being a little late this morning, the traffic was horrendous."

David smiled and asked, "Where did you come from?"

The consultant looked at him quizzically. No one usually questioned him after he gave his usual apology, but he answered, "Along the North Circular road."

"Oh, the same road we came on at 8:20 this morning for this appointment."

Wendy gave David a dig in the ribs and quickly took over the conversation, "Mr Rogers, thank you for seeing us both at such short notice. It's very good of you."

He turned to her, "Not at all dear lady, always happy to help parents, when I can."

The next twenty minutes were taken up with the scanning procedure. David was seated near enough to see the small blob on the screen that represented the life created by Wendy and himself. His mood changed from one of annoyance to wonder. He had missed the scans of his other children. He was a struggling barrister then, unable to refuse work in order to attend a scan. Now he was a struggling silk with no work to refuse!

This was a fascinating experience for him and he realised what he had missed. Although the foetus was still quite small, Mr Roger zoomed in and the baby's body could clearly be seen with arms, seemingly moving in sequence with the ultrasound waves. They could clearly see the heart visibly pulsating on the screen and they heard the steady rhythm of the heart beat through the machine's speakers.

At the end of the session Mr Rogers told them, "Baby is fine! The right size, the right position and a perfectly strong heartbeat. You must both be very happy."

They both agreed they were as he added, "These machines are wonderful these days. The very latest specifications with the ability to record. I can provide you with a DVD of the scan if you'd like?"

Wendy answered for both of them, "Thank you doctor that will be wonderful."

David nodded his agreement, thinking the session was proving of value after all.

Mr Rogers smiled at them both, "Don't worry, it's no problem at all."

He searched in his desk and then put a previously discarded, blank DVD into the machine and pressed a button. In less than two minutes a recording of the whole process was made and he handed it over to David saying, "See my receptionist on the way out would you. I think the cost of the DVD is £50 plus 20% VAT but I can never remember."

CHAPTER 6

NEW INSTRUCTIONS

"Hello sir, how's the father to be?"

It was Tuesday afternoon, 26th April and just over two weeks since the scan and John's new standard welcome to David as he arrived in chambers, was becoming irritating. David just put on a false grin in response and immediately changed the subject. "So, John, how are your efforts to find me gainful employment working out?"

John looked serious for a moment and then grinned back at him, "Funny you should ask that now." He turned to the first junior clerk, Nick Gobright, "Isn't that right Nick?"

Nick grunted something inaudible in response but John had David's interest now and in order to retain it, he waited for David to say something.

"Ok John, you have my full attention, why is it funny that I ask that question now?"

"Well sir, I have just been on the phone to Mr James of William James and Co, a Croydon solicitor. You may have heard of them?"

David had never heard of the firm but rather than show his ignorance he replied, "The name sounds familiar."

"Well they've picked up a decent brief that needs a silk. The client is charged with 'causing the death of a child' and I've persuaded them to give you the brief."

"Excellent John, who's the junior on the case?"

"Since we took Ms Petford-Williams on as a tenant in chambers, she has been doing a lot of work for that firm so I've suggested her as your junior. You worked well together on her uncle's case last year so I thought you'd make a good team again."

David thanked him and asked where Sara was. John looked at his watch before telling him that Sara had been in Croydon Magistrates Court that morning but she had finished before lunch and as it was just after 2pm, she was back now and in the junior's room in chambers.

David ignored the implied criticism about the time he came into chambers. If there was no work to do he saw no reason to come into chambers early and sit around twiddling his thumbs.

He made his way to Sara's room and saw that she was seated next to Sean McConnell telling him about the particularly trying bench of magistrates she had just appeared in front of, "... and then they said they weren't sure of his guilt but they certainly didn't think he was innocent and they hoped he didn't do it again!"

She turned to the door as David walked in and both she and Sean greeted him. After an exchange of greetings and polite enquiries about how everybody was, David spoke directly to Sara, "I hear that the clerks have put us forward as a team in a 'causing the death of a child' case."

Sara looked bemused, "The clerks put 'us' forward?"

David beamed at her as he added, "Well they claim they did, I automatically assumed that my instruction was entirely down to you. Can you tell me a little about the case and the firm of solicitors?"

Sara was still trying to adapt to chamber's life and the fact that the clerks claimed credit for everything that went well and yet claimed that it was someone else's fault when things went wrong.

"Well David, William James is someone I met when I was co-defending with him in Croydon Magistrates Court on a shoplifting case. I was able to show that the store detective, who had arrested our clients, could not have seen what she claimed and was lying and both our clients were acquitted. William told me that he was impressed with my efforts and wanted to use me on his work.

Since then he has instructed me on a lot of Magistrates Court work and a little Crown Court work over the last few months.

Then he picked up this case and asked me if there was a Queen's Counsel I could recommend. Of course, I recommended you, telling him we had worked together and he instructed me as the junior. I drafted the application to extend legal aid for Queen's Counsel, the judge granted the extension at the PTPH which was held last week and now he has instructed you."

David beamed at her, "The PTPH hearing?"

"Yes, it's one of those new digital cases. All the papers are loaded on line. I will invite you to join the system so that you can have access to them. As you know David, we no longer have Pleas and Case Management Hearings, the old PCMHs, we now have Plea and Trial Preparatory Hearings, PTPHs."

David had heard of them but had so far avoided appearing in one or discovering what they were. Over the years, he had attended 'Directions' hearings, then 'Pleas and Direction hearings', which became known as PDHs for short. These in turn had changed into 'Pleas and Case Management Hearings' which became PCMHs for short and now they had changed the name to 'Plea and Trial Preparation Hearings' which were now known as PTPHs. He wondered how long it would be before someone else was no doubt paid a fortune to come up with yet another set of initials to learn, for essentially the same hearing.

Sara did not notice his mind wander and carried on.

"The PTPH was not wholly effective as the Crown Prosecution Service had not uploaded their experts' reports nor had they completed the form properly."

David nodded, the creation of a new name for a hearing had not altered the prosecution's lack of efficiency. If anything, he suspected it had added to it.

Sarah continued with her narrative. "There will be another hearing in just over two weeks and I hope you can be present. The case itself is a difficult one. The prosecution are alleging that our client and her partner effectively starved their own baby to death by failing to provide adequate feeds. They were both arrested and interviewed and our client was charged after the interview. Her partner was not charged straight away as they weren't sure there was sufficient evidence that he was responsible for the baby's care. He then skipped on police bail and has not been heard of since. That is probably good news as I don't doubt his lawyers would try to put all the blame on our client.

The expert reports have been uploaded now and they make powerful reading. We will need our own expert and I have written an advice to extend legal aid and obtain a prior authority so that we can instruct one. The client claims she did feed her baby regularly but the baby was a poor feeder and often refused her feeds and vomited them out, but nevertheless she claims she always persevered. The prosecution are calling a pathologist and a consultant neonatologist. It is a case that will probably be decided on the expert evidence and as I know how brilliant you are at cross-examining experts, I immediately thought it was a case for you."

CHAPTER 7

THE SPIRITUAL VISITOR

"He's a bit wacky but I'm sure you'll get on. He enjoys fine wines and good food, just like you."

David had not returned to chambers that week. The brief in the Rachel Wilson case had not arrived yet and David had just relaxed at home waiting for the weekend. It was now Saturday 30th April and Wendy had agreed to entertain her uncle for a week. He was flying over from Kochi in southwest India, He had apparently lived there for the last fifty years. Wendy had told David a great deal about her uncle Robert over the last few days and he was dreading the visit. She was trying to reassure him now.

Uncle Robert was apparently a spiritual man which meant to David he was a complete time waster. Robert was seventy now and had been a fun-loving hippy in the late 60s. In 1966, aged 20, he had followed his leanings and used his inheritance from his father to fly to India, to live in 'harmony with nature and under the spiritual guidance of a Guru called Darsana'. Her uncle had told her that name meant, 'the auspicious sight of a holy person, which bestows merit on the person who is seen.'

Apparently, her Uncle liked to be known by the name Nashad, an Urdu name originating from Arabia and meaning, 'unhappy' or 'morose'. Wendy had no idea why he had adopted that name and it certainly made David worried about what the weekend would hold.

Nashad had accepted their invite to the wedding and agreed to fly to the United Kingdom for the event. They had fixed the date of 16th July in the Temple. They could not use the Temple Church because of David's status as a divorcee, but they were able to arrange a civil ceremony in the Temple Gardens which was licenced for that purpose. Nashad had decided to come to England three months early in order to, 'acclimatise myself, after spending so long away from the disturbing influence of Western Culture'.

Nashad was due to arrive at 5pm so they had some snacks waiting for him with a couple of bottles of champagne cooling. Just after 6pm and after half a bottle of champagne had been consumed by David, Nashad arrived at their front door.

David had expected someone in traditional Indian attire, but Nashad was wearing a jumper and jeans with trainers on his feet. It made David hopeful that it might not be such a bad weekend after all.

Wendy and Nashad hugged each other. She had not seen him for about ten years when she had visited India for the first and only time and he had shown her around Kochi. Nashad greeted her with a cheery smile, "You are looking so young and radiant my dear."

He then turned to David and with what appeared like a frown, announced, "You look older than I thought you would be."

David's smile disappeared but he tried to recover quickly for Wendy's sake, "Welcome, may I call you Nashad?"

"You can call me anything you like, but I shall only answer to Nashad."

David paused, tempted to make a riposte. Wendy, recognising his expression, quickly grabbed Nashad by the arm and ushered him into their living room.

David soon recovered and offered their guest a glass of champagne. Nashad looked at the half empty bottle David was holding and gave him a steely glance. "I believe in moderation, it is the only way to gain true and lasting enlightenment."

David looked at him coldly, "Would you like half a glass then?"

Nashad replied quickly, "No, a full glass thank you. You see in my many years in the serene lands of happiness, I have achieved true enlightenment and wisdom." He looked David up and down, "I no longer need to follow the rules that others should follow, if they are to attain inner harmony and a true feeling of oneness."

David poured him a full glass, and then refilled his own glass before saying to Nashad, "I know what you mean!"

All of them went outside to catch the last rays of the evening Sun. Wendy and Nashad conversed about relatives and India whilst David made himself cosy, looking longingly in the direction of a second bottle of champagne.

After a few minutes, Wendy announced that she needed to go into the kitchen to see how the meal was. "Nashad, I've made you a lamb baked in spices, just the way I know you like it and I don't want it to burn."

Nashad nodded at her, "Of course my dear, it would be a travesty if one of nature's creatures had died simply for our sustenance and was then too ruined for us to eat. I would offer to help but men of David's and my generation should really rest at this time of the day."

Wendy nodded and quickly disappeared into the kitchen before David could respond. She just caught his words, "Don't worry about me Nashad, I have a long time to go before I reach inner senility."

She heard the emphasis on the "I" and hoped her uncle had not. It was probably going to be a difficult weekend.

David got up from his chair and opened the second bottle of champagne and refilled Nashad's glass before refilling his own. He poured Wendy another orange and mango juice, which had recently become her favourite drink. He then returned to his seat and took a sip of his champagne before looking questioningly at Nashad. After a few seconds of silence, he asked, "I was just wondering, 'Nashad' is an interesting name. I understand it means 'morose' or 'unhappy'. Why did you choose such a name for yourself?

Nashad rose slightly from his seat and clasped his hands lightly as if he was about to impart important and complex knowledge to a person who could not easily understand. "I chose the name because I believe that until I found true enlightenment I was like men of the Western world. Truly unhappy and truly morose. However, I have now achieved enlightenment but I have retained the name as a reminder of my previous state..." He looked around him at the objects in David's room and continued, "... when all I wanted were material goods and random pleasures that could never truly fulfil me."

David nodded and poured himself another glass of champagne, "I see, I'm glad to hear that. I was hoping it was not like that name Darsana, and referred to those who you cast a gaze on."

Nashad looked at him coldly, "I can see that you will never achieve inner harmony."

David took his seat and grinned, "Really, do tell me why?"

"To achieve inner harmony means that you have acted throughout your lives with humanity to others. You and Wendy are lawyers. Lawyers by the nature of their occupation can never achieve that harmonious state."

With a look bordering on contempt, David asked, "Oh I don't think you should dismiss our chances altogether, after all, even you managed to achieve inner harmony."

Nashad was silent for a few minutes before finishing his glass.

David beamed at him, "Robert, can I offer you a refill?"

Nashad held out his glass as David poured him a drink then suddenly stopped as if he was deep in thought. "I'm so sorry," he announced, "I completely forgot you only respond to the name Nashad."

Nashad drank the glass in silence before adding just as Wendy was entering the room with her

55

spiced lamb and couscous, "You are a very pompous man, David."

David raised his eyebrows slightly, "I do so hope and pray that won't stop you attending the wedding?"

CHAPTER 8

BRISTOL

The remainder of the week had been similarly trying with Nashad frequently mentioning how 'young' Wendy looked and yet referring to David and himself as men of 'our generation'. On the following Saturday, Nashad walked down the path towards a taxi which was to take him to King's Cross station and from there to some other unfortunate relative. As he entered the taxi David turned to Wendy and said, "One thing I can say for your uncle, he has given me an interest in where we seat everybody at the wedding. Do you think it will be possible to hire a separate Marquis for him and any other enlightened ones he brings with him?"

Wendy frowned at him, "If you're not careful, you'll not get invited to the wedding!"

Sunday came and in the afternoon David enjoyed a leisurely trip to Bristol on a quiet train. On Monday, he was appearing in an attempted murder trial that was listed for five days. He had not fancied an early trip on Monday morning so he had booked himself into a hotel just five minutes away from the court. He arrived just after 4pm and as the hotel had a swimming pool and gym, he decided to get a few lengths in at the pool as part of a fitness regime that had lapsed long ago.

At 7pm he went downstairs to the restaurant for his evening meal of sirloin steak, large cut chips and a half bottle of Chilean Merlot. Any good he had done for his health in the pool disappeared at the first mouthful of the succulent cut of meat.

At 8pm he returned to his room to deal with some last-minute preparation on the case. He was representing Rod Hammon, a twenty-four-year-old unemployed labourer. David was instructed by a local firm, Lawrence Shine and Co and was leading their in-house solicitor advocate, Daphne Maughan. Unusually, the brief had come through chambers, much to David's delight. It was a straight forward case and David was a little surprised that legal aid had been extended to cover Queen's Counsel.

David knew the facts well. Rod Hammon came from one of Bristol's crime families. He had started an affair with Elizabeth Andrews, the product of a rival crime family. It had been a stormy relationship much frowned upon by both families in something approaching a very downmarket version of Romeo and Juliet.

Rod was not an articulate man and preferred to voice any issues he had with a display of his fists. Elizabeth had been the butt of many such arguments and their relationship had been on and off many times. On 30th October 2015, on the anniversary of them first meeting, the two lovers had met and had a romantic meal in a local Indian restaurant. A couple of dangerously hot curries later and they had then returned to Rod's flat and consumed a litre bottle of vodka together. Sadly, the mood had changed and Rod had resorted to arguing with his fists again. According to Elizabeth's statement, Rod would not let her leave and had locked the front door and told her she was staying the night. However, the amount he had consumed had necessitated a visit to the toilet. Whilst he was occupied, Elizabeth had phoned her brother Ray and asked him to come and rescue her.

Within twenty minutes, Ray and three of his friends were outside the flat kicking the door in. Elizabeth claimed that Rod had immediately phoned his family and told them to come to his aid. He had then picked up a sharp kitchen knife and told Elizabeth, "I'm going to kill your brother and the rest of your fucking family."

The scene was set for a confrontation of the local Montagues and Capulets. Elizabeth claimed not to have seen what had happened next but her brother Ray, had received eight stab wounds and was lucky to be alive. A neighbour, Ashok Patel had seen the incident and claimed that he saw someone who "looked like", his neighbour Rod "hitting" someone in the street.

Ray had made a statement in hospital claiming that he could not remember anything about the incident. Despite it being a crowded neighbourhood, no other person admitted to having seen anything and none of Ray's or Rod's friends had come forward to make statements to the police. The knife was never found although there was a statement from a police officer who had attended Rod's flat that night. No one was home and he gained entry by force. He had searched the place and noted that there seemed to be a knife missing from a knife rack. Rod was arrested a few days later when he returned to the flat.

Rod's instructions to his solicitors were simple. He had a meal with Elizabeth. They had an argument but he had not hit her. The bruises on both sides of her face were when she accidentally tripped in his flat and banged her head on the table and then when she fell further, on the other side of her face on the hard uncarpeted floor. He had not prevented her leaving and had left after her to visit and stay with another girlfriend for a few days. He was not aware that anyone had been stabbed, nor who had committed such a terrible act.

To David it was a straight forward case and should not tax him unduly over the next few days. However, he thought the chances of persuading a Bristol jury that his client was not involved in the stabbing were slim, even though there was no forensic evidence linking him to the stabbing.

At 9 in the morning David entered the court. He had met the client once before and had asked that he be there at 9 for a last minute consultation. At 9:30am his junior, Daphne appeared, walking into the court building nonchalantly, but still the client was not there.

Eventually, at 10:25am, just five minutes before the case was due to start and after several frantic calls by Daphne, Rod Hammon walked into the building wearing the biggest grin his face could manage. David reminded him that he was facing an attempted murder charge and he had wanted to see him early. The client's demeanour did not change, although he made a poor effort to apologise, claiming his mini cab had been late to his flat. As he could have walked from his address to court in thirty minutes, David ignored the excuse.

At 10:30 they were all called into court in front of His Honour Judge Keith Bullington. The Prosecutor, Robin Eves, was a member of the Bristol Bar who was already in court. He quickly turned to David and asked, "Is your client willing to plead guilty to anything, section 20 wounding or actual bodily harm?"

The difference between an attempted murder charge carrying a potential life imprisonment and wounding or actual bodily harm carrying a maximum sentence of five years was considerable. David grinned at the prosecutor and replied, "No, nothing at all."

It was obvious to him from the desperate look on the prosecutor's face that he had witness difficulties and could not prove any offence. Within a few seconds this was confirmed as Robin addressed the judge.

"Your Honour, I regret that we are not in a position to proceed with this trial, at the moment. A number of police witnesses have attended court but the two main civilian witnesses, Elizabeth Andrews and Ashok Patel, have not attended and although the police have been checking there whereabouts, there is no sign of them. I frankly admit that without their evidence I do not have a case. I ask for an adjournment of the case in order that further enquiries can be made."

The judge turned to David, "Mr Brant, do you have anything to say?"

David rose to his feet, "Your Honour, this case was listed for trial three months ago. The prosecution knew the importance of these witnesses and should have made sure that they attended court. I cannot argue against an adjournment until say 2pm for further enquiries to be made but without any evidence that these witnesses are ill or intimidated or have some other good reason for not attending, I suggest the trial should commence today. Mr Hammon has waited for an opportunity to defend himself against these allegations and should not be deprived of that opportunity simply because the prosecution has lost its main witnesses."

The judge adjourned the trial until 2pm to see if there were any further developments stating he would review the matter then.

David left the court room with the still grinning Rod Hammon. He could not help himself ask, "I trust you don't know where the witnesses are?"

Rod's grin widened, "No idea, although I knew my Lizzie would never give evidence against me. Her brothers wouldn't allow it. They don't want a member of their family being called a 'grass'."

"And what about Mr Patel, there's no reason why he shouldn't turn up is there?"

"Not that I know, though I have heard a rumour round the neighbourhood that he's come into a little money recently and taken his family to India on a holiday, but it's only a rumour."

David nodded, not doubting for a minute that the 'rumour' was true and what the source of Mr Patel's recent good fortune was. He left Rod and went to the robing room to get changed.

As he had over three hours to kill, he decided to have a walk around Bristol and enjoy the sights. It was a reasonably sunny day so he walked down to the riverside. As it approached midday he went to Bristol market and bought himself a pulled pork sandwich and walked around eating it, enjoying the experience more than if he had been dining in a five-star restaurant.

At 2pm he was in court to hear the prosecutor say that they had made further enquiries and from what they could tell, the witnesses had deliberately absented themselves and were unlikely to be found in the foreseeable future.

He continued to say that he had thought about applying to read their witness statements under the hearsay provisions of the Criminal Justice Act 2003 but had decided that would not be appropriate as their evidence was the only real evidence against the defendant. Therefore, he was reluctantly, offering no evidence in the case and no doubt the court would like to record a verdict of not guilty and discharge the defendant.

Rod Hammon gave a cursory, unmeant thanks to David and left the courtroom quickly. David watched him go. He had no doubt that would not be the end of the matter. The Andrews' family clearly had their own ideas about justice and Rod Hammon would discover all too soon that the punishment they would mete out, would probably be far worse than any that the court had in mind.

CHAPTER 9

THE OLD PUPIL MASTER

On Monday 13th May 2016 at 9am, David passed through security at the Old Bailey. The case of Rachel Wilson had been listed for what David was told was an adjourned PTPH after stage 1 directions had been made. He had no idea what that meant and decided he must research the meaning of PTPH at some stage. It probably would not matter today as a trial date had already been given of 12th September and there was little else to deal with, so as far as he was concerned, it should be an easy day where he could meet the client and get some initial ideas about her defence.

He had met Sara in Chambers and she had handed him a paper copy of the new PTPH form. "Don't worry David, I've uploaded the original to the digital case system so the judge and the prosecution should have a copy. It looks relatively straight forward. The only real difficulty I see is the section on expert witnesses. We've only just been informed by the legal aid authorities that we can instruct our own expert neonatologist to deal with the case, but we're not sure yet exactly when he will be able to serve his report. He has asked for six weeks before he can serve even a preliminary report and eight weeks to serve a full report as a precaution."

David nodded, it was becoming increasingly difficult to tie down experts to a specific date for a final report, a matter the courts were well aware of, but which did not stop them issuing unrealistic time limits to the defence for the service of such reports.

David quickly read the new form, it was very like the old PCMH form in that it had myriads of questions that were either irrelevant, or no one was in a position to answer yet. He put the form into his bag and they both made their way to court.

At 9:15am David was getting robed in the Silk's robing room at the Old Bailey when a Queen's Counsel came up to him and spoke to him in a lilting Welsh accent, "You must be David Brant QC, representing that scallywag, Rachel Wilson. I'm Owen Jenkins QC. I will be prosecuting you today and at the trial."

Owen Jenkins was a little shorter than David, a large build with a ruddy complexion and a jovial face. David gave him a polite smile in return and commented, "You're here early for a prosecutor!"

Jenkins laughed, "Don't I know it! I've come here from deepest, darkest Wales. I had to change trains at Cardiff from my little country station where the trains seem to leave at deliberately inconvenient times. I had a choice, I could either get to court at 09:00 or 10:20. I thought the latter was pushing it a little for a 10:30 start. There only had to be a sheep on the line and I would have kept you all waiting for another hour and a half!

Anyway, enough about my travel difficulties. I can see from that new-fangled form that your junior has uploaded, that this is a trial. Is there anything we need to discuss before the hearing?"

David nodded, "The only thing to discuss is about our expert report, we need eight weeks to serve one. That should still give you plenty of time for your expert to respond even with the summer break. Do you have any objection to that request?"

Jenkins put a reassuring hand on David's shoulder, "Not at all my boy, not at all. We all understand how these things work. It seems a perfectly reasonable request to me, and, of course, if your report is unfavourable to your client, as I suspect it will be, I don't expect you to serve it at all!"

Fifteen minutes later David was seated in a small conference room on the same floor as the court. He was sipping from a luke warm coffee that Sara had insisted on buying from the canteen. At 9:40am Rachel was brought into the room by their solicitor, William James.

Introductions were made and David took a long look at Rachel Wilson. He had read all the papers served by the prosecution and was aware of the comments Rachel had made on her 999 call and to the paramedics and the police who had arrived at her home. He was concerned that she would be as obnoxious in a consultation with him as she clearly had been in the past.

He was grateful when she appeared subdued and restrained and hoped she would be like that at trial. He was not concerned about how she treated him, he could easily deal with that, however, he was concerned about how a jury might view her. Ideally, he would like the jury to have some sympathy for a mother, who had lost her baby, not loath her as some foul-mouthed, ranting drunk.

In the course of the next hour he took her through the papers. He advised her of the difficulties she faced and that there was a strong prosecution case on the child cruelty charge, "You see the prosecution will be putting the case on the basis that you either starved baby Annie, or knowing that she was seriously ill, you failed to get any medical assistance for her preferring to drink excessive amounts of alcohol. It's not going to be an easy case. I could approach the prosecutor and ask if he would drop the more serious charge of causing or allowing the child's death, if you pleaded guilty to the child cruelty charge."

David watched as tears rapidly appeared in Rachel's eyes and fell down her face. She then blurted out, "I always fed her properly. She was difficult to feed from the time she came home from hospital, but I always carried on until she took all her feed, even if she vomited a little. I never knew there was anything wrong with her until that last night, and that's when I immediately phoned for an ambulance."

At 10:30am they all entered court 7. This was where HHJ Tanner QC was currently sitting. He had been selected by the list office to deal with the PTPH hearing and what was worse, as far as David was concerned, he had been selected to be the trial judge!

They all rose as the judge entered the court, and sat after he had taken his time to plug in his laptop and connect it to a monitor and keyboard and then finally taken his seat as they all stood around. He looked down at counsels' benches and noted David's face beaming up at him. He ignored the expression. He had never had anything good to say about his former pupil and he was not going to exchange pleasantries with him now.

As he looked away towards the prosecutor, he saw from the corner of his eye, David turn and whisper something to his attractive female junior barrister. Her face broke into a smile. Tanner could not hear what was said but had no doubt that it was an uncomplimentary comment about himself.

David turned back to face him, keeping a grin on his face. He loathed Tanner. After all Tanner had tried to destroy his career all those years ago when he was starting off as a young junior barrister. He knew Tanner was a deeply miserable man and suffered from a degree of paranoia, which was why he had deliberately turned to Sarah and whispered, "Smiler, is looking his usual happy self today."

He had no doubt that Tanner would correctly guess that he was making a comment about him, and, importantly, that he could not do anything about it.

The hearing went along the usual lines; the parties were identified, pleas of not guilty were entered, directions were made by the judge and the trial date was confirmed. Tanner had of course wanted to ask a few unnecessary questions to show that he was in charge, not accepting that the parties knew what they were doing. Before pleas of not guilty were entered, he had looked at David and said, "Presumably your client will be pleading guilty to the cruelty charge. The evidence appears to be overwhelming. Either she starved the child, or she failed to get her medical attention, or it was a bit of both."

70

David had risen slowly from his seat to answer the question, "No my lord, we have a full answer to that charge."

He was in the process of sitting down when Tanner bellowed, "Well what is it?"

David's dismissive expression had not changed as he answered, "It does appear on the PTPH form, My Lord, which I am sure your Lordship has read. In summary, my client did not starve her child, nor was she aware of how ill her child was, until she was forced to call an ambulance. Unfortunately, it was too late and the child died a natural death from an unascertained cause that had nothing to do with my client's care."

Tanner gave a look of contempt at both David and the client who sat sobbing quietly in the dock. Knowing that he could not get any further on the question of pleas, Tanner commented, "I see on the form you want eight weeks to serve a medical expert's report."

"That is right my lord."

"Why so long?"

"Your Lordship is aware that under the legal aid rules we have to obtain a 'prior authority' directly from the legal aid authorities, before such a report can be commissioned. Despite putting the application in weeks ago, it has only just been granted. We have identified an expert, but he says he will require eight weeks to report, hence why we are asking for that period of time. If we receive the report earlier we will serve it earlier, but we are, regrettably, in his hands.

In any event the trial is not listed until 12th September, so the prosecution will have over nine weeks to deal with the report before the trial commences. I have spoken to my learned friend for the prosecution and he does not raise any objection to the request for eight weeks for service."

Tanner's face reddened as he responded gruffly, "Your expert will have to move much faster than that Mr Brant. Whatever the prosecution may agree or not agree to, I have to make sure that these cases move smoothly. You will serve your expert's report on the prosecution and the court within six weeks of today, otherwise you will not be allowed to rely on it."

CHAPTER 10
PLANNING FOR THE FUTURE

David stared at Wendy's list of things to do for the wedding, the honeymoon and the forthcoming birth of their child and poured himself another glass of Rioja. The last couple of weeks had been taken up with David and Sarah spending many hours preparing the necessary plans. To David it had seemed a never-ending saga. The day before, the bank holiday Monday, he and Wendy had decided to arrange a seating plan for the wedding meal. He had been surprised just how long it had taken. The politics behind who should sit where and with whom, who had offended who in the past and who was not talking to each other, made the current 'Brexit' debate, the debate on whether the United Kingdom should leave the European Union, look like child's play in comparison. David had been happy when they had come up with a 'provisional plan'. The word 'provisional' had concerned him but Wendy assured him it was only a precaution in case more people provided a late acceptance or some people dropped out nearer the time. He had noted with relish that Nashad was seated several tables away from the wedding party's table.

David had plenty of time at the moment to help with the plans. His other case of attempted murder had been listed the previous week and it turned out to be another short hearing in court, rather than a week's trial. Just a few days before the trial the prosecution had served a video of a CCTV they had suddenly 'found'. The CCTV video had been downloaded from a store's camera that had overlooked the scene, a day after the incident, but it had been wrongly placed with exhibits from another case and only found by pure accident. It clearly showed David's client wielding a knife and threatening others before stabbing the victim. The defendant had taken one look at the CCTV and sensibly asked David to negotiate the best deal he could with the prosecution. It resulted in David's client pleading guilty to the lesser, but still serious charge of causing grievous bodily harm with intent and him receiving a sentence of nine years' imprisonment.

There were no other cases in the pipeline and David was still waiting for his own expert's report in the Rachel Wilson case, so he was not involved in any fruitful work at the moment. Wendy was still busy with her own case work so David had taken on much of the wedding planning himself. For the most part it had been a waste of his time as whenever he came close to making a decision, Wendy would suddenly be available and would unravel his hard work. Still at least this way she could not complain if anything went wrong!

Wendy had managed to take time off for another scan which had been conducted two week earlier.

Again, they had to wait thirty minutes whilst their Consultant, Mr Rogers, negotiated the traffic jams that miraculously appeared the moment he set off from home. The scan had gone well with Mr Rogers saying the baby was fine and everything was on course for the October delivery date. David already had his aged and battered looking credit card ready to pay for a DVD copy of the scan. This time the image was clearer and he could clearly see the baby's arms legs and part of her face in 3D. They had by now been told the sex of the baby. Wendy had asked the usual concerned mother's question, whether he minded having a girl rather than a boy. He truthfully answered he did not care, provided she was healthy.

As usual, David did not bother to go into chambers nor was he often bothered by chambers contacting him. On the few occasions he did go in, the talk was usually about the birth of his child or which way people were voting in the forthcoming Brexit vote. Chambers had for the most part, divided along the lines of the barristers and the staff. The latter wanted to vote to leave the EU. As John Winston said, "We have too many immigrants in this country taking our jobs." The barristers for the most part wanted to stay in the EU. Most were critical of the EU but thought the UK prospects were better within the market. David had followed the barrister's opinions. He disliked Brussels bureaucracy but thought it was still, 'better the devil you know'.

On his last visit to chambers he had found himself in the clerks' room in an argument with John Winston about the subject. The argument went on for twenty minutes until he said to John, "You have a villa in Spain, don't you? Have you thought what will happen to that if we come out of the EU. They might bring in laws preventing foreigners owning their own properties, or you might have to apply for a visa to visit it."

John's face dropped a little as David continued, "I also thought you were planning to retire there? That might not be possible if we come out of the EU."

John had been morose for the rest of the day as David's points struck home. He doubted whether his honestly held opinion would benefit him with the clerks and he was not expecting any new work soon. It was probably better to avoid going in to chambers too much before the vote, which he knew was due to take place on 23rd June.

On 10th June, he finally received a call from John Winston, "Hello sir, I trust you're well, we've not heard much from you recently."

David could not help reply, "Well you could always remedy that by getting some work for me."

John laughed down the phone, "Funny you should say that, that's why I'm calling."

David was taken aback for the moment and he asked hopefully, "A new case John?"

"No, sir. It's the Rachel Wilson case. The solicitors have sent you the defence expert's report. They want you to read it and have a consultation with him and the client next week before they serve it. They said he can only make Friday 17th June. I told them you're busy but said you might be able to make that date."

David smiled at the receiver. He still wondered after all his time at the Bar why clerks always had to lie. Why tell a solicitor, a potential source of work, that he was busy and therefore potentially unavailable? Why not say, truthfully, if not slightly misleadingly, that one of his cases went short recently and he is currently available.

He put the thought out of his mind. He knew clerks thought that solicitors would not brief a barrister who had little work, hence they would keep up the fiction that they are all busy, all the time. Hopefully some new work would be coming soon.

He readily agreed to the date and timing for the consultation and was about to put the phone down when John added, "How's it feel sir? Not long now until you'll be a father again. Ms Pritchard has already asked me to mark some time out of your diary for when the baby's due. I thought it only right to mark out the end of

October and all of November to give you time to bond with the little one."

CHAPTER 11

THE DEFENCE EXPERT

Promptly at 10:00am, Nick Gobright ushered Malcolm Williamson, the Defence Consultant Neonatologist into David's room in chambers. David was already seated at the head of the conference table with his junior, Sara, on his right and the solicitor, William James, on his left.

After the initial introductions were made David announced, "Mr Williamson, we have all read your draft report and that the reports of the prosecution experts, the Child Pathologist, Dr Henry Numan and the Consultant Neonatologist, Mr Robert Peters. Can you begin by giving us a summary of where you agree and disagree with their reports?"

He agreed to do so and for the next forty minutes went through the prosecution reports and his own reports, summarising the findings, translating certain medical terms and highlighting the many points of agreement and the few disagreements he had with them.

At the end of his narrative David asked, "Could I attempt a summary at what you have just told us? In essence, you agree that the cause of little Annie's death is "unascertained" but that dehydration undoubtedly contributed to her death."

He nodded in agreement as he said, "Yes, that's a correct analysis."

"However, you cannot ascertain what was the cause of the dehydration. It could have been as a result of starvation, but equally it could be as a result of some other condition, such as malabsorption or even a chronic infection that was not diagnosed during life and could not be diagnosed after death."

"Again, that's right."

"You have noted that the post mortem was a week after her death and that her recorded weight at the post mortem was less than the last recorded weight when she was alive."

"Yes, that's correct."

"However, you do not believe that weight is relevant as the body could have lost weight between the time of death and the time of the post mortem and so it should be discounted when considering the question of dehydration."

"Yes, that's right."

"Could you help me on one specific point. If you are pressed in court under cross examination to give your preferred cause for the dehydration, what would you say?"

"Well that is never an easy question. I would try to answer it based upon my experience and the knowledge I have gleaned from this case. In my opinion chronic infection is the least likely cause of the dehydration. There would have been other signs present that should have been picked up by the doctors or at least the health visitor who saw the baby, even if the parents did not. In relation to starvation and malabsorption, I would not be willing to commit myself. Both, in my opinion, are equal possibilities."

David smiled, that was enough for him bearing in mind the onus was on the prosecution to prove that Rachel had 'caused' the death of little Annie. He had one further matter he wanted to deal with before he had a consultation with Rachel. "The prosecution state as an alternative that if the parents did not starve Annie, they must have seen the rapid deterioration in her condition and should have obtained medical assistance long before she called the ambulance on the night of her death. What do you say to that?"

Mr Williamson thought for a few moments before opening his briefcase and producing a pink coloured World Health Organisation chart for the expected growth rates of pre-term girls.

He spread the chart out in front of the lawyers and pointed to some plotted marks that he had made. "You will see that I have plotted this chart right back to when the baby was in hospital. You will have seen similar charts in the papers but it does appear that the hospital used charts for ordinary term babies and then tried to plot backwards rather than using these freely available charts that even appear in the red books supplied to all new born babies by the hospital!

If you look here I have plotted her birthweight on the chart. You will see that she weighed 1.4 kilos at birth so she fell between the 50th and 75th centiles on the chart. The centiles just show her position amongst other babies. The 50th centile is in the middle and means that she is of average height, out of a hundred preterm babies born at 30 weeks (which is when she was born), approximately 50 would weigh more and 50 would weigh less than she did. As she was between the 50th and 75th centiles it demonstrates that there was good foetal growth.

You will note that she lost weight after birth and one week later at 31 weeks, she only weighed 1.3 kgs. This is perfectly normal in all babies as they lose fluid after birth and will therefore lose about 7-10% of the bodyweight. This is soon put back and you will see on the chart that the baby had surpassed her birthweight and weighed 1.5 kgs at 32 weeks. This did mean that she had dropped to the 25th percentile point (i.e. 75 babies of her age would weigh more, 25 would weigh less) but there was nothing to worry about.

Thereafter she put on weight in hospital and stayed between the 25th and 50th percentile points until week 36. You will see then there was a drop in her expected weight at this stage. If she had continued on the 25th to 50th percentile point she should have weighed around 2.4kgs but in fact she weighed 2.2kgs which placed her between the 9th and 25th centile. i.e. 75-91 babies out of a hundred preterm babies of her age would weigh more than her now.

This was a cause of concern at the hospital and it is noticeable that at this period she was seen to be bleeding from her bowels. It was suspected that she was suffering from 'NEC', necrotising enterocolitis, a well-recognised and potentially serious bowel condition that affects premature babies.

It was treated appropriately by the medical staff and because it was suspected that the baby was cow's milk intolerant, she was placed on Pepti Junior, a formula milk for babies with cow's milk intolerance. Thereafter she continued to grow but stayed just above the 9th centile even when she left hospital at 42 weeks of age. Then she weighed 3.2 kgs.

Thereafter you will see that she was weighed by the health visitors on approximately a fortnightly basis. At first, she stayed around the 9th centile but after just over one month at home she dropped below it. After about 6 weeks she fell below the 9th centile and was hovering around the 2nd centile. After about 9 weeks she had just fallen below the 2nd centile. After 11 weeks, her weight was approximately half way between the 0.4 and 2nd centiles. Two weeks later, on 1st February 2016, when she was last weighed by the health visitor, she was just above the 0.4 centile."

David butted in, "What exactly is the 0.4 centile?"

"It means that if you took a thousand babies born at the same time as this baby, 996 would weigh more than her."

"That's quite a drop then?"

"It is from her birth weight where she was between the 50th and 75th centiles but the point I make is that the drop was gradual until she was just above the 0.4th centile shortly before her death. It means there was no massive drop in weight that would be obvious. Indeed, she was always putting weight on when she was weighed during her life, however, there was a slow drop through the percentile points. To anyone caring for her day in and day out, she would have been putting weight on, not enough, but it does not suggest that there would necessarily have been any obvious signs demanding immediate medical attention, as opposed to imperceptible changes over time."

CHAPTER 12

THE CLIENT

Mr Williamson left the conference room just after 11am, almost bumping into Rachel who was being shown into the room by Nick Gobright. David had not asked him to stay as he knew his presence would not have assisted her in the consultation, and in any event, he was a busy man with a large hourly rate.

After the introductions and offer of cups of coffee all round, Rachel sat down in the seat opposite David. He waited until she was settled before announcing, "Rachel, we've just been discussing the case with our own expert. Although he agrees with most of what the prosecution experts state, he does disagree with one important aspect. He states that dehydration was a contributory factor in Annie's death and although it could be as a result of starvation, equally, it could be because of what is called, 'malabsorption'.

In other words, Annie's body was not able to take in all the nutrients she was being fed by you which led to the dehydration. Importantly, he states it could have been gradual and she would have put weight on so any changes in her condition would not necessarily have been noticed by you."

Rachel looked blankly at him, so he tried another tack.

"His evidence supports your case that Annie did not starve to death, but died of natural causes."

Rachel now reacted, "That's what I've been fucking saying all along and none of you bastards fucking believed me!"

David looked at her coldly and paused before responding, "Rachel, we understand that you are under extreme stress, but swearing at us will not help you. If you have that attitude in court, the jury will not like you and will probably think that you are capable of anything. In any event, it is not a case that we did not believe you, it's a case that we have to investigate the evidence, so that we can present the best defence for you."

He paused again before slightly raising his voice, "Is that clear?"

Rachel was quiet for a few seconds before replying, "I'm sorry. I didn't mean to swear at you. I know you are all doing your best. It's just so difficult. I'm all alone, Bob's disappeared and I've lost my baby and everyone thinks I killed her!"

David nodded and added, "We understand that." Although he freely accepted to himself he could never understand what she was actually feeling and neither could anyone else unless they were in the same position as her, having lost a child and being charged with her murder.

He decided to deal with her gently throughout the rest of the consultation.

"Rachel, we are here to help you, which is why I need to ask you a few questions. You may have heard that the prosecution has to prove its case so that the jury are sure of guilt and the defence need do nothing."

She nodded as she pulled out a tattered dirty handkerchief to dab at her eyes.

"That is the law but in reality, the jury will want to hear from you and hear your denial that you starved baby Annie. That is why you must be ready to give evidence and ready to deal with the questioning from the prosecution barrister."

During the next hour, he took her through the background to the case, how often she fed little Annie, how often Bob fed her and whether she ever noticed any signs of illness. Rachel answered all the questions frequently dabbing at her eyes with the dirty handkerchief. At the end of the consultation David knew a little more about the case and the difficulties they would face.

He knew the jury would be unsympathetic to Rachel, but at least, he felt, they had an arguable defence.

CHAPTER 13

DEVASTATING NEWS

"Mr Brant, surely you are not suggesting this was anything other than a category one case?"

David had suggested no such thing. It was 4th July and his wedding was just over two weeks away. The last place he wanted to be at the moment was here, in the Court of Appeal, dealing with an appeal against sentence.

His client was Jimmy Nelson, who was no stranger to the courts. He had been convicted of a large number of offences of violence in the past. He had started with a conviction for common assault, then graduated to causing actual bodily harm and then further progressed to causing grievous bodily harm.

On this occasion, he had been charged with attempted murder. He had returned home and stabbed a supposedly close friend, Billy Fencer, in the chest, close to his heart. Jimmy claimed he had acted in self-defence. It was his case that he did not know Billy was there and he had been in the dark when Billy attacked him. He claimed that he picked up a knife that had been left conveniently on a table. The Prosecution claimed this was nonsense and pointed to Billy's evidence that he had been staying in the flat for at least a month with Jimmy's permission. They also relied on Billy's girlfriend's evidence that Jimmy had phoned her on the day of the incident to tell her that he thought Billy treated her, "like shite and I'm going to kill him when I next see him."

The jury had acquitted Jimmy of attempted murder but convicted him of the lesser, although still serious, offence of causing wounding with intent to cause grievous bodily harm. The judge had then sentenced him to an, "extended sentence of 12 years because of your history of violence and my conclusion you are a serious danger to the public."

Normally, a defendant who received a sentence of imprisonment would only serve half the term before being released from prison. He would then be 'on license' for the remaining half, meaning that if he committed another offence during that period he could be returned to prison to serve the remaining term in addition to anything he received for the new offence. An 'extended sentence' as its name implies, meant that Jimmy would not be released after serving half the sentence. Also as the sentence imposed on Jimmy was over ten years, he would have to serve two-thirds of the sentence before he could apply for parole and if he was not granted parole, he could find himself serving the full term of the sentence and then be released on licence.

David had advised on appeal against sentence and settled the grounds of appeal. He had a suspicion that the judge had been influenced consciously or subconsciously, by the fact that during a police interview, Jimmy had admitted that he had been convicted of murder as a teenager, but had then been acquitted on appeal. That evidence had been excluded from the jury's consideration, but the trial judge had heard it.

As usual David's grounds had been submitted to a High Court Judge who clearly thought there was some merit in the appeal as he had given David leave to appeal to the full Court of three judges. Clearly the three Court of Appeal judges that faced David thought differently! They had almost ignored David's submissions and now the senior judge, Lord Justice Simmerson, seized on something he had never argued.

"No, my lord, I am not suggesting that. My argument is that this was a single stab wound and the appellant immediately phoned the emergency services after he had injured Mr Fencer. Those factors, I suggest should put the sentence at the lower end of the guidelines for a category one offence."

"Are you suggesting that your client is not a danger to the public?"

"I am suggesting this was a specific set of circumstances peculiar to the parties and that the learned judge did not need to conclude that he was a danger to the public 'at large'. In any event, the learned judge should have considered that he was passing a lengthy sentence of imprisonment in any event. The public were going to be sufficiently protected by the length of that sentence and there was no need to extend it."

The look the three judges all gave him answered any lingering doubts he might have about the outcome of this appeal.

"Anything else Mr Brant?"

There was not anything else he could realistically argue, "No, thank you my lords."

The judges did not retire to consider the appeal, but the two on the outside rose from their seats and quickly spoke to the Lord Justice Simmerson who sat between them. Within thirty seconds they returned to their seats and Lord Justice Simmerson gave a judgment stating that the sentence was perfectly justified on a man who was clearly a continuing danger to the public at large.

David left the courtroom and immediately bumped into an old friend, Terry Bridges, whom he had known since they were both pupils together. Despite appearing in the same courts in London and the South, he had not seen Terry for at least a year. Although Terry had been at the Bar the same number of years as David, he had never applied to become a Queen's Counsel, readily admitting that his practice did not merit it. Accordingly, after close to forty years as a criminal barrister, he was still called a 'junior barrister'. In practice, it meant he was a lot busier than David and undoubtedly earned more!

Terry had just appeared in an appeal against sentence in front of the Court of Appeal judges next to David's court and had received a similar reception.

"Hey David, good to see you again. Do you fancy a quick pint across the road to wash away our 'Court of Appeal' experience?"

David readily agreed and they crossed the road and went into the nearest pub and ordered a couple of pints. As it was lunch time they also ordered steak sandwiches. Neither was part of David's diet that Wendy had imposed upon him for the wedding, but he felt after the morning he had, he was entitled to a little leeway!

The sandwiches arrived and David took a bite at the same time as hearing his phone bleep. He picked it up assuming it was nothing and noted it was a text from Wendy.

"Hi love, don't worry but I've had to go to hospital, I've bled a little and wanted to check that everything is ok."

David was immediately worried. He downed his pint, took another bite of his sandwich and left

Tony with a, "Sorry mate, we must have a proper lunch soon."

He made his way to a Temple tube station knowing it would probably be another year, or even longer before he met Terry again. He stopped outside the tube station to phone Wendy.

"Hi love, are you ok, how's the baby?"

Wendy sounded unusually calm, "It's ok, I'm waiting to see a doctor but the nurses say it's normal and nothing to worry about. I'm sorry, I know you were in the Court of Appeal today and I didn't mean to disturb your lunch. What were you having by the way?"

He paused before answering, "Just a sandwich. Anyway, I'm making my way to the hospital now so hopefully I'll see you soon."

St Gregory's hospital was near to Moorgate tube station, so David rushed to Temple tube station and within twenty minutes he exited Moorgate station. As he did so he immediately picked up a signal on his phone and he received three increasingly frantic text messages from Wendy.

"The doctor's looking concerned!"

"The doctor says he's not concerned about the bleeding, as that's normal, but"

"He is concerned by the fact that my cervix is dilated by 3 cm. Our baby is making an appearance at just over twenty-four weeks of pregnancy!

In a panic, David made his way to the maternity ward and within another fifteen minutes, he was invited into Wendy's room. As he entered the room he immediately saw Wendy lying on a bed. She tried to give him a reassuring smile, but it was clearly for show. It was a few moments before he realised that the doctor standing next to her was his own son, Robert.

"Hi dad, this isn't my ward or my speciality, but I heard Wendy was here and thought it might be comforting to see a familiar face."

Wendy beamed at him demonstrating that he was right, as David nodded a thanks to him. He then turned to Wendy, "What's this I hear that our baby wants to have a summer rather than an autumn birthday?"

Wendy continued to smile at him but he could tell she was deeply distressed. "Yes, she's keen to come out. I have asked if there is any way they can keep her from making an early appearance, but they say there's not. There's a risk that because my cervix is so dilated that there is an infection down there and it will be better for our baby to come out and take her chances in the outside world rather than continue to grow in a potentially infected environment."

David nodded, he was lost for words. He had no idea what was best for the baby.

Wendy's expression changed slightly as she continued, "There's an added problem though. St. Gregory's is an excellent hospital with excellent doctors and nurses."

She smiled at Robert as she said this.

"Unfortunately though, they do not have an intensive care unit for babies who are born under 30 weeks of age. Our little girl is only just over twenty-four weeks, so we have to be transferred to another hospital. Apparently, St Basil's near Wembley can take us and we're waiting for an ambulance now."

David collapsed into the nearest seat. His morning in front of crotchety Court of Appeal judges was nothing in comparison to this. He knew Wendy was struggling to keep her emotions intact and he had to say something reassuring. All he could think off was, "Is it safe to travel by ambulance in your condition?"

Wendy's brave countenance finally changed and she stopped smiling and wiped away a tear from her left eye, "There's always a risk darling, but we have no choice. The sooner we get to St. Basil's the better."

CHAPTER 14

THE NEW ARRIVAL

An hour later and Wendy and David were in the back of an ambulance, travelling as quickly as late afternoon London traffic would permit, with the blue light flashing and the siren wailing as they made their way from Moorgate to Wembley.

It was a surreal experience. He had cross-examined many paramedics in the murder cases he had conducted and always assumed that the ambulances were the modern affairs seen on the television. This ambulance was distinctly an old rickety one with dubious suspension. David was seated on a cold steel seat without a cushion, but fortunately Wendy was on one of the collapsible beds that had been wheeled into the ambulance and looked reasonably comfortable.

There was one female paramedic with them in the back, completing pages of documentation on all the 'jobs' she had done that day. She rarely looked up during the journey even though Wendy was connected to various instruments measuring her and their baby's vital signs.

Infuriatingly, there were no windows so David could not see where they were or gauge the progress they were making. He cursed every time the ambulance stopped for traffic, wondering why the idiot drivers did not get out of the way of an ambulance that was clearly on an emergency call. Meanwhile he held Wendy's hand and tried to calm the situation with what he hoped were amusing comments but which in reality were simply banal.

After what seemed an eternity, but what was actually less than forty minutes, the ambulance pulled in front of the Neonatal unit's entrance of St. Basil's hospital. Wendy was immediately rushed into the wing and placed in a room with a large bed and various machines, whilst she waited for doctors, nurses and a midwife to appear.

There was a comfortable chair in the room and David collapsed into it feeling completely exhausted. Wendy raised an eyebrow as if to say, 'it's not you who is about to give birth!' Wisely he did not say anything and simply looked around the room to take everything in. It did not help his mood when he saw a discarded bloody dressing in the floor of what should have been a sterile room and he wondered if the move between the hospitals was really a good idea.

Fifteen minutes later the male midwife arrived. He told them he was from Jamaica, which was obvious from his strong accent. David was momentarily concerned at the fact that the midwife was male, but he soon put the thought out of his mind. It soon became clear he knew what he was doing.

The midwife told them it was a busy time of the year for the unit so no doctors were immediately available, but there was nothing to worry about, he had delivered many premature babies and the doctors would be on hand when the baby arrived.

Both David and Wendy had many questions that they wanted to ask. Uppermost was, what were the chances of a twenty-four-week-old baby surviving, but the midwife refused to be drawn, stating that they must do everything they could to increase the baby's chances. He pointed out that at twenty-four weeks the baby's lungs would not be sufficiently developed so they would need to give two injections of steroids, twelve hours apart so they would not want Wendy giving birth for at least twelve hours.

He also explained how the sides of the baby's lungs would 'stick' together as the baby had not produced the necessary lubricant, 'surfactant' and they would have to inject some directly into the baby. He did go through a number of processes that would be necessary but David took little of it in.

It was strange that he had cross examined many medical experts in his career, becoming sufficiently knowledgeable on numerous areas to conduct lengthy and effective cross-examinations. Here though he could not think of any questions other than the ones the midwife refused to answer.

After about an hour a doctor arrived, Dr Laddie, who examined Wendy. He was late twenties and had probably only fully qualified a few years earlier. Again, he would not be drawn on the questions that David and Wendy wanted answering. He echoed what the midwife had said, they needed to focus on delivering the baby and giving her, her best chance of survival.

David and Wendy stayed in the room over the next eighteen hours. Wendy was brought some hospital food, David made one visit to the public canteen to purchase a beef curry for himself. Both slept badly. Both were clearly worried about the situation which had kept them awake and in addition, David had found the chair that had been allotted to him to sleep in was totally unsuitable.

In the early morning, after the last dose of steroids, Wendy had been given a drug to induce labour and so had started to suffer labour pains.

After a fretful night, nature took its course and at 11:07am on 5th July 2016 little Rose Louise Brant was born. 'Little' was perhaps an understatement. Rose weighed a bare 605gm at birth, 1lb 5 ounces. She was so small that she could easily fit into the palm of David's hand. The only good that had come from the situation was that the actual labour was a short one and Wendy did not suffer full labour pains.

It was clear when Rose was on the way and the midwife acted very quickly. Just before she arrived, the room was miraculously filled with doctors and nurses who all seemed to have a function and carried it out frenziedly, as David looked on helplessly.

After he appeared, her umbilical cord was cut and Rose was placed in what looked like a sandwich bag. He was later told that doctors had discovered how useful these were in premature births for reasons he never really understood. A tube was inserted into her mouth whilst a doctor pushed a syringe like object up and down generating air for Rose whilst her signs were checked. She was then rushed away to be intubated, have a tube inserted through her mouth into her lungs so that a machine could do the breathing for her.

Wendy was clearly exhausted by her ordeal and needed rest. As she turned her head away from them, Dr Laddie approached David and said in a cheery voice, "Come with us so you can be with your daughter."

David meekly followed. The confidence he displayed in a courtroom had no place here. As they left the room with a nursing sister, Sister Watts, Dr Laddie placed his hand on David's shoulder and announced, "I do have to tell you a few facts now. The chances of a baby of just over twenty-four weeks surviving, are about 50/50,"

David looked at him crestfallen, he had just witnessed the miracle of birth and now he was being told he could toss a coin to see whether Rose lived or not!

Dr Laddie had not finished and he continued in a matter of fact way, "Also, if she does survive there is a high risk, again about 50/50, that she will suffer severe health problems. These can range from blindness, brain damage due to bleeding in the brain, hearing loss, or even, cerebral palsy."

David just looked at him open-mouthed. The chances of Rose being healthy had fallen to one in four. Having delivered this devastating news, Dr Laddie patted him on the shoulder and entered a room through a door marked ICU 1. David was about to follow when his right arm was grabbed by Sister Watts, "Mr Brant, the doctor has to tell you those things, that's his job. But he is telling you about all the babies born here. This is your baby and your baby is different. You have to be positive for her and your partner. I will not have any glum faces in my ICU, so come on, smile and let's see your baby together."

Strangely the pep talk worked and David felt better. Of course, the doctor had to give him the statistics, but lots of babies were born premature for all number of reasons, including the fact that a number of parents were drug addicts and had poisoned their babies. Surely, Rose's prospects were better than that. He put a smile on his face, thanked the sister, held his head up high and walked into the ICU 1 room to catch a glimpse of the latest addition to the Brant family.

CHAPTER 15

THE FIRST FEW WEEKS

On the night of Rose's birth, Wendy was moved to a private room on one of the wards in the main hospital. David had insisted on paying for the room as he thought she needed the rest and would need easy access to bathroom facilities, rather than having to traipse through a cold hospital ward trying to find some that were not being used. He had not been concerned at the £170 a night charge for the room, although he had wished that they could have provided him with something other than yet another uncomfortable chair to sleep in. He was sure that when the NHS ordered chairs for patient's rooms the specifications included a line to the effect, 'Make as uncomfortable as possible.' He was convinced that the idea was to discourage visitors staying for any length of time!

On the following night, he had returned to their flat, ostensibly to obtain some clothes and items for Wendy, but mainly so he could have a comfortable night's sleep and carry out some necessary tasks at home.

Their wedding had been arranged for Saturday 16th July 2016, but that obviously had to be cancelled now and everyone had to be contacted.

Neither would be able to forgive themselves if something happened to Rose whilst they we're getting married or drinking champagne and exchanging pleasantries with others at a wedding reception.

He also had to cancel the Honeymoon which had been a week's cruse around the Mediterranean followed by a week's stay in Sorrento on the coast of Naples in Italy. It was important that he did spend as much time with Wendy and Rose as possible so he had to make sure that he had no cases or essential paper work in the forthcoming month. The latter proved very easy as the clerks were happy to tell him there was nothing in his diary for the foreseeable future!

Rose lost weight in her first week just like little Annie and they were assured that was normal in all babies as they lost moisture and there was nothing to worry about in that regard.

There were of course other worries. Rose needed to be intubated to survive. They knew that she needed oxygen for her lungs to grow but they were also told that it had to be carefully regulated. Oxygen was a poison, whilst it helped Rose's lungs grow, it could be poisoning other organs like her eyes. Many pre-term babies in the past had survived only to be blinded by being given too much oxygen. An eye test was carried out in week two and it was found that Rose had scale 1 damage on a scale of 1-4. Again, they were told that this was normal in pre-term babies and she would probably correct herself, but nevertheless, the information just added to their growing list of concerns.

An x-ray was carried out on her skull and they were told there had been some bleeding into the brain. Again, they were told this was normal in pre-term babies but it would have to be monitored in case it did not clear and caused long term damage.

After a week in the hospital wards, Wendy had moved into a house in the hospital grounds, run by a charity that had donated the property to be used by the parents of children who had to stay in the hospital for a number of weeks or months.

Another three weeks had passed and just before David was due to return to work, Dr Laddie announced the 'great news'. Rose had 'graduated'. They were now ready to remove the intubation tube and try her on something called CPAP. She would still need oxygen, but it would now be delivered through a mask that would be attached tightly to her face.

David and Wendy were not allowed to watch the procedure being carried out. There was a clear concern amongst the medical staff that if Rose did not take to CPAP, she would have to be reintubated which could cause further damage to her lungs and they did not want the parents around to witness that. It did not help David and

Wendy's worries but fortunately, no such emergency took place and Rose continued to grow with the use of the CPAP mask.

David returned to work and started to prepare the Rachel Wilson case. It was strange but he saw the case in a different light after Rose's birth. After all, little Annie had been a preterm baby and had first been intubated and then placed on CPAP, before being discharged. He lost a degree of objectivity as he thought how cruel it was that she had been through so much, struggling to hang onto life and then having her young life taken from her due probably to dehydration and worse, possible starvation!

It took him some time to put such thoughts out of his mind and concentrate on the defence case, now with the added advantage that he knew some of the terms and procedures referred to in Annie's medical papers because he had come across them in Rose's case.

He visited the hospital as frequently as he could and stayed a few nights in the week when he could. He tried to find good restaurants around the area to take Wendy to in order to take her mind off the fact that Rose's hold on life was still precarious.

Like most expectant mothers, Wendy had expected to meet other mothers of children and form bonds in ante-natal classes, which could last for years. Of course, she had never gone to such classes because Rose had been born too early. Wendy only saw the mothers of sick preterm babies and the atmosphere was distinctly depressing.

There was one family who were clearly drug users. They had been allowed to stay in a private room in the hospital at no cost, so they could be near their child who was born premature, blind and with a withered left foot, all probably as a result of the mother's heavy intake of class A drugs.

The parents were expelled from their room in the hospital when it was found they were smoking cannabis in their bedroom and the communal bathrooms where other mothers changed their babies' nappies.

Wendy eventually became friendly with Janet, a forty-year old mother who had been trying for ten years for a baby and finally resorted to IVF treatment. Her daughter Julie, had been born at 28 weeks with a hole in the heart. She was in the incubator next to Rose and the mothers saw each other every day.

Sadly, Julie was operated upon twice but with no success and Wendy had listened tearfully through a screened curtain to her friend's stifled cries, as the feeding tubes and oxygen tubes were removed one by one from the child's slowly dying body. She had found it particularly difficult when the doctor announced, 'We are just leaving the morphine tube in, so that Julie doesn't struggle as she passes over.'

Janet immediately afterwards moved from the hospital and Wendy never saw her again.

Wendy was fortunate to then make friends with Angela and Richard Whitgift who were staying in the same house as her and on the same floor. They had a son called Robin. He was born at 26 weeks but was in a worse condition that Rose because he was born with his stomach on the outside of his body. There was no explanation for this condition as the parents did not use drugs or abuse alcohol nor did they smoke. They seemed to David, when he met them, to be perfectly decent people whom fate had chosen for particularly undeserved treatment.

Angela explained to Wendy that Robin had been in the hospital for four months already. Miraculously, it seemed to Wendy, he had been operated upon and his stomach reinserted into his body cavity with Manuka honey being used as a topical medicine to reduce infection. Although his progress was slow and he was not out of harm's way yet, he was growing and digesting milk and his parents were hopeful he would grow up normally.

Richard had to make the long journey to work to Uxbridge from the charity house every morning and so he set off very early. It meant that Wendy and Angela became close friends and had their breakfast together in the house before visiting their babies at the same time, who were in the same baby care unit, just a few incubators apart.

David had been happy with the arrangement. It meant he felt a little less guilty about not spending as much time at the hospital because of the amount of work he now had to conduct on the Rachel Wilson case.

Strangely, he spent little time at home now. Normally he preferred to work from home, but he had found it easier to work in chambers recently. It was probably because his home life was in turmoil and he could not stop thinking about Wendy and Rose when he was there. At least when he was alone in his room in chambers, he was not constantly reminded of Rose's struggles, even if he did think about them both frequently.

On 16th August at 11am, David was again alone in his room in chambers, working on Rachel's case when he received a call from Wendy. Rose had been on CPAP for ten days now and had been progressing well so he was not unduly alarmed to see she was phoning.

He answered the call with a cheery, "Hello love, everything ok?"

He suddenly noted the hesitation at the other end of the line, "No, it's not David. I'm sorry I had to call you, I'm just feeling so depressed. You may have to brace yourself for this. I think we're losing Rose."

David was stunned into silence and could not speak for a few seconds. Everything had been going so well, what could possibly be wrong. He realised he had to say something comforting, but all he managed was, "Wendy, darling, just tell me what's happened?"

"I was feeding her this morning. As you know I feed her my expressed breast milk through a feeding tube. I don't know what happened, whether I knocked her mask or breathing tube or what, but suddenly she turned blue. It was obvious she wasn't breathing. The alarms sounded and the doctors and nurses rushed into the room and took her from me. The CPAP clearly wasn't enough for her and her whole body stiffened and turned a horrible blue colour. They tried to intubate her but couldn't. They then ushered me out of the room. They've closed the curtains round her.

Oh David, I'm terrified, I'm sure we've lost her."

He knew he had to summon up more confidence than he actually felt.

"Wendy, try not to worry. I'm sure this is one of those setbacks we were told to expect. As we were told at the start, it's two steps forward, then one or two steps back every day, sometimes it's three steps back. I'm sure you didn't knock her mask or breathing tube. It's probably just become dislodged and they thought it better to intubate her to be on the safe side. It can't be an easy or pleasant procedure putting a tube into a baby's lungs and I seem to recall that they have to paralyse the baby to do it so they probably wanted you out of the room so they could do it properly."

She paused for a few seconds in thought before adding, "I'm worried though, what if she's been starved of oxygen for a long time? What if she's brain dead or brain damaged?"

Now he paused before answering, realising that both were realistic possibilities.

"I'm sure she's not, if there is any problem we'll deal with it when it arises. You see if they'll let you go back in now and check on what's happening and then tell me."

They both put their phones down and David was surprised to see how white his knuckles were from gripping the hand set so tightly. He had not even held little Rose yet. He had been reluctant to do so whilst she was attached to so many tubes, for fear he might knock them! It was something he had never expressed to Wendy, telling her there would be plenty of times for cuddles when Rose was stronger.

He had to acknowledge, he loved Rose from the moment she arrived. He had enjoyed seeing her grow little by little and liked seeing her open her eyes and stare at him when he spoke to her, peering over the CPAP mask which hid so much of her beautiful face whilst having the added effect of distorting it. He realised he had never felt so low in his life, even during that horrible period of his life when he was going through the rigours of a divorce, with his own children blaming him for the breakup.

Were they really going to lose Rose at this stage after she had fought so many weeks to stay alive?

CHAPTER 16

FURTHER EVIDENCE

David waited on the end of the phone for an agonising twenty minutes, unable to conduct any further work, trying to amuse himself by doodling in a notebook. The Rachel Wilson trial had suddenly become wholly unimportant. Eventually the phone rang and he picked it up gingerly, worried about what to expect.

Immediately he heard Wendy's reassuring voice, "Hello love, they think everything is ok. They thought Rose needed intubating again and it took longer to insert the tube this time. You were right, they had to paralyse her with a drug so that she wouldn't move. They don't believe there will be any permanent damage but they want to keep her under observation for the next few days."

He put on his calmest voice in reply, "I'm sure everything will be okay love, as I said, it's one of those setbacks we have to expect every so often. Today is three steps back day, tomorrow we will take one or two steps forward again."

They finished their call as Wendy wanted to be by Rose's side and keep an eye on her. As he placed his own phone away, he noticed that despite not being the slightest superstitious, he had involuntarily crossed his own fingers and was firmly touching the wooden top of his desk!

There was no one else in the room but he still spoke out loud, conscious of how many times he had used the phrase 'I'm sure' today. "I'm sure everything is going to be all right…"

He hesitated before adding, "… isn't it?"

Over the next few weeks, further checks were carried out on Rose in the hospital. It seemed she was none the worse for her ordeal and she progressed, although there were one or two further setbacks during this period, some more worrying than others, particularly when the damage to her eyes was recategorized to a class 2. Again, they were told this should right itself in time, but that did not placate their concerns.

After a week, the tube had been taken from her lungs and she was put back on the CPAP breathing mask. The doctors said they were happy with her progress, although she was not putting on as much weight as they hoped. Discussions were then had about introducing cow's milk to her diet in addition to Wendy's breast milk. Wendy was very reluctant to allow the introduction of anything else to Rose's diet whilst she seemed to be progressing and the decision was put back whilst her low weight gain was monitored.

David had taken a back seat in all these discussions deciding these were really decisions for Wendy. She was producing sufficient breast milk for Rose and as everyone said, 'breast was best', he did not want to support the doctors against her, even though it had been explained that there would be more calories in a cow's substitute milk and it did appear that Rose needed more calories.

Meanwhile the case of Rachel Wilson was about to commence and David had to spend more time preparing for trial. Because of Rose's current predicament, he spent extra time reading the medical notes about Annie's treatment in hospital, to see if there was anything that might help Rose or at least help him to understand the hospital care plan.

He was slightly concerned that in the last two weeks, the prosecution had served two new witness statements. One was from a Thomas Adams that had been taken at the end of July. He said he knew both Rachel and Bob and he remembered seeing them both in their local pub, 'the Bull's Head' at 9:30pm on the night Annie died and Annie was not with them.

The solicitors had taken Rachel's instructions and she said he was lying. Bob had gone to the pub that night but she had stayed at home with Annie. When asked why Thomas Adams was lying, she claimed that he was infatuated with her and had 'tried it on' numerous times including in July and she had rejected him each time. She said he was making these false allegations because he wanted to get back at her for rejecting him. He was a 'hard man' who was used to getting his way.

The other statement was from Bob's mother, Joan Harwood. Worryingly, she stated she was very concerned with the way Rachel had looked after Annie and had tried to give advice but it had been constantly rejected by Annie.

Again, Rachel's instructions had been taken on these points and she claimed that Bob's mother had always disliked her and thought Bob could do better. She was making up these lies because they did not have a good relationship and because she blamed her for Bob going to prison when he assaulted her.

It was an unfortunate development so near to the trial, but not an unusual one in David's experience. Frequently the Crown Prosecution Service served devastating statements just a few days before trial, even though the statements had been taken months before. David knew that the jury might have some difficulty in believing that Thomas came forward and lied, simply to make things bad for a woman who had spurned his advances. They might also struggle to believe that Joan had come forward to lie about Rachel in this way just because her son could do better.

David did advise that the solicitor make some enquiries in the local pub to see if any of the staff or locals remembered that night. He knew after such a long time it was unlikely anyone would remember Rachel not being in a pub on a certain night. They were far more likely to remember if she had been there, and such enquiries could harm her case. Nevertheless, he still thought the enquiries should be made.

On 12th September, the trial began in the Bailey. A further expert report was served by the prosecution just a week before the trial responding to the defence expert's report. In essence Mr Peters stated there was nothing in the point raised by the defence and he was 'surprised' it had been raised by an expert in this field! Although he conceded that he could not rule out malabsorption as a possible cause of the dehydration, he could not state it was as likely to be the cause as starvation, which in his opinion was by far the most likely cause.

The report came as no surprise to David, Mr Peters came across as one of those experts who was dogmatic and would not easily accept an opinion that was contrary to his own. He wondered whether he might be able to shake him under cross-examination and at least gain some concessions. Only time would tell.

CHAPTER 17

THE TRIAL

The case was listed at 'not before 2pm' on 12th September as His Honour Judge Tanner was dealing with a number of other cases in the morning. David had a lie in and arrived at the Old Bailey at just before 1pm. Sara was already there and he was pleased to find that the solicitor and the client were there as well.

The first person he saw was Owen Tudor Jenkins QC, who was putting his robes on when David walked into the robing room. He was met with a beaming smile.

"My dear boy, it is so good to see you again. I presume you have seen my expert's detailed response to your scurrilous defence report?"

David beamed back in return and added, "No, but I have seen your very late, remarkably short, and terribly dismissive response to our timely, lengthy and perfectly reasonable expert's report."

Owen laughed, "I take it from your answer that there is no late change of heart on the part of your lady and I was wise to book rooms in London for the duration of the trial?"

"Very wise, I hope you've booked somewhere nice?"

Owen grimaced as he replied, "I'm afraid not. Rather uncharitably the Crown Prosecution Service refuse to pay my hotel expenses, stating a London Silk could prosecute this case. As they asked me to prosecute this case because of my experience with 'causing or allowing death' charges, I was a little galled at their parsimonious attitude! My clerks booked me into a Bed and Breakfast establishment in Clapham. I was mortified to find it does not even have a bar that opens during the week!"

He raised his hand to his brow as he added, "Oh, the sacrifices we barristers must make in these times of austerity."

They continued chatting in a friendly fashion about what steps they needed to take before they went into court. Owen had agreed to exclude any photographs of the deceased child from the jury bundle but warned that the photographs may become relevant in time. He promised to give David sufficient notice to allow him to make an objection, should he seek to rely upon them later. They finally agreed that there was only one issue that they needed to discuss with the judge before the jury was sworn and that was whether Owen should be allowed to play Rachel's 999 call to the jury.

Owen conceded, "I will confess that I was in two minds whether to play it. It is clearly prejudicial to your client although it is probative of her state when she was supposedly caring for her child.

But I have a rather keen CPS solicitor who, remarkably, has read these papers and an equally keen junior, Simon Hunter. I don't know if you know him, he is from London chambers, somewhere in King's Bench Walk, a prosecution set I understand and he is very ambitious. Both are very keen that I play the tape."

David tried to persuade him otherwise but was unable to do so and after a further consultation with the client, at 2:05pm he was ushered into Court 7.

There was a further five-minute delay until HHJ Tanner QC came into court and took his seat, followed by the usher who was carrying the judge's papers and laptop. As usual he scowled at David and then smiled as Owen rose to his feet to address him.

"My Lord, we are almost ready for a jury, although there is one matter we seek your Lordship's ruling upon before we commence."

He paused as Tanner's expression returned to a scowl as he turned towards David. "And what is the point Mr Brant that will delay us swearing in a jury?"

Owen sat down as David stood up slowly to address the judge. He slowly pulled his gown over his shoulders and shuffled a few papers before addressing his former pupil master, "Simply this my lord, we know you will have read the papers in the minutest detail and you will of course have noted that my client made a 999 call to the ambulance services when she discovered that her child was not responding to her attempts to wake her. We have no objection to that call being referred to and indeed an edited summary being placed before the jury. However, we do object to the tape being played in its entirety.

Our client, understandably, was in a terrible state at the time of the call and her frustration and fear clearly comes across in the language she involuntarily used. The issues in this case concern whether she starved her baby to death or failed to obtain medical assistance when it would be obvious that it was needed. Her state and the language she used to the emergency operator are wholly irrelevant to those issues and if the tape of the call is played, it may unfairly prejudice the jury against her, in a case which is already fraught with emotion. Hence we object on the basis that the prejudice in playing such a call far outweighs any probative value the call could possibly have."

David sat down and Owen began to stand to respond. HHJ Tanner immediately waved his hand indicating that he should remain seated, "I have read all the relevant papers in this case, although not in the minutest detail, which is not required nor is it the function of a trial judge. I consider that the call is relevant to the issues in this case. It shows the defendant's demeanour and state at a time she should have been caring for her child. I can foresee that there may be a degree of prejudice, but it is insignificant and I will warn the jury against it.

I have no doubt Mr Brant that you will be able to make the points to them that you have made to me."

He then snidely observed, "Clearly I have more confidence in the good sense and fairness of an English jury than Mr Brant does. Now let's get on and get a jury sworn."

CHAPTER 18

THE OPENING

The jury panel of fifteen potential jurors came forward slowly and seemingly, reluctantly, into court. David immediately noticed there were ten women and five men. The selection he knew was random, but it always seemed in rape cases and cases like this filled with emotion, that the panels had far more women than men.

After the jury were selected there were now nine women and three men going to sit on Rachel's case. David had already warned Rachel that he had no right to challenge jurors and so those who were randomly selected were going to be the jurors unless Rachel actually knew one of them.

Owen began his opening address to the jury by introducing the defendant and the barristers in the case and explains that the defendant was in a relationship but they would not be trying her boyfriend as he had breached his police bail before being charged and had not been seen since. He also handed out jury bundles and he explained that the latter were for their assistance and contained; a copy of the indictment, containing the charges she faced and some of the medical documents from the case. It also contained a timeline, which he told them was designed to assist them. It began with little Annie's birth on 12th August 2015, her discharge from hospital on 4th November 2015, went on to document the visits by the health visitor, and then to the day of her death on 19th February 2016. It ended with references to the arrest, interview and charging of Rachel.

"Let me turn now to the tragic facts of this case. As the charge on count 2 makes clear, it concerns the death of a child, in fact a six-month old baby. A baby who had struggled to come into this world as she was born premature, a baby who struggled to survive in a hospital because of her tender age and condition, a baby who eventually fought against the problems of prematurity and was allowed home to live with her mother and father.

You will hear that sadly her ordeal was not over and by the age of six months, she lost her tender grip on life. It is the Crown's case that she lost her grip because the parents never looked after her adequately. She needed all that a young baby needs, the care and love and attention of doting parents, but because she was born prematurely she needed more, much more. All of which had been explained to the parents by doctors at the hospital where little baby Annie was born.

The parents claimed that they understood and signed all the necessary pieces of paper to allow them to take little Annie home.

You may well be aware, those of you with children or grandchildren, that hospitals these days provide the parents of new born babes, with little red books that list; inoculations, growth, weight and the like and provide charts that can be completed to demonstrate whether a child is putting on the expected weight. There is of course a great deal of difference in children. Some are born very small, some are born very large, but all tend to fall into a position on these charts and with some individual variation, they tend to follow an expected growth and weight line."

He asked the jury to turn into their bundles to page 25 where they would find Annie's plotted positions on a red chart.

"You will hear from a health visitor, Melissa Head, who visited the family as frequently as they would allow. Often on her visits, an excuse was made by the parents as to why she could not see Annie. However, she persevered and did see little Annie on a regular basis and weighed her and kept a record of those plots.

You will see from those plots carried out by professionals in the hospital, that whilst she was in their care, little Annie followed a roughly expected growth line and a weight line and although she changed from birth, she appeared to be healthy, certainly for a pre-term baby.

However, you will see from the plots carried out by Melissa Head who visited little Annie at her home, that once she was released from hospital, Annie no longer followed the expected growth and weight lines and fell through the different centile positions. In medical terms, although she was gaining weight, she was not advancing at the correct rate.

Melissa Head last visited the family on Monday 25th January this year. She managed to gain access. She will describe Annie's state to you and the advice she gave to the parents. She also weighed little Annie and took measurements of her height and head circumference. Little Annie weighed just 4.3kg. That meant she was now just above what the doctors call the 2nd centile.

She was weighed again when the post mortem was carried out. She weighed 4.5kg. That would have been her weight at the time of her death and would place her just above the 0.4 centile."

David looked up from his papers at this point and looked towards Owen who noticed the glance but ignored it and carried on, "The question you will want to ask yourselves is why? What happened after she was released from hospital into the care of her parents that meant she failed to put on adequate weight or grow at the expected rate?

We suggest the answer from the evidence you will hear, is clear. Her parents failed to feed her or look after her properly. They would have seen her slowly withering away and yet they did nothing to help her. They did not provide her with adequate feed and when it must have been obvious she was suffering. They also failed to obtain medical assistance for her when it was obvious that she needed it.

We do know of only one attempt to obtain medical assistance, but by then it was far too late. On 19th February of this year at 10:04pm, Sadie Potts, an emergency operator, received a 999 call from a clearly distressed individual. I am going to play that call to you soon. You will hear what the defendant had to say, some of which was very unpleasant. You will no doubt want to consider that she was undoubtedly distraught at the time and this may have affected her demeanour, but you may think it obvious she was drunk and you may want to consider whether she sounds drunk and was in any fit state to look after a six-month old child?

Ladies and gentlemen, paramedics arrived quickly but could do nothing to assist poor little Annie who was clearly dead. It was noted by them that rigor mortis had already set in. You will hear from one of the paramedics, Andrew Biggs, that when he arrived the defendant was drinking large glasses of vodka and was abusive to him saying words to the effect, 'What you fucking looking at? You should be helping my baby.'

It was clear to the paramedics that little Annie was long dead. There was no hope of helping her. They tried to break the news to the parents saying they were sorry but there was nothing they could do for her, but they were met with the comment from the defendant's partner, "You're sorry you bastard! If you'd got here sooner, she would've still been alive!"

In cases of this type the body is taken away and a post mortem carried out, to try and determine the cause of the death. A week later a post mortem was carried out by a child pathologist, Dr Henry Numan. You will hear him give evidence before you. He states that the cause of death was unascertained but a contributory factor was dehydration.

This is a standard way that pathologists report. As a result, an expert report was obtained from a consultant neonatologist, a doctor specialising in premature babies. Again, you will hear from him. Essentially, he will tell you that in his opinion, death was as a result of dehydration. He considers that this could be as a result of little Annie not absorbing enough nutrients from her milk intake, but this is unlikely as she was not suffering any such 'malabsorption', as it is known, when she was in hospital. He then goes on to consider the other horrifying possibility. That she was starved by her parents. This he concludes is what happened in this case. These parents wilfully neglected their child preferring to drink copious amounts of alcohol rather than feed little Annie the small amount of milk she needed. You will see that count 1 on the indictment deals with this wilful neglect. Count 2 deals with the causes of that neglect namely that the wilful neglect caused the death of the child.

You will hear from another witness who may be able to assist you on this point. He only came forward recently, no doubt unaware of the potential importance of his evidence. His name is Thomas Adams. He knows the defendant and her partner very well as he lives nearby and has seen them regularly. He will tell you that at about 09:30pm on 19th February 2016, he saw the defendant and her partner in a local pub, called, 'the Bull's Head' just one hundred yards or so from their home. Both appeared to be drunk and were dancing to music played from behind the bar. They did not have little Annie with them. We know no one else was looking after little Annie that night. It appears that they left her alone in their home whilst they went out drinking and dancing in a local pub.

Poor little Annie was left abandoned in a dark, cold house, with no on to hear her pitiful fading cries. She was neglected, starving and helpless, when she finally gave up her last dying gasp of breath!

CHAPTER 18

THE 999 CALL

There was complete silence in the court as Owen finished his opening. David quickly scanned the jurors' faces, there were a couple of women dabbing handkerchiefs at their eyes and one man who looked a ghastly shade of green. It was a powerful opening and David worried the case might been lost before he had said a word.

As he was thinking of how to defuse the emotional atmosphere in the court Owen announced that he would commence the prosecution case by playing the 999 call. David picked up a pen and noisily scribbled a note in his counsel's notebook. It was a meaningless gesture only carried out because he wanted the jury to see that he did not seem fazed by the evidence. In reality he thought the 999 call was one of the most damning pieces of evidence in the whole case, potentially demonstrating a wholly uncaring attitude on the part of his client.

He again watched as the jury listened to the tape that was now being played loudly in court. He tried to avoid grimacing as Rachel could be heard slurring, 'How can I fucking calm down, you fucking bitch, my baby's not breathing!'

The jury now seemed to all sit upright in their seats, some occasionally glancing towards the sobbing Rachel, with impassive faces.

Mercifully the tape ended and the judge announced that as it was close to 4pm he would adjourn the case for the day.

David watched the jurors leave court, several giving Rachel a cold look as they filed out of court. It was not a great start to the case.

He returned to chambers with Sara, but neither wanted to discuss their day in court. They both knew that the opening represented the high point of any prosecution case. The evidence was rarely as compelling as it appeared on paper but the 999 call had clearly had an effect on the jurors.

David did not stay long in Chambers. He wanted to go and see Wendy and Rose. He knew at this time of day the quickest way there would be by tube, so he made his way to Temple tube for the journey.

By 6pm he was entering the Neonatal unit of the hospital. Rose had progressed from the ICU unit and was now in a unit called the High Dependency Care Unit. She was still on CPAP and kept in an incubator but at least it was step in the right direction.

As he entered the doors and washed his hands, as the signs forcefully directed, he saw that there were curtains around Rose's bed. He had an initial concern but almost immediately he heard Wendy's laugh and he realised there was nothing to worry about and that Rose was presumably having an early evening feed.

He peered around the curtain and saw Wendy holding Rose with her back to him, with a nurse, standing next to her.

Wendy smiled at him, "Hello David, this is Angelina Potento. She's Rose's nurse in the High Dependency unit. Angelina is from Italy. We were just talking about you."

His own smile dropped a little, "Yes, I heard the laughter!"

Wendy gave Angelina a conspiratorial wink. "It's nothing to worry about. Rose has had a great day."

She turned Rose slightly so he could see her face. The CPAP mask had gone and now Rose had a cannula fixed to her face by small plasters decorated with teddy bears. Wendy completed the details, "It's great that she's come off her CPAP and has progressed to having oxygen through a cannula. It's so much less invasive and doesn't screw her face up like the mask did. You can still see the effect of the mask on Rose. It's made her little eyes bulge, but Angelina has told me that's normal and Rose will soon be back to normal. She's progressing so much that they think she'll be moved to the next unit down, the Special Care Unit."

David nodded and gently touched Rose's head. "Good girl, hopefully you'll be coming home soon."

Wendy hesitated before saying anything. "I think we are some way off that yet. The doctors do have one concern and that is that Rose is not putting on enough weight and has dropped a centile."

David stood rigid for a second. Suddenly thinking of what happened to little Annie. Wendy saw his expression and quickly added, "They say it's not too worrying as they should be able to correct it, but Dr Laddie wants a word with us on his rounds, which should be anytime now."

Angelina left them and David enquired, "So what did you two find so amusing about me?"

"Oh nothing. Angelina just asked, who did I think Rose looked most like and I said you. Then we talked about her not taking enough feed and I quipped, 'She doesn't take after her father in that regard!"

Wendy noticed David's smile drop from his face so she quickly added, "Don't worry I was only joking."

He involuntarily sucked his stomach in as he noticed Angelina looking at him across the room. No more hospital food for him then. His thoughts wandered for a moment, it never ceased to amaze him that the food in the hospital canteen was all fried, with chips being a major seller. The alternative was limp salad that always looked like it was the least healthy meal on offer and well past it's sell buy date.

For the next half-hour, they discussed his day whilst Wendy gave Rose a 'skin to skin' cuddle with an almost naked Rose resting on Wendy's breasts. They were told that these cuddles helped the baby regulate her own skin temperature and in any event, Wendy found them an excellent time to bond with Rose.

At 6:30pm Dr Laddie entered the unit with a number of students and nurses. He did the round of all the babies in the unit before stopping at Wendy's side.

He cheerfully greeted them before turning back to his group and saying, "We are really happy with Rose's progress. Obviously, there's a long way to go yet, but little Rose has done very well and is advancing at a rate that we never believed possible a few short weeks ago."

He turned to the grinning parents, "You must be so happy that Rose is off the CPAP and now is breathing air through the cannulas with the assistance of a little oxygen?"

They both said they were, but David could not help add, "Can you tell us what the situation is with her weight. I understand she has dropped a centile?"

Dr Laddie nodded, "She has dropped to just below the 9th centile but it's not a great worry. She was only just above the 9th centile when we last weighed her, last week. We do think she needs something in addition to breast milk though. I know Wendy does not like the he idea of giving a milk substitute but we really think she needs it. We still want her to have breast milk but we would like to add some more calories to it.

Breast milk is certainly best but it never has the same calorific content as a breast milk substitute. We want to put her on a combination of 50% breast milk and 50% of a product called Infatrini which is very high in calories, and see if that helps her grow."

They had further discussions with the doctor before they agreed to try out the new combination to see if it helped Rose put the weight on that she needed.

At 8pm David left the hospital and returned to his home where he started to look through the Rachel Wilson's papers. He had never heard of Infatrini despite having concentrated on Annie's care in hospital and at home. It was certainly not mentioned in her medical notes and he wondered if that had any significance?

CHAPTER 19

THE PARAMEDIC

On the Tuesday morning, when the jurors had all taken their seats in court, Owen announced that his next witness was the paramedic Andrew Biggs.

A few minutes later Andrew Biggs was in the witness box and was sworn and had dealt with a few preliminary questions from Owen. Owen then asked, "Mr Biggs, tell us what you observed upon your arrival at the defendant's home."

"Certainly, we had been informed that a baby was in the house and was not breathing, so my first concern was to get to her and try and make sure she was still alive and could be stabilised before we took her to hospital, so I was not really spending a great deal time looking at my surroundings. However, I did notice that the house was cluttered and dirty. It looked like it had not been cleaned in weeks. I almost fell over some weights that had been carelessly left in the hallway and as I came in I noticed the stairs were covered in objects; baby toys, curtain rails, clothing, all were serious trip hazards."

"I understand that you made your way to the sitting room where the defendant, her partner and the little baby were. What did you see when you entered the room?"

"Well that room was dirty and cluttered as well. There were objects all over the place. I noticed two half full ashtrays and a really strong smell of smoke as I entered the room. I also saw that the female occupant of the room was sipping from a large tumbler of what I assumed was vodka."

"Why did you assume that?"

"There was a half empty bottle of vodka on the table next to her and after her partner had refilled his glass from the bottle the female refilled hers."

"Did either of them speak to you as you entered the room?"

"Yes, the female did. She noticed me looking at the vodka bottle and she said, 'What you fucking looking at? You should be helping my baby.'

I was a bit surprised as I'd only just entered the room."

"What did you do?"

"I could see the baby was a bluish colour and looked stiff. I had no doubt that the baby was already dead and this was confirmed within a few seconds of me examining her. Rigor mortis had set in all her limbs, her torso and her jaw. Hypostasis was also present."

Owen intervened and feigned ignorance with a one word question, "Hypostasis?"

"Sorry, that's where after the heart stops pumping blood around the body, the blood tries to find the lowest point in the body. Due to gravity that is usually the part of the body that is in contact with the ground or object the body ids lying on. It leaves a purplish mottled colour to that part of the body. Nevertheless, I went through the necessary procedures."

"What did the defendant and her partner do?"

"They just carried on drinking from the vodka bottle."

"You had a colleague with you in the ambulance, Geoffrey Gilroy. Did he enter the house?"

"Yes, he came in shortly after me."

"Did he take any part in trying to revive the child?"

"No, there was no point, it was obvious she was dead.

"Did there come a time when you told the defendant and her partner that the baby was dead."

"Yes, it's always a difficult moment but I told them I was sorry, but we had lost her."

"Why did you say 'sorry' and 'we' had lost her?"

"They're just expressions. I was trying to make it easier for the parents. As far as I was concerned the baby was dead before we arrived, probably before the 999 call was made."

"What was the parents' reaction to your telling them, their child was dead?"

"The male seemed to speak for them both. He shouted out, "You're sorry you bastard! If you'd got here sooner, she would've still been alive."

"How did that make you feel!"

"I was hurt, we'd got there as soon as we could and there was nothing we could do."

Owen nodded for the benefit of the jury and paused for a few moments before asking, "Were you still there when the police arrived?"

"Yes, we were."

"What was the parents' reaction to the police?"

"I was surprised. They were both quite aggressive. I think it was the female who called a young male Pakistani constable, a 'Paki cunt'."

Owen had finished his questioning and before he sat down he asked the witness, "Please remain there, my learned friend, Mr Brant may have a few questions for you."

David nodded a thank you to Owen and then looked towards the witness. In reality he had little to ask. Rachel had wanted him to blame the witness for her child's death because they had taken ten minutes to get to the house. He told her he had no intention of attacking the paramedic. The evidence suggested that Annie was dead by the time the 999 call was made and in any event, it would alienate the jury if he attacked a paramedic who had simply been doing his job. Eventually and reluctantly, Rachel had agreed to leave the conduct of the cross examination in David's hands.

"Mr Biggs this was clearly a distressing incident?"

"Yes, it was."

"But sadly, one you come across quite regularly in your work?"

"I've not personally seen many dead babies before, but I have seen many dead people and, sadly, children."

"And no doubt you have come across many grieving relatives and friends?"

"Yes."

"In your experience, you must have noted that grief affects people in many ways?"

"Yes, certainly."

"Some are calm, almost detached?"

"Yes."

"Others react by swearing, throwing things, even reaching for a bottle of spirits and trying to drink their sorrows away?"

"Yes."

"A perfectly decent, honest, upstanding, polite person can suddenly become a drunken ogre due to the effect of grief?"

"Yes."

"Particularly when their child or baby has died?"

"I suppose so."

"I note you made a witness statement in this case two weeks after the incident."

"I believe so."

"Did you rely on any notes that you had previously made?"

"I had an incident report log but it only details times and the procedures carried out."

"Did you note any swearing by either parent in that log?"

"No, that wasn't relevant to the log."

"I am sure we all understand that. Does that mean that the first time you were asked to recall who said what was two weeks after the incident

141

when you made a witness statement to the police?"

"Yes."

"You say that it was the male who said, 'You're sorry you bastard! If you'd got here sooner, she would've still been alive'."

"Yes."

"You also say, that "The male seemed to speak for them both."

"It seemed to me he was."

"How?"

"Pardon?"

"How was he speaking for both? Did my client say anything, or nod agreement?"

"I don't think so, it was just an impression."

"So, he could have been just speaking for himself."

"I suppose so."

"You also told the jury, "I think it was the female who called a young male police constable, a 'Paki cunt'?"

"Yes."

"It follows from your words, 'I think', that you cannot be sure whether it was her or the male who said those words?"

"No, but Caroline told me the Asian officer said it was the female."

David paused for a few seconds, "Caroline?"

Andrew turned to the prosecution benches and looked at the officer in charge of the prosecution case.

David followed his gaze, paused and looked at the jury, "Are you telling us that Detective Sergeant Caroline Leadbetter, the officer in charge of this prosecution case, has discussed the evidence of another witness with you?"

Andrew hesitated before replying, "I wouldn't call it a discussion, she just said it when I told her I could not remember if it was the male or female who said it."

"And is that your evidence, that you cannot remember who said it?"

"Yes."

"So, it may have been the male who uttered those words?

"Yes."

David turned to the judge, "My Lord, I had consented to the officer in the case remaining in court during the witness's evidence as the only part I had thought she played in this case, was in interviewing my client and putting the papers together for submission to the Crown Prosecution Service. It appears from this witness' evidence that she may have played a more significant role than that and I ask that she leave court and not return until she gives her evidence."

Tanner looked towards Owen who stood and said, "I have no objection to that course in the circumstances."

Tanner turned to the officer, "Very well officer, will you leave court please."

A slightly red faced Caroline Leadbetter rose from her seat behind Owen and bowed and left the court.

David waited until the court door was shut before continuing with his questioning.

"Yes, thank you. Now Mr Biggs, I want to ask you about the house. How long were you inside the house for?"

"Probably about thirty minutes."

"You entered through the front door, travelled through the hallway and went into the living room. Did you go elsewhere, for example the baby's nursery?"

"No, I remained in the living room until I left."

"So, you are unable to tell us what state the rest of the house was in?"

"That's right."

"Now you describe the house as 'cluttered and dirty'. Obviously, you are referring to the few parts that you saw?"

"Yes."

"Presumably, your main interest was not on checking the cleanliness of the house, but upon seeing whether you could save the life of the child?"

"Yes."

"There is a difference between 'clutter' and 'dirt'. My client fully accepts that her house was cluttered with her treasured belongings and her partner's junk, but denies the house was dirty. May it be that you saw clutter and assumed dirt?"

"Well I remember seeing the two half full ashtrays in the living room."

"But no ash was on the floor or the settee?"

"Not that I can remember."

"And you could not say when they had started smoking that night. Whether it was after they had discovered their child was unresponsive, for example?"

"No, I can't."

CHAPTER 20

THE POLICE OFFICER

PC Tanvir Sidhu entered the court room and made his way over to the witness box. He had rarely given evidence before in court and then only in a Magistrates' Court. He had never given evidence before a jury in a Crown Court and certainly not in the Old Bailey and he was nervous. He had arrived at court early and gone to the Court's Police Room where he had seen many senior officers who were awaiting their turn to give evidence in the various courts.

He had admitted his nerves to them and been told by one particularly helpful officer, a Detective Sergeant Tony Roberts from what used to be called the 'Flying Squad' and was now named the less attractive, 'SCD7'. He told Tanvir that he should not worry particularly as his evidence did not sound controversial.

"Just remember," he helpfully added. "Judges at the Old Bailey can be a crotchety lot. They like police officers to address them properly and call them 'Sir.' None of this poncey, 'My Lord' or 'Your Lordship' that the pompous barristers use."

There were a few murmurs of agreement from around the room. Tanvir was happy to receive the advice. His own desk sergeant in Croydon who had not seen the inside of a courtroom for years had told him to call the judge, 'Your Lordship' or 'My Lord.' It helped to meet people that went to the Old Bailey regularly so he did not make any mistakes which would demonstrate his inexperience.

Once he was sworn he gave his name and then turned to HHJ Tanner and added, "Sir," with a beaming smile. The judge looked at him with contempt and Tanvir assumed that this was one of those crotchety judges that Tony had warned him about.

Owen saw the glance and intervened quickly, "Now officer, we know and it is not disputed by the defence, that you visited the address after the paramedics had just arrived. Tell His Lordship and the jury, in your own words, what you saw when you arrived?"

Tanvir had noticed Owen's emphasis on the words, 'His Lordship', this was clearly one of those pompous barristers that Tony had also told him about. He turned away from Owen and addressed the judge, "May I refer to my notes, sir, that were made at the time?"

Tanner turned red, stopped typing and slammed his right fist down on the bench. "Why is it that every time a young police officer gives evidence in this court, he fails to address the judge properly. Do they not train young officers anymore? Officer, the proper mode of address to a judge of the

Central Criminal Court, is 'My Lord' or 'Your Lordship.' Do you think that you might be able to get that right in the future?"

Tanvir was stunned. He was about to say that he had been told to address the judge in this way when he realised he had been set up by the officers in the police room. "Bastards" he muttered under his breath.

Tanner looked at him, "What did you say?"

Tanvir remembered where he was, "Nothing, sir." He noticed Tanner getting redder and quickly added, "Sorry, My Lord."

Owen again tried to assist, "Officer, you were asking His Lordship whether you could rely upon your notes that you made about this incident. When were those notes made?"

"Shortly after I arrived back at the police station, within an hour of the incident itself."

"Were matters still fresh in your mind?"

"Yes sir." Tanvir paused before turning to the judge, "My Lord."

Tanner glared at him, "You address counsel as 'sir'.

"Yes sir, My Lord."

Owen again intervened, "Did you accurately record what occurred in your notes?"

"Yes, sir."

Owen turned to the judge, "May the officer refer to his notes My Lord?"

Tanner nodded but snarled at the officer, "You may refer to your notes officer, but do not read them out. They are there to assist your recollection, not to replace it."

Tanvir nodded and started to read out his notes, "At approximately 10:10pm I received a call on my police radio to attend 12 Addiscombe Drive, Croydon where it was reported that a young child may have died. I immediately drove to the address arriving at about 10:20pm. I ..."

Tanner slammed his fist down onto the bench once more, "Are you trying to antagonise me officer?"

"No sir, My Lord."

"Then why when I tell you not to read your notes out, do you do just that?"

"Sorry, My Lord."

Owen tried again with an implied criticism of the judge, "I don't believe that any of this is disputed by the defence, and I have been told that I can lead your initial evidence officer, but we will take it slowly. Please just answer my questions officer?"

"You arrived at the Defendant's house at about 10:20pm?"

"Yes sir."

"What did you notice when you entered the house?"

Tanvir looked at his notes but looked away from them before answering, "I noted that the house was very cluttered and dirty and smelt strongly of cigarette smoke. I had to climb over some weights in the hall and push other items out of the way so I could gain access to the living room."

"When you entered the living room what did you see?"

"I saw two paramedics trying to resuscitate a baby. One of the paramedics then said words to the effect that the baby was dead and I remembered both parents being abusive towards him."

"What did you do?"

"I tried to calm the situation down by telling the parents that we were all there to try and help them."

"Did that calm the situation down?"

"Not at first, I recall that the female defendant called me a 'Paki cunt'."

"How did that make you feel?"

David was on his feet immediately, "I did not object when my learned friend asked the paramedic a similar question but I do object to my learned friend continuing to ask professional witnesses how they felt. It can have no relevance to the any issue the jury has to determine."

Tanner nodded in agreement, "I agree, Mr Jenkins, please cease from asking that question again, it has no relevance whatsoever to any issue in this case. Officer, please do not answer that question."

Tanvir nodded a quick response, "Yes, My Lord."

David sat down and passed a quick smile to Sara. Normally Tanner would not have supported the objection just saying something like, "let's get on." However, because he was still smarting from Owen's implied criticism, he had supported the objection.

Owen nodded, "Of course My Lord. Officer, did you say anything in response?"

"Yes sir, I told her there was no reason to use offensive and racially abusive language. We were all there to help."

"Did they calm down?"

"How long did you stay at the address?"

"About another 20 minutes. I waited until the paramedics had removed their equipment and left the property with the dead baby and the defendant in their ambulance."

"Did you have any further dealings with the case?"

"No, sir."

Owen told his to stay there and sat down as David rose to question him. David had seen how the jury had reacted to the judge's dealings with the officer and could see that they clearly had some sympathy for him. He was not going to antagonise them by attacking the officer in any way.

"Officer, this was a traumatic incident for everyone involved, including yourself?"

"Yes, sir."

"Obviously, you did not make a note at the time when you were in the house, you made your notes about an hour later?"

"Yes sir, but the matters were still fresh in my mind."

"Officer, you will be aware that many officers have cameras attached to their bodies these days so that we can have an accurate record of what is said in circumstances such as this?"

"Yes sir, but I did not have a bodycam with me that night."

"So, we have to rely upon your recollection which clearly is not as good as a bodycam."

"I did my best sir and I believe that I have accurately recorded what happened."

"Officer, the evidence you gave earlier was that you, 'saw two paramedics trying to resuscitate a baby. One of the paramedics then said words to the effect that the baby was dead and I remembered both parents being abusive towards him'. You did not record any words used by either parent?"

"No sir."

"Can you remember what was said now?"

"Not after this length of time sir."

"What I suggest happened is that you arrived as one of the paramedics was saying that the baby was dead and it was the father who shouted abuse at him?"

"I believe it was both of them."

"But you cannot tell us what was said?"

"No, sir."

"I also suggest that you were racially abused as you have told us, but it was the male who shouted those words, not the female?"

"No, I am sure it was the female. I'm not lying sir."

"I am not suggesting you are lying but that in this very trying and difficult situation you have made a mistake?"

"No sir, it was the female who racially abused me."

"Let me ask you about the state of the house. When you arrived, you were concerned that there may be a dead or dying infant in the house?"

"Yes sir."

"You were not concerned about whether the house was clean or not?"

"No, sir."

"It is accepted that the house was cluttered and smelt strongly of cigarette smoke, but I suggest it was not dirty. You are only assuming this because of the smoke and clutter?"

"No sir, it looked dirty to me."

"What was dirty?"

"I can't be specific, it was just an impression."

"So, you cannot give us any example of seeing any dirt?"

"No, sir."

CHAPTER 21

THE HEALTH VISITOR

After the officer left court, the judge called a halt to the proceedings for lunch. David and Sara made their way to the Old Bailey advocate's canteen to see what was on offer. He settled for an omelette and Sara for a salad sandwich and both retired to the advocates' benches to eat them.

After consuming some of his surprisingly tasty omelette, he was the first to speak, "How do you think the case is going?"

Sara put her half-chewed sandwich down on her plate before responding, "Well you have made some inroads into the witnesses but it was a good opening speech yesterday by the prosecutor, coupled with that horrible 999 call by our client. I can see certain members of the jury are already looking at her with ill-disguised contempt."

"Oh, I don't think there is any disguise in their contempt at all. They loathe her, as would most people. We have little chance of changing their opinion on our client. We'll have to appeal to their sense of fairness and work on reasonable doubt. After all, the Crown may still have some difficulty proving deliberate or neglectful starvation in this case."

Sara nodded but added, "That might change this afternoon when the health worker gives evidence!"

At 2:05pm Melissa Head walked into court and entered the witness box. She was in her late thirties and was wearing a dark suit. She took the oath and gave her name to the court.

Owen beamed at her and asked her to make sure she spoke up so all the members of the jury could hear her. He then asked, "I understand that you are a 'health visitor', how long have you been involved in that line of work?"

Owen was momentarily stunned by the answer, "I'm not a health visitor."

"I'm sorry I thought that was your job title."

"Actually, my title was, 'Safeguarding Nurse for Children', but I resigned after this case. I didn't want to be responsible for the health of anyone else's young children, after young Annie died."

"I see. Well can you tell us, how long you were a 'health visitor' or 'Safeguarding Nurse for Children', before you resigned?"

"I was in the post for six years. Before that I was paediatric nurse for ten years."

"So, you had spent a considerable amount of your career dealing with children?"

"Yes."

"What age group?"

"As a nurse, from babies to early teens, as a health visitor, from babies to five year olds."

"I believe you were assigned to Annie Harwood when she was born?"

"Yes, I became the health visitor for Annie."

Owen could not resist asking, "You mean a Safeguarding Nurse for Annie?"

She frowned at him as she replied, "Yes."

"What was your role?"

"My role was to assist families to raise their children from birth to five years of age."

"What would this involve?"

"This would involve making home visits as well as having regular group sessions at various locations around Croydon, to discuss families with other health professionals."

"Did you keep notes of your visits and these meetings?"

"Yes, the NHS have a computer system that I have been trained on which is called `System One'. The system records patients' details and allows health visitors and others to input directly onto the patient records, any visits, correspondence or interactions they have with them.

"When do you make these records?"

"As soon as possible after making an interaction, or receiving correspondence or having a meeting."

"Can you tell us about the visits you made to see Annie? I suspect there will be no objection in the circumstances to you relying on the notes you made on System One."

David nodded in agreement and Melissa opened a thin blue file that she had in front of her.

"I first contacted the mother on 30th October when Annie was still in the hospital. I was unaware of her discharge date and I wanted to make an appointment to see her as soon as possible after she went home."

"Where was her mother, the defendant at that time?"

"She was at home. I've recorded the time as 09:50am. She told me she had just got up, she was feeling a little run down and would not be going to see Annie until later in the day."

"What did you arrange with her?"

"I asked her to contact me the moment Annie came home so we could arrange the first home visit. She agreed to do so."

"Did she contact you when Annie came home?"

"No. I phoned her two weeks later on Friday the 13th November to see if Annie was home yet and she told me Annie had been home for seven days!"

"So, what did you do?"

"I arranged to see her the following week on Monday 16th November at 10am."

"Did you see her on 16th November 2015?"

"Yes and no. I attended the home for my pre-arranged visit to see Annie but on my arrival her mother was on her way out. She told me that she was going to visit her own mother who was ill. She had Annie with her in a pushchair. The mother said that Annie was fine. I did see her quickly but had no opportunity to check her or weigh her."

"Did anything cause you any concern?"

"I thought that she was not rapped up enough for the cold weather and I suggested that the mother put a jacket on her and cover her with a blanket."

"Did the mother agree to do so?"

"She said she would but she was in a hurry. She did say her mother had bought some clothes for Annie and she would put those on her when she got to her address. She then left."

"Did you arrange to meet her again?"

"Yes, I told her I would normally see her fortnightly but because I could not see her this time, I would come back the following week on 23rd November."

"Did you see her on that day?"

"I did, I arrived at 10:05am. Both the mother and father were present at the home. It looked like they had just got up as he was wearing pyjamas and a dressing gown and she was in a nightie. She was feeding Annie when I arrived. She told me that was Annie's first feed of the day. I was a little surprised as I would have expected her to be fed before that time."

Owen looked at some notes that he had before continuing, "Did you notice anything about the state of the house?"

"I did. The house was terribly cluttered. The hallway seemed to be used as a storage area and the living room was full of items."

"What type of items?"

"Papers, bottles, gym equipment, ashtrays."

"Did you give any advice to the mother and father?"

"I did notice a smell of smoke in the living room. I did advise the parents not to smoke in the presence of Annie. I also advised that they might want to make more space for her in the living room, so that she could be changed and would have a place to sleep during the day."

"How did they react to this advice?"

"I recall that the father glared at me and said nothing. The mother told me that they did not smoke around Annie and if they wanted to smoke they would go outside or smoke in the kitchen."

"But you noticed ashtrays in the room?"

"I did and I mentioned that fact to them. The mother told me they were from the previous night when Annie was upstairs in her room."

"Did you ever see Annie's room?"

"No, I was never invited upstairs. The only rooms I saw were the hallway and the living room."

"You also measured Annie and weighed her. What was her weight on this occasion?"

"Her weight was 3.6 kgs."

Owen directed her and the jury's attention to the jury bundle and the World Health Chart that had been completed by the prosecution expert.

"We can see that would put her just about on or slightly above the 9th centile."

"Yes."

"Did you arrange to see Annie again?"

"I did, I arranged to come back at the same time in two weeks' time on 7th December."

"Did you visit on that day?"

"I did."

"Did you see Annie?"

"No, when I arrived, no one answered the door. I tried a number of times because I saw the bedroom curtains of the room above move and I was sure I saw the father's face look out for a moment."

"What did you do?"

"I had other appointments which I went to."

"Did the mother or father contact you about this abortive visit?"

Melissa looked down at her notes, "I have a record that at just after 11am the mother contacted me by phone. She said her mother had been taken ill again and she had to visit her urgently. She had taken Annie with her. She was apologetic that she had not contacted me earlier. I did ask her about her partner saying I had seen him in the house and I was surprised that he had not opened the door to me to tell me this. She told me he was ill as well and had to stay in bed."

"Did you arrange another visit?"

"I did. I could not see her again that week because I had many other visits and meetings booked. I did arrange to see her on 14th December at 11am."

"Did that visit go ahead?"

"It did. I saw the mother and Annie. The father was not present."

"Did you examine Annie?"

"I did, she appeared to be generally well though she had a runny nose. I advised that she be kept rapped up and given Calpol if necessary and if her symptoms worsened, to take her to the GP's surgery or the Accident and Emergency department of the local hospital. I also weighed her and found that she now weighed 3.9 kgs."

"As we can see from the chart in the jury bundle, this means she had fallen from the 9th to the 2nd centile. Did this concern you?"

"Not overly, children do move through the centile points. I assumed that she was adjusting to life in the home environment away from the hospital."

"Nevertheless, did you ask any questions about her feeding Annie?"

"I did and she reported that she fed Annie every 2-3 hours and that she would wake her up for feeds if necessary."

"When was the next visit?"

"The next visit should have been two weeks later on 28th December, but because of the Christmas and New Year break, I did not see her again until 4th January 2016."

"Did you weigh her on that occasion?"

"I did and she weighed 4.2kgs."

"That means she had fallen below the 2nd centile, did that not cause you concern?"

"I was a little concerned about her weight but generally she looked heathy. I asked the mother again about feeding and she said that Annie's cold had been worse over Christmas and she had not wanted to eat much and had thrown up after some meals. I told her to take Annie to the doctors if this continued but she said Annie was better now and was feeding properly."

"When was the next visit?"

"I saw her next on 18th January 2016 when she weighed 4.3kgs."

"Did that concern you?"

"Not at the time, she still seemed generally heathy and she was still putting on weight."

"You saw her for the last time on 1st February 2016 when we can see that she weighed 4.4kgs. Did that weight concern you?"

"Again, Annie seemed generally healthy and she was putting on weight. I was concerned that she was not putting on enough weight, so I made a note to fully review the situation on my next visit."

"Now that should have been two weeks later on 15th February, but there was no visit that week. Why was that?"

"I was on annual leave that week, my husband had booked a holiday in Spain for our tenth wedding anniversary, so I rearranged the visit for the week following, the 22nd February."

"Of course, we know that Annie died on 19th February, so that visit never took place."

Melissa looked down at her feet, "No it did not. I wish I had never gone on holiday and seen her on 15th February. I might have been able to save her."

Owen nodded and looked at the jury before continuing, "So the last time you weighed her was on 1st February 2016 when she weighed 4.4kgs. And we know that at the time of her death she weighed just 4.35kgs which means that she lost …"

David rose to his feet, "I do object to that, we know no such thing."

The judge responded as quickly picking up the jury bundle that was in front of him, "I thought the timeline was agreed Mr Brant. It clearly states

166

that the child weighed 4.35kgs at the time of her death!"

"In fact it does not, My Lord, the timeline only provides the weight at the time of the post-mortem. The child's body was not weighed at the time of her death. It was only weighed a week later at the time of the post mortem after the body had been refrigerated. We will produce expert opinion that there would be some loss of weight in that time and consequently the child would have undoubtedly weighed more than 4.35kgs at the time of her death and maybe significantly more. Unfortunately, we are unable to estimate the exact weight."

The judge looked to Owen for assistance. Owen paused before responding "Very well, I'll withdraw the question for now and await this evidence with interest."

He then turned to a Melissa, "Thank you, that concludes my questioning, will you wait there, there will be some questions from my learned friend."

David noticed the jury observing him when he stood to cross-examine. They were probably wondering what he was going to ask. He had the same dilemma. He had prepared a certain line of cross examination that was critical of the health visitor, but he could see the jury were showing some sympathy for the witness. After all she had given up her job and career because of Annie's death and no doubt had blamed herself for missing signs. He knew he would need to take a very subtle approach.

CHAPTER 22

CHALLENGING THE ACCOUNT

David gave Melissa one of his best beaming smiles and was met with a stony frown. He wondered whether he should try a stony expression in future, maybe she would smile?

"Ms Head, I am going to ask you questions on behalf of Rachel Wilson, the mother of Annie."

He noticed how the witness bristled a little at the mention of Rachel's name but he ignored her reaction and carried on.

"You have told us about your considerable experience with children of all ages from babies to early teens."

"Yes."

"In your sixteen years of experience you must have come across many children and indeed many parents?"

"Yes."

"I suspect that no two were alike?"

"I wouldn't say that, there are considerable similarities between families."

"Yes, but each one has its own particular problems or issues. A premature birth, a child born with birth defects, stressed parents, loving parents, parents who do not seem to care?"

She nodded and replied, "You do meet all types as a nurse and safeguarding nurse."

"But as you say, there are similarities?"

"Yes."

"Parents react in different ways to children, don't they?"

"I don't know what you mean."

"Well it's well known that some mothers can be very happy when a child is born, others can suffer from depression, post-natal depression."

"Yes, I have come across both many times."

"There is also probably a difference between the parents of a first child and parents who have had many children before?"

"Yes, most parents who have had children before know what to expect. New parents tend not to have much idea, unless they have been around big families with younger siblings."

"Rachel Wilson was a new parent with no previous experience of having children?"

"I believe so."

"Well I assume it's in your file that you have in front of you."

She screwed her eyes up at him and gave him a dismissive look, "Yes, it is."

"Thank you. You are also aware from that file that she had left her parent's home at the young age of sixteen?"

"Yes."

"We don't need to go into details but she alleged that her step father had been sexually attentive towards her?"

"Yes."

"He had raped her?"

Owen rose quickly, "My learned friend did say he would not go into details, I cannot see what relevance these questions have!"

David quickly responded, "They are highly relevant to her life experiences and knowledge of parenting that she received from her own parents."

The judge was not impressed, "Move on Mr Brant."

David nodded, "Of course, My Lord."

He had made the point to the jury and hopefully obtained some small degree of sympathy for his

171

client, so he was happy to move on to his next question and not argue the point.

"Ms Head, were you aware that Rachel Wilson had an abusive partner?"

"I was aware that there were allegations of physical abuse."

"He beat her regularly and she even had to visit hospital on a number of occasions?"

"I believe so."

"That was the environment that she was taking Annie into when she left hospital?"

"Yes."

"When you first contacted her on 30th October 2015, Annie was still in hospital?"

"Yes."

"She did not know when Annie was going to be discharged at that stage?"

"I don't believe she did."

"You asked her to contact you when she took Annie home?"

"Yes."

"Of course though, there are many things going through any mother's mind when taking a baby home, but especially a mother taking a pre-term baby home?"

"Obviously."

"Thank you, and no doubt you can confirm, from your experience, that mothers don't immediately contact the Health visitor the minute they arrive home? I suspect that you have had to initiate the calls on many occasions?"

"I did, probably on 90% of the occasions!"

"So, the fact that Ms Wilson did not immediately contact you on her arrival home was the norm in your experience?"

"Yes."

"Now a first visit was arranged for 16th November 2015 at 10am but unfortunately was not effective. You have told us she was leaving home at the time you arrived?"

"Yes, she said she had to visit her mother."

"I wanted to ask you about that. Firstly, you have recorded the time of the visit as 10:05am, might it have been a little later than that at, 10:15am and you have recorded the time wrongly?"

She adopted a stern expression, "No, I always record my times accurately!"

"I'm going to suggest that you've made a mistake about that."

"No, I did not."

"This was a very quick meeting on the pavement outside her house lasting no more than a few seconds?"

"Yes."

"It would be easy to make a minor mistake about the time of a meeting that effectively did not take place?"

"I do not believe I made a mistake."

"I suggest that you made another mistake as well. She did not say she was visiting her mother. She told you she was visiting Bob's mother."

"I have it in my notes that she said she was visiting her mother."

"I presume you have no recollection now and are relying entirely on your notes?"

"Yes."

"Do you accept that you may have made a mistake?"

"I don't believe so, I always tried to be accurate in my notes."

"I have no doubt about it, but we all make mistakes."

"I don't believe that I did."

"She told you on one visit that she had had no contact with her mother since she left her mother's home aged 16?"

Melissa quickly looked down at her notes. After a few seconds, she found the entry she was looking for.

"Yes, she did, but it was not on this occasion. That was on the visit on 14th December.

"Did you point out the apparent inconsistency with, what you thought, she had said a month earlier?"

"No, I did not."

"Very well, in any event you did see her on 23rd November 2015?"

"Yes."

"You have told us that the house was cluttered."

"Yes, it was."

"Did you notice that many of the items looked like they may have been associated with the male occupant, items such as gym equipment, bottles of beer, sports magazines, for example?"

"I did not associate them with either a male or a female." She paused for a few seconds before she added with a slight smile, "After all I use gym equipment and I have read sports magazines and I have drunk the odd bottle of beer!"

175

David beamed at her, tempted to say 'touché', but he decided to ignore the implied rebuke.

"The house was cluttered, but it was clean, wasn't it?"

"I don't think a cluttered house can ever be described as clean!"

David could see how this was going. She clearly did not like his client and was not going to be helpful. He picked up his own copy of the System One notes.

"Well shall we try and rely on your notes, in which you always strive to record matters accurately! Can you look at the notes for the 23rd November?"

She turned to the necessary page as did members of the jury.

"You have recorded there, 'The house was cluttered but generally was clean save for the ashtrays in the living room which had not been emptied.' That was recorded by you?"

"She looked at the note and frowned, "Yes it was."

"Indeed, on every one of your visits, where you gained access to the house, you recorded that the house was clean?"

He gave her time to look through the notes which also gave time for the jury to take the point on board.

Eventually, she responded with, "Yes, I did record that."

"Now you have told us you noticed a smell of smoke in the living room on 23rd November and noticed the ashtrays and you gave advice that they should not smoke around Annie?"

"I did."

"As you have told us, the father frowned at you when you gave this advice, it was the mother who explained that they did not smoke around Annie."

"Yes."

"You weighed Annie on this occasion and as you have told us she weighed 3.6 kgs. That meant she was on the 9th centile and certainly did not give you any cause for concern?"

"No, it did not."

"As you have said, the visit arranged for 7th December did not proceed. According to your notes, Rachel Wilson did contact you about this and told you her mother had been taken ill. Again, I suggest that you made a mistake in your notes and she told you Bob's mother had been taken ill and she had to visit her?"

"No, I've recorded that she said her mother."

"The next visit on 14th December did go ahead?"

"Yes."

"On this occasion, Rachel Wilson was alone with Annie. The father was not with her. Did Rachel Wilson appear more relaxed on this visit, more open in her answers to you?"

"I don't know if I would say 'more open' but she did appear to be more relaxed and she did say a lot more than she had on my previous visit."

"Yes, because on this visit she told you about her step father raping her …"

Owen now frowned at David, who ignored him and continued, "… and she told you how she had not seen her mother since she was sixteen and how her partner Bob hit her and was abusive towards her?"

"She did tell me all those things."

"She was hardly likely to have told you that her partner hit her in front of him, so I suggest she was more open with you?"

"I suppose so."

"Again, you weighed Annie on this occasion and she weighed 3.9kgs. I don't believe we have been told this, but am I right in my understanding that when babies are weighed, all their clothes including their nappies are taken off?"

"Yes."

"So, on each occasion you had an opportunity of fully examining Annie's torso as well as her head?"

"Yes."

"You have told us that you were not concerned about her weighing 3.9kgs, as you put it, you thought she was, 'Adjusting to life in the home environment.'"

"Yes."

"You saw her again on 4th January 2016, on 18th January 2016 and 1st February 2016?"

"Yes."

"On each occasion you weighed her?"

"Yes."

"Again, she would have been naked and you would have had an opportunity of examining her?"

"Yes."

"On each occasion your opinion was that Annie was generally healthy and putting on weight, albeit less than was ideal."

"Yes."

"If you had seen any signs that suggested Annie was malnourished or being starved, you would have taken steps to remedy that situation, which could have included taking Annie away from her parents and placing her into care."

"Yes."

"The fact that you did not, shows that on your visits, you did not consider that Annie was being mal nourished or starved, but was being looked after adequately, otherwise you would have intervened?"

"Well I ..."

David interrupted her, "If you had seen any signs of her being starved or malnourished, you would have intervened?"

Melissa finally and reluctantly answered, "Yes."

"It follows that you saw no such signs and your opinion at the time was that she was being cared for adequately?"

With a look of obvious reluctance, she finally answered, "Yes."

CHAPTER 23

THE HOSPITAL DOCTOR

Melissa Head had been the last witness called on Tuesday and the rest of the afternoon was taken up with the junior for the prosecution reading out the statements of witnesses that the defence did not require to attend court. David had not gone to the hospital to see Wendy and Rose because Wednesday had been set aside for the prosecution to call important medical evidence and that meant that he had a lot of preparation that evening.

He had received an update about Rose's condition. She was doing well although it was too early to tell whether she was putting on more weight as a result of taking breast milk mixed with Infatrini.

At 10:15am on Wednesday morning, Dr Malik Ahmad entered the court room and made his way to the witness box. Malik had been born in Luton to a relatively poor Pakistani family who ran a local grocers shop. Malik had shown himself to be very intelligent at school and the family had spent as much as they could on his education. They had not encouraged him to enter the family business, his younger brother had that role thrust upon him as Malik had gone to Imperial college in

London to train as a doctor. The course had taken six years followed by postings in a number of hospitals around the south east of England until he had finally been offered a job as a Registrar in St Barnabas hospital in Croydon in the Neonatal department. He had loved the work; researching the latest techniques to save preterm babies, always a developing area, and his presence had helped the hospital achieve the status of one of the best neonatal hospitals in London. All his colleagues at the hospital, including the senior consultants in his department, recognised his abilities and he was also renowned for his confident, but caring air, when he dealt with parents and all the difficulties they faced.

The work was difficult at the hospital, particularly when it became clear that a preterm baby was not going to make it and he had to tell the family and sit with them as a baby was detached from life support, but overall he enjoyed the experience of putting everything he had into trying to save a new born life and giving a preterm baby every chance to have a normal life.

He now looked at; the judge frowning at him as he walked into court, the array of barristers observing him suspiciously and the blank faces of what appeared to be an unfriendly jury and he wished he had gone into his family's grocery business and his brother had become the doctor in the family.

He read through his witness statement and the hospital notes the previous night and could not see any hint that he had failed baby Annie in any way. However, this was a court of law and he had heard horror stories of doctors being ripped to pieces in cross examination and a confident doctor who entered the court believing he had done nothing wrong, frequently would leave the court with accusations ringing in his ears and full of self-doubt.

He nervously took the oath and gave his name to the court before staring blankly at Owen.

Owen could see that the doctor was nervous. He was acutely aware that a jury could mistake nervousness for incompetence and decided he needed to reassure the witness.

"Dr Ahmad, thank you so much for coming today. I am sure we all know how busy doctors are in NHS hospitals and that you would rather be back saving the lives of young preterm babies than being here. I am sure we will all limit our questioning to the essentials so that you can return to your important work as soon as possible."

It seemed to have the desired effect as Malik visibly seemed to gain an air of confidence in the witness box.

David looked at Owen and nodded in apparent agreement. Owen's comments were wholly inadmissible. He had effectively given a character reference for his own witness and suggested that lengthy questioning was inappropriate and might put a baby's life at risk. Of course though, David could not object as the jury no doubt agreed with every word!

Owen took the jury bundle and asked Malik to turn to the World Health Organisation pink chart, the WHO chart, listing Annie's weight.

"Dr Ahmad, it is not disputed by any party in this court that Annie was born on 12th August 2015 and was about ten weeks preterm?"

Malik checked his notes before answering, "Yes, that's right."

"I believe that you were involved in her care from the very beginning?"

"Yes, I was the doctor on duty the night she was born and I was called to the delivery room when the midwife believed that she was ready to arrive."

"Was she able to breath on her own when you arrived?"

"Although she was of an age where she should have been able to breath on her own, probably with the aid of oxygen, it was obvious that she could not and I took the decision to intubate her, that is, place a breathing tube directly into her lungs. Once that was done and she was breathing, I moved her immediately to ICU."

"How long was she intubated?"

"For a week, then the tube was removed and she was placed on CPAP."

"CPAP?"

"Yes, it stands for 'continuous positive airway pressure'. It's where a breathing mask is attached to a baby's face tightly over the nose and mouth, to try and make a seal and then mild air pressure is used to keep the airways open."

"How long was she on CPAP for?"

Another week and then the mask was removed and nasal cannulas were fitted so that she could breathe normally, but with some assistance from a small amount of oxygen."

"Would these procedures have any effect on her long-term health?"

"Her lungs might be weaker than other children but generally she should have been able to lead a normal life."

"I want to turn to her weight. She was regularly weighed in hospital?"

"Yes, it is standard procedure to ensure that she is gaining weight and keeping roughly to one of the centiles you see on the WHO chart you have shown me."

"Let us look at the WHO chart together."

Everyone turned to the necessary page in the jury bundle as Owen continued, "We see from the chart that when Annie was born she was of normal weight for her preterm age, 1.3kgs, which placed her somewhere between the 50th and 75th centiles?"

"Yes, though we don't refer to 'normal' weight. Each baby is different."

"I stand corrected. In any event, we see that she lost weight after birth. I understand that is 'normal' for all babies?"

Dr Ahmad smiled in response, "Yes, that is normal."

"We can see from the chart that she did put on weight rising to 1.5kgs but she also dropped a centile so that she was just above the 25th centile after two weeks. Was that worrying in any way?"

"No, these things happen in hospital as the baby finds her own growth pattern."

"Now she stayed above the 25th centile until week 36 when she dropped a centile point again and was now 2.2kgs. Was that a concern at the time?"

"We were concerned at the time but more because we had noticed bleeding from her bowels. We assumed that this was as a result of 'NEC', necrotising enterocolitis, a potentially serious bowel condition that affects some premature babies.

Her mother had tried to express breast milk in the hospital, but could not produce enough, so we had put Annie on formula milk. The formula is a standard one based on cow's milk. We presumed that Annie was cow's milk intolerant so we changed the formula to a formula called Pepsi junior and the condition cleared. Thereafter she put on weight at a steady rate and stayed above the 9th centile until she was discharged from hospital care after 12 weeks, weighing 3.2 kgs."

"Doctor whilst you were caring for her, did you carry out any tests to see if she was suffering from chronic infection or malabsorption, that is a condition that may have prevented her from gaining weight at a consistent rate?"

"No, we did not. Clinically there was no reason to do so. There was no evidence of chronic infection and no sign of malabsorption. That could have been an explanation for her loss of expected weight gain at week 36 but we believed it was cow's milk intolerance and when we changed her formula, she continued to thrive."

"So, you saw no signs of her suffering from malabsorption or chronic infection?"

"No, we did not."

Owen thanked him and sat down as David stood to question him.

"Dr Ahmad, I too do not want to take up too much of your valuable time but I have a small number of questions that I wish to ask you on behalf of my client, the mother of Annie."

"Of course." Malik was feeling very confident now, this had been easy so far.

David turned to the WHO chart, "As we see, even in hospital over a period of twelve weeks, this baby fell through two centile points from between the 50th and 75th centiles through the 25th and 50th centiles, down to a level between the 9th and 25th centiles?"

"Yes, that's correct."

"Now we know that she was found to be, 'bleeding from her bowels' in hospital and you believed that this was due to the condition NEC brought about by cow's milk intolerance?"

"Yes."

"Just assist me please, when you say 'bleeding from her bowels' what you mean is that blood was seen in her stools?"

"Yes."

"You decided to put her on Pepti junior milk?"

"Yes."

"As she had not gained weight at the expected rate, it meant she was not obtaining sufficient calories that her body needed?"

"Yes."

"Why not put her on a substitute milk that contained more calories, such as Infatrini?"

Although the court was cold, Malik felt beads of sweat appear on his forehead.

"We considered that Pepsi junior was sufficient."

"Did you ever consider using Infatrini?"

"No."

"Is there any reason why it couldn't have been used in this case?"

"Not that I can think off. It is a prescription only milk but that is the only difference to ordinary milk formula"

"Of course, obtaining a prescription is not a problem in a hospital, you could have written one.

"Yes, I could if I had thought it necessary."

"But you never considered prescribing Infatrini?"

"No."

"It provides about 50% more calories than Pepti junior, doesn't it?"

"I believe so."

"Infatrini is advertised as being suitable for babies who suffer from a range of conditions."

David turned to his notes and picked out a piece of paper, 'Faltering growth, gastrointestinal problems, malnutrition, Undernutrition'. It even states that it is suitable in cases of malabsorption. I can show you the paper if you want?"

"No, I accept it can be used in those cases."

"Yet you never thought about using it in this case?"

"No."

"It is also more convenient for mothers to use, isn't it?"

"I'm sorry, I don't know what you mean."

"Well it's in liquid form so a mother does not have to carefully measure out powder and boil kettles."

"Yes, I am aware it is in liquid form but it would still have to be placed in warm water to heat it."

Are there any side effects of Infatrini?"

"None, that I'm aware of."

"So, there was no reason why it couldn't have been prescribed in this case?"

"No."

David put his notes aside, "Very well, could the fall in centile points have been as a result of something other than cow's milk intolerance, for example, an underlying condition meaning that she did not absorb nutrients as she was expected to?"

"I don't believe so, as I've said her initial weight loss is expected in babies and her subsequent weight loss, we believed, was due to cow's milk intolerance."

"Yes doctor, I appreciate that is what you believed, but could her fall through the centiles have another cause, such as failure to properly absorb nutrients, in other words, malabsorption?"

"Well, I suppose it could, but I don't believe it did."

"In any event, you last cared for her when she was 12 weeks old. After that time, she could have suffered from chronic infection or malabsorption and you would not have known about it?"

"Well of course, anything could have happened after she left our care."

"And indeed, an underlying condition that had not been diagnosed at the hospital, could have worsened?"

"Well yes, but we do not believe we misdiagnosed any conditions."

"Yes, but we all know that hospitals do miss underlying conditions, maybe because they are not serious at the time or are not displaying the symptoms that they later do?"

"Sadly, that does happen."

"Can you help us, were there any other conditions that existed in Annie that might have led to bleeding in the bowels?"

Malik quickly looked at his notes, beginning to get slightly worried as to where this was leading, "I don't believe so."

"I take it you have never been served with a copy of the post mortem report in this case?"

"No, that wouldn't normally happen, unless there was some criticism of her care at the hospital."

"Please understand me doctor, there is no criticism of you or the other medical staff at the hospital. I am suggesting that an underlying condition may have been missed because the symptoms were not sufficiently acute to have been diagnosed at the time."

"I see."

"Now, I just want to quote from one part of the pathologist's report. He will be giving evidence about this later today. My lord will find the report at page 576 of the exhibits, the jury, as is normal, do not have a copy of the report."

Tanner turned to the page without a word of acknowledgment.

David continued, "At paragraph 34 of the report it reads, 'The small and large intestines showed no abnormality other than a Meckel's diverticulum, measuring 4 cm on the antimesenteric border of the ileum.'

Can you assist us as to what that is?"

Malik noticed the sweat running down his right cheek and he raised his hand to wipe it as he answered the question, "Yes, a Meckel's diverticulum is an abnormal sac or pouch, a bulge in the small intestine present at birth and is therefore a congenital health issue. The ileum is the final section of the small intestine. The mesenteric side of the ileum is where the blood and nerves come from and exit and the antimesenteric border is the opposite side, furthest away from the blood and nerves."

David nodded, "Thank you doctor, would I be right in thinking that a Meckel's diverticulum can cause bleeding in a baby's stools?"

He paused and thought for a few seconds, "Yes it can."

"And so, this could have been the cause of problems in week 36, rather than NEC, or cow's milk intolerance?"

"It could have been."

"And of course, the symptoms could have worsened after Annie left the hospital?"

"That is possible, though generally a Meckel's diverticulum does not cause any problem."

"But it can?"

David picked up the notes he had made, "It can cause; blockage of the intestines, bleeding into the intestines resulting in bloody stools, inflammation of the intestines, pain or discomfort ranging from mild to severe, nausea and vomiting, anaemia and in extreme cases it can be life threatening?"

"Yes, in extreme cases but I saw no sign of the conditions you refer to."

"Apart from the bloody stools?"

Malik hesitated before answering, "Yes, we did see those, but that condition stopped when we changed her milk."

"But as you have already told us, her condition could have clearly worsened once she left hospital?"

"Of course."

CHAPTER 24

DISTURBING NEWS

The rest of the morning was taken up with two minor witnesses who gave evidence. David allowed Sara to cross examine them whilst he looked at his notes for the cross examination of the pathologist who was due in the afternoon.

As they finished early David suggested to Sara that they avoid the canteen food and go out for a sandwich. He took her to one of his favourite lunch time wine bars, which was hidden down a side street a few hundred yards from the Old Bailey and which was never discovered by witnesses or jurors.

He ordered a steak sandwich and a small glass of Malbec. Sara ordered a more calorie conscious tuna sandwich and a sparkling water.

After their food and drink had been delivered and almost finished Sara asked a question about his cross examination that had been nagging her.

"David, I know you thoroughly prepare your cross examination, almost writing out all your intended questions. You sent me a final version of what you intended to ask the doctor yesterday. As you know I went through it and suggested a few possible additions. However, nowhere did you

195

include any questions about Infatrini. Indeed, I'll be honest, I've never heard of Infatrini until you mentioned it. Why did you ask the doctor about it?"

David finished the last bite of his sandwich and drained his glass before answering.

"It wasn't planned, indeed I'd never heard of Infatrini myself until yesterday. Rose's doctors want her to have Infatrini mixed with breast milk because it's has extra calories. I confess I wanted to have the doctor's opinion whether there was a downside to Rose having it. The questioning had little to do with this case, but I doubted anyone but you would realise that!"

She smiled at the compliment, "Actually, I thought it was a good point in Rachel's case. If they had prescribed a higher calorie milk in the hospital and she had gone home taking that, Annie might not have died!"

David nodded, "I realised that only after I'd asked the question. Of course though, it doesn't deal with the prosecution's case that Annie was starved. It wouldn't matter how many calories were in the milk if she wasn't being given any!"

Shortly afterwards they returned to court and as they still had fifteen minutes before the court sat for the afternoon, David decided to phone Wendy to check on how things were at the hospital.

He was surprised when a tearful Wendy answered the phone and he quickly asked, "My God what's happened, is Rose ok?"

"She is now. We had a scare this morning when she couldn't catch her breath. Rose has been moved to the Special Care Unit overnight. Just as I was entering the unit and was washing my hands, I suddenly heard her gasping for breath."

"But she's alright now?"

"Yes, she's fine. Her breathing is normal now and she's started on the Infatrini so they are hopeful she will put on a bit more weight."

He let out a breath of air in relief, "Thank God for that."

He paused and then added, "If Rose is ok why are you so tearful?"

He heard a few sobs from the end of the line.

"Oh David, you're going to think me such an idiot, you'll never forgive me!"

He was beginning to get worried now. Had she had an affair? What could possibly be wrong? Although he tried not to be, he was a little colder when he next spoke, "Why don't you tell me what has happened?"

She sobbed again before answering, "It's my lovely diamond engagement ring. I was wearing it today when I went into the Special Care Unit. I took it off to wash my hands and then I saw Rose was gasping for breath. I quickly ran over to her leaving my ring on the sink. It was half an hour later that I remembered it. I went back and it was gone. They took all the hospital bins apart, which are under the sink, just in case it had fallen into one of those but it wasn't there. As I sat with my back to the sink I never saw who took it. There's no CCTV in here and it could be anyone, one of the druggie mothers, a cleaner, even a doctor or a nurse, though I doubt it's one of the latter two."

David was silent for a few moments, thinking about the loss and the work involved in three-week murder trial that had paid for the ring. Of more concern to him was the fact he had declined paying the relatively small premium to get the ring insured.

There was a lot he would like to say at this moment, but wisely he did not. He satisfied himself with, "Don't worry about it, I'll be getting you a wedding ring soon. Have you contacted the police?"

"Not yet, I will later today but we both know it will be hopeless, the ring will have been sold to a pawnbroker or someone similar, a long time before the police arrive."

"I know but we should go through the steps of reporting it. I'm annoyed at myself that we never took insurance out on it, like they suggested in the shop!"

Wendy sounded more cheerful now but was still clearly tearful, "David, thank you for being so understanding. I thought you would call me such an idiot for leaving it on a sink."

"Of course not, I can understand you were distracted through fear that Rose was unable to breath. Anyway, I've got to go now, it's almost 2pm, I'll come and see you tonight after court."

He politely did not remind her that he had advised her not to wear the ring in the hospital because there were so many 'undesirables' around!

He walked towards court 7 inwardly fuming. God how he hated the criminal classes! The scum that could take a mother's engagement ring away from her when her preterm baby, living in a Special Care Unit, was struggling to breathe!

As he was having the thought he came across Rachel gloomily entering the court. Momentarily he wondered what she would have done if she had come across Wendy's ring in the sink. He did not doubt for a moment she would have taken it!

Rachel turned and saw his expression, he immediately assumed a professional look, and dismissed his uncharitable thoughts, "Good afternoon, Rachel, I know it's difficult for you, but try to cheer up a little, the jury may misread an unhappy face for a guilty one. I believe the case has gone very well for you so far, and we have a lot more points to make on your behalf."

CHAPTER 25

THE PATHOLOGIST

At 2:10pm the court sat again and Owen called Dr Henry Numan, the prosecution's pathologist, to give his evidence.

He entered the court with his usual confident air. He had given evidence on hundreds of occasions in the past and to him, a visit to court was just like a day in the office would be for most people. He had not got dressed up for his court experience, but wore his old tweed suit with a dickie bow tie. It was his only attempt at whimsy.

He was soon sworn and Owen took him through his impressive credentials.

After a few minutes of dealing with all his qualifications, the medical papers he had written and revealing that he had given evidence on hundreds of previous occasions, he volunteered that he was, "A full time forensic pathologist whose work mainly involves conducting post mortems. I tend to become involved in cases where police have some interest, as was the case here."

Owen took him through his findings at the post mortem. Although he gave his account clinically, it was a difficult time for some members of the jury, who remembered that he was dealing with the post mortem on a baby.

Dr Numan continued, "I weighed the body before the post mortem and recorded the weight as 4.35kgs."

Owen quickly interrupted, "We know that the body was not weighed at the time of death but only a week later at the time of the post mortem. Would the body have lost weight during that week?"

Dr Numan thought for a few moments before answering, "It is possible that there was some loss of weight but I would have thought it would be negligible."

Owen looked quickly towards David and gave him a wry smile before he turned back to Dr Numan and asked, "You examined the body, did you find any marks that were consistent with a cause of death?"

"No, there were no abnormalities consistent with a cause of death. I checked the body for evidence of marks and injuries and I found a scar on the outer aspect of the left upper arm consistent with a vaccination site 0.5cm across and roughly circular. I found no other marks of old or recent injury on the body. However, I did find signs of extensive nappy rash."

Owen nodded, "Is there any significance in that finding?"

"Not really. It's caused by the effect of the child's urine coming into contact with the skin. It cannot have had any relevance to the cause of death."

He paused before adding, "Although it might be some evidence of neglect of the child."

"Was rigor mortis present when you saw the body?"

"No, but that is not surprising as the post mortem was carried out a week after death. I did notice hypostasis on the left side of the face and on the back. The jury is probably aware that hypostasis is the effect of gravity on the blood after blood circulation has stopped. The blood pools to the lowest point leaving a purplish mark. In this case this was consistent with the child lying in that position at the time of death."

"You examined the internal organs did you find anything that might have caused death?"

"No, apart from the presence of a Meckel's diverticulum, which is of no consequence, there is no evidence of any developmental abnormality."

"Please assist us with your reference to a Meckel's diverticulum. We have heard that this is an abnormal pouch growing in the small intestine, is that right?"

"Yes, it's a slight bulge in the small intestine. This one was 4cm long."

"You say it is of 'no consequence', what do you mean?"

"I could not see anything to suggest that this caused any problems to the child. There may have been some minor discomfort during life, but in my opinion it could have played no part in the child's death."

Owen nodded and then looked down at his notes before asking, "Can you assist us as to the state of the child's eyes?"

Henry, turned over a few pages of his report, "Certainly, the eyes were of a slightly sunken appearance. I did note that there were no petechial haemorrhages present in the white of the eyes or on the inside of the eyelids."

"Can you explain the significance of that finding?"

"Yes, petechial haemorrhages are the small red or purple spots on the skin or in the whites of the eyes, caused by a minor bleed from broken capillary blood vessels. It's a frequent finding when someone has been asphyxiated, strangled or suffocated. The absence of such a finding does not mean that the person was not asphyxiated, strangled or suffocated, just that there is no evidence to support such a finding."

"Was there any evidence to support a finding of asphyxiation, strangulation or suffocation?"

"None that I found."

"Did you conduct any further examination of the eyes?"

"Yes, I dissected both eyes."

David noticed that a young male juror who was in the front row of the jury had turned a shade of light green. He wondered if to say anything but decided not to. This evidence was difficult for anyone to listen and to and he wanted it to end as soon as possible.

Owen had his back to the jury as he examined the pathologist and had not noticed the young man nor had the judge who was taking a careful note of the evidence.

"What did you find?"

"I examined the vitreous humour of the eyes. I noted that it contained raised levels of urea and creatinine."

"I shall ask you the importance of that in a moment. Did you find anything else in your examination?"

"Yes, I also found positive evidence of streptococci in the middle left ear. The type that can cause meningitis."

"Now, can you tell the jury your conclusions in this case?"

"Yes, certainly. I could not find a clear cause of death. There were no marks or injuries that could have caused death. There was no evidence of any toxicological cause or contribution to death. There was no evidence of ingestion of poison or a dangerous household product.

I could find no abnormalities in the child's organs save for the Meckel's diverticulum, which was irrelevant in my opinion.

I could find no evidence of disease or infection that might have caused death although I was concerned at finding streptococci in the middle left ear. This is a virulent organism and could contribute to death in a baby. It would have been of more significance if traced in blood cultures that were taken, but it was not. Nevertheless, it was a possible contributor to the child's death and cannot be absolutely excluded. However, I am unable to propose it as likely cause of death, even on the civil standard of proof, the balance of probabilities.

On the other hand, the visible sign of the sunken eyes did suggest a degree of dehydration in the child before death. My examination of the vitreous humour of the eyes confirmed this finding. During life, the kidneys clear the urea and creatinine from the body. Dehydration can interfere with the effectiveness of the kidneys. The fact that raised levels were found in the vitreous humour supported a finding of dehydration during life.

Also, the extensive nappy rash concerned me. It could not have caused or even contributed to the death of the child, but if a child is dehydrated, the urine is more concentrated with higher levels of ammonia than normal and this could have caused the extensive nappy rash seen on the child, when it came into contact with the skin. In my opinion it is likely that dehydration contributed to death.

Indeed, to use the rather legalistic formula, it was a significant factor that in my opinion was more than a minimally contributing factor to the cause of death. It may have been the only cause of death, although I am unable to conclude positively that is the case."

Owen thanked him and sat down, just as David was about to start his questioning a note was sent from one of the female members of the jury. Tanner quickly read the note and looked towards the young male in the front row who looked like he was going to be sick.

"Yes of course, we'll take a fifteen-minute adjournment now."

CHAPTER 26

AN INTERRUPTION IN THE EVIDENCE

The adjournment took over an hour in all. The young juror sent a note saying he could not carry on. The talk of dissecting the eyes had made him ill. After a quick discussion with counsel the judge had the juror in court.

Everyone watched as the juror came into court and sat alone in the jury box. He had a distinctly milky green pallor and looked like he was physically ill. It was not the first time this had happened in one of David's cases, what surprised him was that it was always male jurors who could not deal with this type of evidence.

HHJ Tanner either did not notice or worse, was not moved by the juror's plight.

"Now young man I have had your note which states you do not think you can continue in this trial. I do not understand why this issue is raised now. You were told early on in the trial what the case was about. The charge of 'causing death' was read out to you. I cannot understand why you could not have told us then of your concerns. These trials cost a great deal of public money and

I am loath to discharge a juror at this early stage of the trial"

David whispered to Sara, "It's his best 'man-up" speech, given with his usual emotional detachment."

Tanner noticed David but could not hear him, "Did you want to add something Mr Brant."

David rose slowly and gave a look of sympathy towards the juror who, if it was possible had turned even paler and looked like he was going to vomit, "Not at the moment My Lord, I was just asking my junior her opinion on whether we should ask that this juror be discharged as the burden of continuing in this trial does seem to be having an adverse effect on his health."

Tanner turned red, "Mr Brant, whether a juror is discharged or not will be my decision. I am minded to insist that he continues to sit as a juror or be considered in contempt!"

The juror immediately got up and ran out of the courtroom and through the door to the jurors' room emitting loud groaning noises followed by the slamming of an internal door.

Owen took the opportunity to address Tanner, "My Lord, the prosecution does not consider it appropriate that this juror continues to sit on this case. We share your lordship's concern that he should have raised this matter earlier, but looking at him and hearing the sounds we could all just hear now, and bearing in mind that we still have to hear the cross examination of the pathologist and the examination and cross examination of the neonatologist, we suggest justice would be better served by discharging this juror and continuing with just eleven jurors."

Tanner became even redder but knew he was in difficulty as it was the prosecution's suggestion, so he turned to David, "And I suppose you agree Mr Brant?"

"Yes, My Lord."

It was a simple decision for him. He would not want someone sitting on the jury who was going to be physically ill. Putting aside the effect on the juror, the other jurors would no doubt feel sympathy for him being forced to continue to sit on the case and continue to hear distressing evidence and there was only one person they could take that out on consciously or subconsciously, and that was Rachel!

Tanner gave him his usual look of loathing, "Very well, but we will sit late tonight so that we can finish the next witness so that he is not caused the inconvenience of coming back tomorrow!"

The juror was discharged without being forced to return to court again and at just before 4pm, Dr Numan returned to the witness box.

David rose from his seat and began questioning.

"Dr Numan, the post mortem took place a week after death, is that usual?"

"It's not unusual these days, but it's not ideal."

"Why?"

"Well it all depends on when the body is refrigerated, whether there is any deterioration or not. Ideally a post mortem should be sooner rather than later."

"In this case, you weighed the body at the time of the post mortem?"

"Yes, I did."

"The weight was slightly less than the last weight recorded a few weeks earlier when the child was alive. Is there any significance in that?"

"Any reduction in a child's weight at this age is concerning and might demonstrate in itself dehydration or a lack of being given adequate food or milk."

"Of course, and no doubt we could agree on that if the weighing was carried out when the child was alive or immediately after death and not a week later?"

Henry frowned slightly as he replied, "I accept there may have been some loss of weight before the post mortem was carried out, but it is impossible to quantify. There are no studies that I am aware of that deal with such loss."

"But there could have been such a loss?"

"Yes, but I doubt it would even be a hundred gms!"

"If the child had weighed one hundred gms more at death than on the day of the autopsy, it means she weighed more than the last time she was weighed in life?"

"Yes, by 50 gms or so, not a great deal."

"No but it would have meant she remained roughly on the same centile point?"

Henry quickly looked through his own charts before answering, "Yes, or just below it."

"Let me ask you about another subject. Rigor mortis in young children. We have heard that when the paramedics arrived, rigor mortis had begun to set in?"

"Well I'm not sure that's a proper description, it was certainly present though I cannot say 'it had begun to set in'."

"Very well, rigor mortis was present. Now despite the television and books telling us that you can use rigor mortis to assess a time of death, in fact it is notoriously unreliable because there are so many variables?

"That's right, body weight, the ambient temperature where the body is found and factors like that."

"Including the age? It's right isn't it that it is notoriously difficult to assess in young children?"

"Yes, it is."

"In a baby, rigor mortis could have started well within an hour of death?"

"It could."

"Similarly, with hypostasis, this can occur quite quickly after death."

"Yes, it can. The blood stops circulating around the body at the time of death and then tries to find the lowest part in the body. It can occur quite quickly."

"Now in your first report for this trial, you concluded that the cause of death was 'unascertained'. You did state that death could have been contributed to by dehydration but did not list that as a cause of death. You then had an opportunity of reading the report of Robert Peters, the consultant neonatologist, also instructed by the prosecution. You then served an addendum to your report, now listing the cause of death as 1A unascertained and 1b, dehydration. Why the change?"

213

"Mr Peters is an expert who has spent many years dealing with the newly born. I deal with the deceased who range in age from babies to the very old. I read his report and considered that his opinion on dehydration fitted the known facts. I had already considered that it may have been a factor, now I concluded that it was."

"But you still listed the cause of death as primarily 'unascertained'?"

"I wouldn't say 'primarily'. These reports are mainly statistical. In my opinion dehydration may have been the only cause of death."

"But you cannot say that it was?"

"No."

"I want to ask you about possible causes of death. Firstly, dehydration. That could have been a cause of death?"

"Yes, as I've said."

"As you've also said, you cannot categorically state that it was."

"No."

"And if it was, you cannot say what the cause of the dehydration was? It could have been that the child was not being given enough to eat or drink but equally it could have been as a result of the child not absorbing the food she was given, because of malabsorption?"

"Yes, though I saw no signs of malabsorption."

"But you wouldn't would you at a post-mortem?"

"Not necessarily, but if she suffered from malabsorption, I would have expected it to be noticeable in life. For example, the child would be prone to vomiting or having chronic diarrhoea."

"Did you ever check to see whether that was the case?"

"I was never instructed that it was."

"Did you check though?"

"No."

"We have heard that the child was suffering from nappy rash. That is as a result of the ammonia in the child's own urine being in contact with the child's skin."

"Yes."

"If a child is suffering from dehydration, you would not expect any urine to be expelled?"

"If no fluids were being introduced to the child, I would not expect urine, but if some fluids were introduced to the child, albeit an inadequate amount, I would expect some urine to be produced."

"Enough to cause the nappy rash seen in this case?"

"That is difficult to answer. I wouldn't like to give an opinion on that."

"Very well, I won't press you on that. The child could also have suffered from an overwhelming infection in life that can occur at this age and would not necessarily have been seen at the post mortem?"

"That is true."

"Such an infection could cause a child to absorb less fluids even if an adequate amount of food and milk was being given to the child?"

"Yes."

"You did in fact find evidence of a virulent virus in this case. Streptococci were present and as you have stated, you cannot rule that out as a cause of death, even though you do not believe it was the cause."

"Again, that is true."

"You also found a Meckel's diverticulum in this case?"

"Yes."

"That can cause blood in the stools and in a severe case, can lead to malabsorption?"

"Yes, but I saw nothing in this case to indicate that it caused any problem to the child. I ruled it out as having no relevance."

"But by the nature of your examination, you cannot say what it was like when the child was alive?"

"I disagree, I saw nothing to suggest it played any part in the child's death."

"Indeed, to be fair you don't know, that is why you concluded the cause of death was 'unascertained'?"

"Yes, though dehydration, through whatever cause, could have been the sole reason for the child's death."

"But you are not able to conclude that is the case?"

"No."

CHAPTER 27

THE NEONATOLOGIST

David had concluded his cross examination of the pathologist quickly. It was clear to him that he was making little headway, he was only hoping that the jury had not realised this.

The following day, the case did not start before 12pm as the judge had to sentence four defendants in an armed robbery case and he had told the jury not to come to court before 11:30am.

At a few minutes after 12 everyone was in court, when Owen announced that his next witness was the Consultant Neonatologist, Mr Robert Peters.

A few minutes later Robert Peters entered the courtroom carrying a large file. He did not look either right or left as he strode into court, but simply entered the witness box, took the oath before the usher had said anything and then gave his name.

Owen opened his mouth to address him, but Mr Peters spoke first, "I presume you would like me to give my qualifications first?"

Owen was taken aback, it was the first question he was going to ask. He now desperately tried to think of another one but as it was customary to take expert witnesses through their qualifications first, he resigned himself to a, "Yes, please do."

Robert took them through an impressive list of qualifications which took him ten minutes to read out. He covered his basic medical qualifications, then his advanced medical qualifications followed by his clinical and academic experience as a neonatologist and finally referred to a list of papers he had published in medical journals in the United Kingdom and abroad, on the subject of the treatment of preterm babies. Owen waited patiently until he had finished before asking his first question.

"Mr Peters, I understand you have prepared a number of reports relating to this case?"

"Yes, that is right. I have prepared two reports for this trial and a further report for social services dealing with failings in this case by those professionals responsible for the care of the child."

Owen seemed slightly taken aback, "Sorry, you prepared a report for social services dealing with failings by other professionals?"

"Yes." The witness looked surprised that Owen was not aware of the report. After a short pause, he continued, "I concluded there were a number of failings here. The health visitor should have noticed that the child was falling through the centile points, the local general practitioner should have kept a closer eye on the child's health and the hospital, where she was born, should have arranged to have more contact with the child after she was discharged from their care."

Owen gave an involuntary nod, "I regret that I was unaware of this report and I suspect my learned friends are as well?"

David stood up and addressed the judge, "That is right, for obvious reasons I would like to see this report before I cross-examine the witness. I would like to know what conclusions were reached about the 'failings' of the professionals in this case!"

Owen quickly responded, "I would like to see the contents of the report as well before I continue to examine the witness. I wonder if I might have an adjournment so that copies of the report can be obtained?"

HHJ Tanner turned his usual shade of bright red as he answered, "No, no, no, the Crown Prosecution Service should have been aware of such a report, as should you. It is customary to have consultations with experts before trial! We have already lost time today and I am not going to have the jury sitting around aimlessly until 2pm whilst the prosecution get their act together. You can continue to examine-in-chief before lunch and then we will take an adjournment when copies of the report can be supplied to Mr

Brant to allow him to read it and cross-examine promptly at 2pm!"

Owen tried to object but Tanner was adamant and eventually he reluctantly continued his questioning.

"Mr Peters, I understand you never examined the child's body and have prepared your reports on the basis of documents, reports and photographs supplied to you?"

"Yes, that is true. I am not a pathologist so there was no reason for me to examine the body. I received a considerable volume of records, both from the time when the child was in hospital receiving care as a premature baby and then from the time she received care after discharge from the hospital. I also had Dr Numan's helpful pathology report so I had sufficient information to prepare a detailed examination of the records that were in my possession."

"We know that baby Annie was born prematurely at 30 weeks. Other than being a premature baby, did she have any abnormalities?"

"No, she had the kind of problems which babies born at that gestational age frequently have and therefore she needed to be cared for in the baby unit of the hospital for a number of weeks."

"So, there were no abnormalities of any significance that were recorded at the time of her birth?

"That's correct."

"Was there a period of time in hospital when she had respiratory problems?"

"Yes, but that is normal in premature babies whose lungs are immature. She was intubated, that is a breathing tube was inserted through her mouth and into her lungs, but that was only for a few days. She was then placed on something called, 'CPAP' which is a kind of breathing support mask which forces air into the lungs. Again, she was only on that for a few days before being able to breath herself without any additional assistance."

"Did she make good progress in the neonatal unit?"

"Yes, there was an episode when blood was seen in her stools. This is a potential risk in babies caused by necrotising enterocolitis, an inflammation of the bowel. In fact, it was never clear that she was suffering from this condition as it was also believed it might be as a result of an intolerance to cow's milk. As a result, her feeds were changed and, as a precaution, she was given a course of antibiotics and the condition resolved."

"No further concerns were raised by the medical staff and baby Annie was discharged from hospital at 42 weeks, so two weeks after her expected delivery date?"

"That's correct. From my reading of the notes, she could have been discharged earlier but I presume the doctors had their reasons for continuing to monitor her in hospital, although they never made a note of those reasons."

"Were there any concerns expressed by the doctors when she was finally discharged?"

"None, apart from the obvious fact that she had been born prematurely."

"Now, the jury has seen the charts and heard on numerous occasions; her weight at birth and throughout her time at hospital. I will only deal with two readings. We know that at birth she weighed 1.4 kilos at birth so she fell between the 50th and 75th centiles on the chart. When she was discharged from hospital she weighed 3.2 kgs and was just above the 9th centile. Is there any significance in that?"

"There is no real significance in the birth weight in my opinion. Birth weight is affected by a number of factors, mainly what occurs in the womb. It does not necessarily have any relevance to a baby's growth.

However, a fall of two centile points in hospital from the 50th to the 9th would normally be of concern. However, in this case we are aware that the episode when she had blood in her stools would have caused either weight loss or at least a slowing of growth and put her on a lower centile."

"Was her weight gain normal or at least satisfactory, when she was in hospital?

The witness hesitated slightly before answering, "It was and that is important. Most problems that affect babies cause problems with weight gain and so paediatricians use weight gain or loss to determine whether a child is healthy or not. Here, after the new milk formula was introduced the child did grow at a normal rate, although that was not the position in the beginning."

"Did that change once she left hospital?"

"It did, from the time the baby was discharged from hospital her growth was inadequate."

"She was still putting weight on though?"

"Yes, but the whole purpose of the centile charts is to enable health professionals to see if a baby is developing normally. Some babies are designed to be very small, some are designed to be large. It doesn't matter which centile you're on, as long as you're following the same one. What does matter is when your growth is failing to follow one of the centile lines. It is of particular concern when the growth is crossing the centiles lines. In that situation, the baby is growing at a significantly less than normal rate.

That is what happened here. The baby crossed a number of centile points from the time she was discharged from hospital."

"Is there a generic term that medical specialists use for this?"

"Yes, it shows that there was a 'failure to thrive'."

"What can cause a 'failure to thrive?"

"There are a number of possible causes, but the most obvious, and top of the list, is an inadequate intake of food, for whatever reason."

"Is it possible to work out what would have been an adequate intake of milk at around the time Annie died?"

"Yes, a rule of thumb is that a baby should take 150-200mls of milk every twenty-four hours per kg of weight. Baby Annie was 4.4 kgs when she was last weighed alive. That means she should have consumed 660-880 mls a day. Some people still refer to fluid ounces. There are roughly 30mls to the fluid ounce so she should have consumed approximately 20 to 30 fluid ounces a day. Of course, these are approximate and babies do vary considerably. Some will want more and some less."

"In the case of Annie and her failure to thrive, if the mother said she had provided 20 to 30 fluid ounces of milk a day to her baby what would you conclude?"

"I would conclude that either the mother is not correct and she was providing considerably less milk or there was a serious underlying condition with the baby."

"Such as?"

"The baby could have been suffering from a chronic infection or malabsorption, where the body does not absorb the nutrients in the milk."

Owen looked towards the jury as he asked, "Was there any sign of a chronic infection or malabsorption?"

Mr Peters also faced the jury as he answered, "None that I am aware of."

Owen paused for the jury to consider that point and satisfied that they had, he continued, "The child's body was weighed again at the time of the post-mortem. We have heard that the body had lost weight from the last time Annie was weighed. Admittedly the post mortem was carried out a week after death. Do you know if the body would have lost weight during that period?"

"This is not really my field but I would be surprised if there had been any significant weight loss. The refrigeration process would have stopped any significant deterioration of the body."

"If the weight recorded at the time of the post mortem was the weight at the time of death, it would mean that baby Annie had lost weight in the last few weeks of her life. What would that signify to you?"

"She should have been putting weight on, not losing it. It is an important fact on any reading. A baby's weight is made up of 75% of water, the bones, organs and everything else comprise the remaining 25%. The weight of the brain, the muscle and everything else does not dramatically change on a daily basis. However, the amount of water in the body can fluctuate significantly. Clearly, what was being lost here was water. The baby was suffering dehydration."

"What could be the cause of such loss?"

"There are really only two ways that that can happen. Either the baby has been losing water either from, for instance, diarrhoea or vomiting or from other secretions. For example, by very severe gastro-enteritis, or because the baby is not being given an adequate supply of fluid. Indeed, almost zero feeds which seems to be the case here."

"We have heard from Dr Numan that there may be some weight loss between the time of death and the post mortem but no more than about 100 gms. That would mean there might have been some minor weight gain between the last time baby Annie was weighed and the time she died. Something approaching 50 gms. Would that have been the expected weight gain over that period?"

"No, not at all. It should have been nearer 200 gms in that period of 18 days."

"Does that weight increase, albeit it a small one, rule out dehydration?"

"No, not at all, insignificant weight gain could still occur when there is dehydration."

"What signs would you expect in a baby suffering from dehydration?"

"An obvious sign would be sunken eyes, which were present here. Also during life, the mouth and mucus membranes would be dry and the baby's skin may be courser and might feel warm. The baby may have had a temperature as she would not be able to produce sweat and cool herself down."

"Would these signs be noticeable to a parent?"

"Most definitely."

"What would happen over time?"

"The baby would get weaker. She would sleep more and move less. She would cry less due to the weakness. Eventually her extremities would become cold as her circulation failed. The breathing pattern would probably change as acid would build up in the bloodstream causing gasping or groaning. Eventually the baby would fall into a coma, stop breathing all together and die."

"You have told us what the possible causes of dehydration may be; namely, insufficient intake of fluids or a serious underlying condition. From what you have seen, is there any evidence of a serious underlying condition in this case?"

Again, the witness turned and faced the jury, "No, I could find no evidence from the post-mortem or from any of the documentation that I have seen that there was a serious undiagnosed problem."

"In your report, which the jury does not have, you made a specific reference to the cerebrospinal fluid, the white cell count and the red cell count. Was there a particular reason for you noting that in your report?

"Yes, it was important to consider whether the baby might have died from meningitis, that is an acute infection of the membranes lining the brain. The way to exclude that is to look at the cerebrospinal fluid. In fact, there was no evidence of acute meningitis."

"One issue that has been raised in this case is malabsorption. Did you consider that?

"Yes, I did."

"Having examined all the necessary reports and documents, what conclusions did you reach in relation to malabsorption?

"Malabsorption, is when the bowel fails to obtain the essential nutrients from food or milk. It is uncommon but when it does occur it can cause a baby to fail to gain weight."

"What are the signs of malabsorption?"

"One of the main signs is chronic, almost explosive diarrhoea. This will recur throughout the day flooding the nappy."

"How noticeable would this be to a parent?"

"It would be very obvious to the parents that there was something seriously wrong with the baby and that she needed medical attention."

"Was there any evidence of such chronic, explosive recurring diarrhoea in this case?"

"Not to my knowledge. There is no reference to this in the papers."

"So, what is your conclusion about malabsorption?"

"I do not consider there was malabsorption here."

"You have examined all the papers in this case and had an opportunity of reading the defendant's interview. In any of the papers you have considered, have you seen any reference to severe diarrhoea or vomiting that might account for the weight loss here?"

"No, none whatsoever. In my opinion, the cause of death in this case was dehydration caused by an inadequate fluid intake. At the very least that was a major contributing factor in the baby's death."

CHAPTER 28

CHALLENGING THE EXPERT

"Well, that was a waste of a good lunch hour!"

David put Mr Peters' social services report down on the table and looked at Sara.

"I have just spent forty-five minutes reading this sixty-page report and all it does is reiterate what he has already written in his prosecution reports. I bet he charged twice though!"

Sara smiled, this had been a relatively peaceful lunch without her having to engage in the usual small talk with David. She liked him a great deal and had a great deal of respect for him professionally, but of late his conversation had always been about Rose and how Wendy was coping with the stress.

Sara had her own worries at the moment, such as; would she receive enough money from the Bar to pay the extortionate rent on her minute London flat, or would she have to forgo luxuries, like food and heating! She did not need to be burdened with David's worries as well. If she heard him say, 'it was all two steps forward and occasionally three steps back', one more time, she would scream!

At least now he was talking about the case and she was happy to discuss that.

"Isn't there anything in the report that you can use?"

David bit a chunk out of his stale sandwich and masticated a little before replying, "Not really. The only thought that comes to mind is how critical he is about every other professional in this case. Everyone got it wrong according to him, apart from himself, of course."

David thought for a few moments before adding, "I suppose we could make something out of that!"

At 2:05pm they were back in court when David asked his first question of the witness, "Mr Peters, you have given an expert opinion on the likely cause of death in this case."

"Yes."

"I have just been looking at your impressive list of qualifications and I note that 'pathology' does not appear in the list. Am I right in thinking that your qualifications are of a clinical nature not a pathological nature? That is, you deal with the living, not the dead?"

"Sadly, in my line of work you do see a number of babies die."

"I dare say, I imagine it does not matter how good the doctor is, sadly babies still die?"

"Yes."

"And I suppose the same applies to parents. However, good the parents are, sadly babies can die under their care?"

"Of course."

"However, getting back to my first question, which you have not yet answered, your expertise is as a clinician dealing with live patients, not as a pathologist dealing with the dead?"

"That is true, but in dealing with the living you are spending a great deal of time trying to make sure they survive, so there is a crossover in the disciplines."

"But you are not a qualified pathologist, qualified to conduct autopsies and report on the cause of death?"

The witness was clearly annoyed as he responded, "No, but I feel qualified to give an opinion in this case."

"Of course you do, but it may be important for the jury to know that you do not hold any qualifications in the area in which you give an opinion!"

The emphasis on the words 'you' in the comment, was not missed by anyone in court. David continued before the witness could respond, "Moving on, I am grateful that I was supplied with your sixty-page report to social services over the luncheon adjournment. I believe that you allowed your own copy to be copied for my use, so thank you for that. Having read through it, it is noticeable that you are critical of every professional who had dealings with Annie?"

"I don't believe I criticised everyone."

"Really, can you think of anyone who didn't receive your criticism?"

The witness paused for a few moments before answering, "I cannot recall now, but I don't believe I was critical of the hospital staff who cared for the baby after her birth."

David turned to one of the pages in the report that he had flagged during lunch, "I note at page fifteen of the report you had this to say about the hospital consultant, 'In my opinion, the diagnosis of necrotising enterocolitis, NEC was wrong and further tests should have been carried out to establish whether the baby suffered from this condition before a course of antibiotics was prescribed'."

"Yes, I recall that. I have always been concerned about the overprescribing of antibiotics, particularly to babies, but I was criticising the consultant, not the doctors with day to day care."

David flicked through the report to another page he had flagged, "Well what about this on page 23 of the report, 'I am surprised that the hospital doctor kept the baby at the unit until her 42nd week. It seems to me that she could have been discharged at least two weeks earlier and I note that no notes were made as to why she was not discharged at that stage'."

"That was more of a comment than a criticism."

"I wonder if the hospital doctors saw it that way?"

Owen rose slowly to his feet, "I wonder if my learned friend could confine himself to questions, rather than comments!"

David beamed at him, "Of course, I will try."

The judge looked at him sternly, "And you will succeed!"

David continued without responding, "You were critical that the hospital did not monitor Annie once she left?"

"Yes, there should have been outpatient appointments arranged to check on her lungs, her eyes and hearing, but I could not find any evidence that such letters were sent to the mother."

"You were critical that her GP had not arranged to see Annie after her discharge?"

"Yes, I was. The records show that the hospital did send him a letter recommending that he contact the mother, but I cannot see anything to suggest that he did."

"You were critical of the health visitor who you state had 'irregular timed' appointments to see the baby and 'never appeared to notice that the baby was falling through the centile points'?"

"Yes."

"You have also been supplied with a copy of the defence expert's report in this case and you are critical of him, stating, 'I am surprised that any expert witness could produce such a report'."

"I was surprised."

"Is that because his expert opinion disagrees with yours!"

"No! It is because I do not believe that it is a professional report and is biased towards the defendant."

"And the same criticism cannot be levelled at you, that your findings are biased towards the prosecution?"

"No, I have given my opinion in accordance with my duty to the court."

"And finally, of course, you are critical of Annie's mother's care of Annie."

"Yes."

"Might it be that just one or two of these people that you have criticised, exercised proper care and you are using the benefit of hindsight and being too critical?"

The witness bristled now, "I do not believe so."

"Very well, let me deal with another matter then. To reach your conclusions, you rely heavily upon the pathologist's report, don't you?"

"I do."

"Of course, if there were any mistakes in his report or findings that might well affect your conclusions?"

"I'm not aware of any such mistakes."

"You are aware of the defence expert's conclusion that it is not safe to use a body's weight at post mortem, after it has been refrigerated for a week, in order to determine the weight during life?"

"I saw that in the report. I am not in a position to deal with that matter as I have not seen any studies to support this."

"So, you do not criticise the defence expert's findings in that regard?"

"I am in no position to do so."

"In your report, you rely heavily on the weight at death to suggest that there had been a loss of fluid and consequently dehydration, which caused death."

"Yes, I do."

"If the weight were out by any significant degree, would that change your findings?"

"It would depend on the 'degree'."

"If the body lost 200 or 300 gms between death and post mortem for example?"

"It might make a difference, but I know of no reason why a body should lose so much weight in such a short period of time."

"Assuming that baby Annie did die of dehydration, you have listed two potential causes of that dehydration. Firstly, she may not have been given enough fluids, secondly she may not have absorbed what she was being given."

"Yes, in broad terms."

"You favour the former, namely, that she was not being given enough fluids?"

"Yes, I do."

"If she was not being given enough fluids would you have expected her to produce much urine?"

"No, I would not. She would produce some, but it would be concentrated."

"Would she have produced much excrement?"

"I would not expect her to have done."

"Were you aware that when the police searched the property a number of nappies were found which contained excrement and/or urine?"

"I was aware nappies were found, I am not aware how long they had been in the house!"

"If they were from the night she died would that change your conclusion?"

"It might. As I stated, I would expect some urine and some excrement, but not a great deal if the baby died from dehydration caused by a lack of fluid intake."

"Before lunch, in answer to my learned friend, you stated that you would have expected almost zero feeds to be given to the baby before her death?"

"Yes."

"Are you aware that the pathologist found traces of unmetabolized medium chain triglyceride (MCT) in her urine?"

"I recall there was some reference to that."

"MCT is an ingredient found in enriched feed, in this case Pepti junior milk?"

"Yes, I believe so."

"Which suggests that she was being fed Pepti junior and was not receiving zero feeds?"

Mr Peters hesitated before answering, "It might, I am not sure how long MCT may remain in the body after being taken. It could be days."

"Didn't you think it might be worth finding out before you suggest that Annie had 'zero feeds'?"

"She may have had reduced feeds, it does not alter my conclusion that she died from dehydration as a result of not having adequate feeds."

"In relation to her feeds, her mother was advised to give her Pepti junior milk?"

"Yes, in hospital."

"Clearly at that time she was not putting on weight adequately which is why there was a change of milk formula?"

"Yes, that's right."

"She could have been given a higher calorie formula such as Infatrini?"

"She could have."

"Do you know why she was not prescribed Infatrini?"

"No, I assume that the hospital doctors considered Pepti junior was sufficient and I note that she did put on sufficient weight after the change in formula."

"Let me deal with malabsorption. You found nothing in your investigation to suggest that baby Annie died from malabsorption?"

"No, I did not."

"But you cannot exclude it as a possible cause of dehydration and therefore death?"

"No, I cannot."

"The reason being that some tests that can be carried out during life cannot be carried out after death and as those tests were not carried out, you cannot rule out malabsorption?"

"That is right."

"Indeed, malabsorption is one of the important causes of failure to thrive in babies?"

"It is."

"You are aware that the pathology report noted that the baby had a Meckel's diverticulum?"

"I do recall that."

"And Meckel's diverticulum can be linked to malabsorption?"

"Meckel's diverticulum is relatively common and is nearly always insignificant. Rarely does it cause problems."

"Yes, but what happens when it does?"

"It can cause an obstruction in the small intestine which could result in a baby vomiting and becoming acutely unwell."

"And in some cases, death?"

"Yes, but I do not think it was the cause of death here. I think it is irrelevant."

"You have told us that in the case of malabsorption you would have expected chronic diarrhoea?"

"Yes."

"Isn't it right that chronic diarrhoea is not found in every case, only in 9 out of 10 cases?"

"There are no certainties in medicine, except that we all die at some stage, so I won't say that you will have chronic diarrhoea in every case, but I doubt it is as low as 9 out of 10 cases."

"But there can be cases of malabsorption where there isn't any chronic diarrhoea?"

"Yes, but it would be extremely rare."

"And there must be cases where there will be some diarrhoea but not of the excessive nature that you have described?"

"Probably."

"Consistent with the nappies that were found at the house by the police?"

"Well, I don't know what state the nappies were in."

"But it follows that if there could be cases of malabsorption where there is no excessive diarrhoea, there could have been malabsorption in this case?"

"I suppose so, but I still consider that this was a case of death being caused by dehydration due to an inadequate intake of fluids."

"I see in your report that you state doctors adopt an expression, 'common things occur commonly and rare things occur rarely?"

"Yes.

"Is that how you approached this case?"

"Yes. You look for the most common cause because as the saying goes, they occur most commonly."

"But rare things do still occur?"

"Yes, but only rarely."

David looked down at his notes, he was about to speak when Tanner asked, "Have you many more questions for this witness Mr Brant?"

David looked at the blank page in front of him, "I do have another topic to cover My Lord, which will probably take some time."

"Very well, we will break there, it is very nearly 4pm and I have a very important meeting to attend tonight with members of the Sentencing Guidelines Council."

He turned to the witness, "I am sorry Mr Peters but I shall have to ask you to come back tomorrow to complete your evidence. Will that be inconvenient to you?"

Peters responded immediately, "Well it is actually, I'm due to address a meeting at Birmingham University tonight and shall be staying in the Halls of Residence tonight in Birmingham..."

Tanner cut him short, "Then we will start a little later tomorrow."

He turned to the jury, "Ladies and gentlemen we shall start a little later than normal court time, we shall start promptly at 10:30am so that we cause the least inconvenience to the witness and allow him to get here from Birmingham. Thank you. You may all go home now."

CHAPTER 29

INTERESTING INFORMATION

David boarded the tube from St Paul's station and made his way towards Wembley changing at Liverpool street. He was exhausted. He always found cross examining experts tiring, but the experts in this case had been particularly difficult, not least because he had so little to put to them and he judged that although he had appeared confident in his questioning, in reality he had made very little progress. This was not a case where there was a simple solution and an obvious answer to the prosecution's case. Rachel claimed she had not starved her daughter but the medical evidence suggested that she had and it did not help her case that she had previously exhibited a laidback attitude to parenting.

In reality he had no further questions for Mr Peters but he had welcomed the opportunity to adjourn his cross-examination just in case anything new occurred to him overnight.

He tried to put the case behind him for now, as he opened his free newspaper that he had picked up at outside St Paul's station. However, when he turned to page 5, he noticed that there was a report on Rachel's case stating, 'Doctor claims mother starved her child to death'. There was a quote from the evidence of Mr Peters that he had given in the morning, 'In my opinion, the cause of death in this case was dehydration caused by an inadequate fluid intake. At the very least that was a major contributing factor in the baby's death.'

David put the newspaper down. There must have been five or six murder cases being tried at the Bailey at the same time as his. One was a gangland slaying of three drug dealers using an Uzi sub machine gun. Why had the newspaper decided to pick up on Rachel's case which wasn't even a murder allegation?

He put the newspaper down and closed his eyes. Maybe he could get a few minutes' rest on the tube!

After forty-five minutes, he arrived at the hospital and made his way to the Neonatal Ward. He had not seen Wendy or Rose in the last couple of nights and was looking forward to seeing them both.

As he walked through the main door to the unit the receptionist, Mary, smiled at him. "Good news Mr Brant, Rose has been moved to the Special Care unit. At this rate, she'll be home soon!"

He was already aware that Rose had been moved to the unit but he thanked her anyway and after receiving instructions where the unit was, he made his way there with a bunch of flowers and a box of chocolates he had bought from outside Wembley Park station.

He noticed Wendy first as he entered the room. Rose was nuzzled up to her with her cannulas resting on Wendy's shoulder. She was having more 'skin to skin' contact and was making a low snoring sound with occasional rasps of breath. To him, they made the perfect image of serenity.

"Hello darling." Wendy said in a hushed voice, "Try to be quiet as Rose has only just dropped off. I don't think she liked her first two days in this unit and she has cried a lot and has only just gone to sleep"

He nodded and replied in a hushed tone which he thought was quieter than Wendy's, but he was immediately met with a, "Shush, don't use your courtroom voice in here!"

Wendy's gaze turned towards the flowers and the chocolates and her face lit up before she put on a frown and whispered, "Are those for me? You shouldn't have bought me chocolates, you know I'm on a diet trying to get my weight down to what it was before I became pregnant. Hospital food and chocolates don't help!"

He was beginning to feel really welcome and wondered why he had not gone straight home. He was used to Wendy having a go at him in the early morning. As he had told Graham in chambers, he often felt like he was in a Disney film, he would go to bed with a dazzling beautiful Princess and wake up with Grumpy! He had even bought her a mug for her tea which was emblazoned with the words, 'I'm not a morning person.'

She soon explained that she had been awake all night because of Rose and was feeling worn out herself. Rose had progressed to the Special Care unit which meant she was getting better, although she was still on oxygen and the doctors had said that when she was finally discharged home from hospital, she would still be on oxygen. That meant she would have to have large cylinders of oxygen installed in the house and would have to be attached to a small cylinder when she went out. They could not say how long this would last.

As Wendy was explaining the ramifications of Rose having oxygen at home, Dr Laddie and a number of medical students entered the unit on their rounds. David waited to talk to him until he stopped next to Wendy and Rose and addressed them, "Hello all, and how is our little patient today?"

He spoke much louder than David had but noticeably, Wendy did not say anything about the volume and simply told him that Rose had not slept much since her move.

He nodded before replying, "That's not unusual when a baby is moved from one unit to another. They sense the change of environment. Don't worry, she's sleeping now and I suspect she will soon be back to her normal sleep pattern."

David took the opportunity to ask about oxygen, "I understand that you are suggesting that when Rose is finally discharged, she will be released on oxygen for an indefinite period. Why is that?"

Dr Laddie looked at his students as he replied in his best didactic tone, "Rose was very premature when she was born and her lungs were not properly developed. She has chronic lung disease and needs the oxygen to help her lungs develop.

It is likely to be a long process. We cannot say how long she will need oxygen for. In some patients, it is only a few weeks, in others it can be over a year. The oxygen will not only help her lungs develop, it will enable her to have a more active lifestyle and even do basic tasks better like eating."

David looked at him and asked, "Eating?"

Dr Laddie returned his gaze, "Yes, it takes an effort to eat and digest. That's why babies often fall asleep after a meal even when they are only having milk. The oxygen will allow her to breath better which in turn will mean she feeds well. That will result in her lungs growing as well as the rest of her body. Hopefully she will then come off the oxygen in the near future when her lungs are sufficiently developed."

David suddenly had a thought, "Are you saying that in some cases a lack of oxygen at home could result in a baby failing to thrive.

Dr Laddie again looked at his students, "Certainly, if the baby needed oxygen and was discharged from hospital without it."

CHAPTER 30

A FURTHER OPPORTUNITY

Sara was starting to panic. It was already 10:25am on Friday morning and there was no sign of David. She was outside court 7 waiting for him. She had phoned his mobile several times already but had just reached his answer phone. Having seen Tanner in action on numerous occasions now, she had no doubt that he would make her cross-examine the witness if David was not there. Although she considered herself a good barrister, for her call, and that she probably was more able than most with her experience, she knew she did not have the skill to deal with Mr Peters, a difficult expert witness whose evidence was crucial in this trial. In any event, she had no idea what to ask. She thought David had covered everything in his cross examination and there were no topics left to raise.

Tanner would be doubly annoyed at David not being there and her explaining that she had no questions for an expert witness who had travelled half way across the country to be here today and yet was not needed. Where was David?

Her thoughts were disturbed by the tannoy which suddenly boomed out, "Would defence counsel Mr

Brant QC and Ms Petford-Williams, please attend court 7 immediately, the judge is waiting."

A few seconds later the doors to the court opened and the usher came out, "Ms Petford-Williams, the judge is waiting to come in and I'm sure I don't need to tell you, this judge can get very impatient if he is left waiting!"

Sara nodded and took another hopeful look at her phone before switching it off and slowly making her way into court. She was unsure what to do. Should she apply for a short adjournment to find out where David was? Should she ask a few irrelevant questions of the witness? Or should she just give her apologies and say that she had no further questions?

A few seconds later she rose from her bench as the judge walked into court. He took his seat as he was handed his computer and papers by the usher. She felt uncomfortable as he constantly stared at her like some wild predator about to pounce on an unsuspecting prey.

Once his computer was plugged in and turned in he addressed her sharply, "And where is Mr Brant this morning?"

She was about to reply when the doors to the court opened and David strolled in. She had never been so relieved to see anyone in her life.

David slowly walked to his seat announcing as he came, "Sorry My Lord, I was on the phone to the defence expert receiving some important information that is relevant to the questioning of this witness."

Tanner's already ruddy expression took on a deeper shade of red, "Mr Brant, why couldn't you take instructions before now, I told you yesterday I wanted everyone here promptly for a 10:30am start. I will not have witnesses and jurors kept waiting because counsel waits until the last minute to take instructions!"

David looked at his watch which read 10:32am "I do sincerely apologise for keeping the court waiting for two minutes, but the information only came to light last night and although I tried repeatedly, I was only able to contact the defence expert at 10:00 this morning. However, I am ready to resume cross-examination now and I suspect that in the long run, the information I have received may actually shorten the trial."

Tanner stared at him disbelievingly but knew there was little he could do in the circumstances and further argument would just waste more time. He made a mental note to deal with this clear insubordination in another way, "Very well then, but do not let it happen again."

David beamed at him in response, "I am sure it will not."

Five minutes later the jurors were brought into court as Tanner addressed them, "Please take your seats quickly ladies and gentlemen. I'm sorry that we have a later start today, defence counsel Mr Brant, was unavoidably delayed so we have lost a little time."

A few faces looked at him in a bemused way, this was one of the least delays they had experienced in the case so far so they did not know why the judge was bothering to mention it.

Once everyone was seated and Mr Peters had returned to the witness box, David resumed his questioning.

"Mr Peters there is one topic I did not deal with yesterday and which I would like to turn your attention to now. When Annie was born, it's right isn't it that she suffered from chronic lung disease?"

"Yes, most babies who are born prematurely suffer from chronic lung disease. Their lungs have not suitably developed in the womb."

"In hospital Annie's breathing was assisted from birth by mechanical means, namely at first; she was intubated, a breathing tube placed into her lungs, then she was put on CPAP and an air mask was attached to her and air forced into her lungs in order to open them. She then had cannulas fitted to her nostrils so that she could be given a constant flow of air, finally these were removed so she could breathe normally?"

"Yes, I believe so."

"Was there ever any concern that she might have been removed from mechanically assisted breathing too early?"

He hesitated before responding, "Not to my knowledge, no."

David picked up the hospital records that were in front of him and turned to address the judge, "My Lord, these papers are not in the jury bundle but do appear in the papers that were served by the prosecution electronically. The reference is Exhibit page 1972."

Owen turned to his junior who immediately turned to the exhibit on his computer screen and showed Owen. Tanner was a little slower but within a few seconds was looking at the same document.

David gave the witness a copy of the relevant page and continued, "Do you see the reference at the bottom of the page, I cannot tell who the Doctor is because he has scrawled his name in illegible writing, but his comments have been written in bold. Will you read them to the jury please?"

"Yes, they read as follows: 'I am concerned that we may have discontinued the oxygen too soon as

255

the child still has breathing difficulties. This must be monitored and reviewed if necessary'."

David looked at the juror's faces. Most were showing some interest in the point. There was only one older male in the front row who clearly was not and indeed seemed to be muttering to himself. David ignored him and turned back to the witness, "To your knowledge, did such a review ever take place?"

Mr Peters hesitated, "I regret that I do not recall this note. I have no doubt I must have read it as I read through all the hospital notes. I probably considered it irrelevant to the issues I had to deal with."

David made a noticeable gesture of raising his eyebrows to the jury, "Will you indulge me for a little time please. I have considered all the hospital notes and there is no reference to Annie's case being reviewed with a view to reinstating her use of oxygen."

Mr Peters nodded, "I am not surprised, it is unlikely that she needed oxygen and the hospital staff did not realise it!"

David paused for a few seconds before stating, "Unfortunately, mistakes do happen in hospital. Indeed, you have been very critical of the care shown by a number of medical staff in this case?"

"Yes, there were some areas of care that were lacking, but failing to diagnose a baby's need for oxygen is unlikely to be one of them!"

David looked at the notes he had taken from his telephone call that morning with Malcolm Williamson, the defence expert.

"But it may have been."

Before the witness could reply, David immediately asked, "If a need for oxygen had not been properly diagnosed, what would have been the consequences to Annie?"

Mr Peters paused before answering, clearly thinking through the question.

"Well the baby would have shown obvious signs of breathing problems. She may have had flaring nostrils or suffer from tachypnoea, rapid shallow breathing, as she tried to take in more air. She may have shown signs of laboured breathing and wheezed a lot. She would probably have been more susceptible to respiratory illnesses. She may also have suffered from Cyanosis, where her skin may be more bluish in colour as she would have less oxygen in her blood and she may also have suffered from apnoea, episodes of her stopping breathing altogether."

David nodded and asked, "Would she have any difficulty eating?"

Mr Peters again thought through the question before answering, "She would probably have had less energy and therefore it may have led to problems feeding her."

"Which could develop in time to a failure to thrive?"

"Yes."

"A dropping through the centile points?"

"Yes."

"And, in an extreme case, death?"

Mr Peters paused again before answering, "Yes, in an extreme case."

CHAPTER 31

THE PUB WITNESS

After Mr Peters had finished giving evidence the judge adjourned the case. The court's list office had listed a separate case in his court and given it an 11:30am hearing time.

David took the opportunity to take Sara upstairs to the Bar Mess for a coffee. He bought the coffee and some chocolate biscuits. He felt that a little luxury and the resulting extra calories, were justified in the circumstances!

Sara munched on her biscuit and sipped at her coffee before she informed him, "You gave me a scare this morning David. I thought I was going to have to cross-examine Mr Peters and I didn't have any of the information you just used!"

"Yes, sorry for that. I only became aware of the issue about oxygen last night when I went to see Rose and Wendy in hospital. I was then up until 2am reading through the medical reports trying to find out anything about breathing difficulties. I found that one reference by accident. It did not appear when I did a computer search because the note was in handwriting and was not picked up. I had given up on the search and was just checking for some further material relating to

Annie's hospital care, when I came across the reference. It turned out to be a useful one."

They returned to court at 12:00pm after receiving a court tannoy. Tanner was already sitting in court when they arrived.

Owen waited until the jury had returned to court and then announced that his next witness was Thomas Adams. There was a wait of a few minutes before Thomas Adams entered the courtroom. David noted that he was about 35 years of age, six feet tall and quite muscular, a benefit no doubt from his employment in the building trade.

As he passed the dock he quickly glanced in that direction and saw Rachel's pleading eyes. He just smirked and quickly turned away, and made his way to the witness box.

After the preliminaries were over, Owen asked him, "Do you know the defendant in this case, Rachel Wilson?"

"Yes, I do."

"How do you know her?"

"We live in the same area and I've seen her in the shops and in our local pub, 'The Bull's Head'."

He added quickly, "I don't know her very well, just enough to say 'hello' to."

He looked slightly nervous and turned slightly and looked up to his left.

David followed his gaze. The witness was looking up towards the public gallery that was high up, behind the witness box. Like all the public galleries in the Old Bailey, the entrance was separate to the main building and the public gallery was therefore completely separate to the court room. As a result Thomas could not see anyone from his position but David could see the public gallery and could see a number of people in it. He noted that there was a newcomer today, a woman in her late thirties who was similarly straining and trying unsuccessfully to see the witness box.

Owen carried on without noticing any of this, he had been reading the witness' statement and was keen to ensure that everything in the statement was brought out before the jury.

"How long have you known the defendant?"

"As I said, I don't know her that well. I first noticed her about two years ago, when she was in the Bull's Head. She was with her boyfriend. She seemed drunk to me and was making a lot of noise. That's why I noticed her."

"How often do you think you saw her after that?"

"I probably saw her in the pub weekly, usually on a Friday night. I saw her at the local shops occasionally, probably a couple of times a month, usually at the weekend."

"I want to take you to a time in February this year. We know that her baby, little Annie, died on Friday 19th February. Had you ever seen her with the baby?"

"I'd seen her at the shops with the baby a few times, just before Christmas last year and just after."

"Did you ever speak to each other?"

He looked distinctly nervous now and shuffled his feet in the witness box as he answered, "Just a quick, 'Hello' or 'Hi'. Nothing more than that."

"I want to ask you about the night that Annie died. Did you see her that night?"

"I did."

"Where was she?"

"I saw her in the Bull's Head with her boyfriend, Bob. They were both dancing together and singing loudly."

"Do you remember what time this was?"

"I know it was in the evening, I stop work on Fridays at about 5pm and I did that night. I went home to change and have a bit to eat. It was probably about 6:30pm I went to the pub. I was there about an hour or so before I saw her and Bob come in."

"Did they have the baby with them?"

He could not help himself as a grin spread over his face, "No, they were alone."

"Did you see them leave the pub that night?"

"I don't think I did. Friday night is a busy night and the pub gets crowded. I remember seeing them at about 9:30pm. They seemed very drunk, as usual, and were dancing and singing loudly, but I don't remember seeing them after that."

"Was the baby with them at that stage?"

"No, I've never seen them take the baby to the pub!"

Owen looked up from the witness statement, "How often did you see them in the pub from November of last year until February of this year?"

"Probably, almost every Friday night."

"And the baby was never with them?"

"No."

"Just one final matter before my Learned Friend asks you some questions. How can you recall that you saw them in the pub on Friday 19th February rather than on any other Friday before or after that date?"

"Well, I saw Rachel at the shops the following week. She was in tears and I asked her what was wrong. She said her baby had died on the Friday night and what was worse was the police were charging her with killing it. It was then that I remembered I'd seen her in the pub that Friday night."

Owen looked at him slightly quizzically, but sat down thanking him. David immediately got up from his seat but paused, looking at the woman in the public gallery for a few seconds. He waited long enough for a few members of the jury to follow his gaze.

The judge observed him and added impatiently, "Are you going to ask any questions Mr Brant, or shall we let this witness go?"

David turned towards the judge, "Thank you My Lord, I do have a few questions."

He turned and faced the witness, "Mr Adams, are you married?"

The grin disappeared from his face and he visibly squirmed, "I don't know what that's got to do with anything?"

"It's a simple question Mr Adams, it requires a 'yes' or 'no' answer."

The witness looked at the judge for assistance but as the judge ignored him, he answered, "Yes, I am."

David looked into the public gallery again, "Did you come to court with your wife today?"

Again, the witness squirmed and looked to the judge and the prosecutor for assistance but as none was forthcoming he quietly answered, "Yes."

"And is your wife in the public gallery today?"

David could see that the woman in the public gallery was blushing as David and now a few members of the jury stared at her.

"I don't know, I can't see her." The witness smirked, he thought that was a clever answer.

David nodded in agreement, "I understand that you cannot see her from your position but surely your wife told you she would go to the public gallery whilst you gave evidence?"

"I can't remember."

"Really, well let's see if I can help you."

David looked at the woman, "Does your wife have red hair and was she wearing a green coat today?"

Again, there was no assistance from the judge or prosecutor so the witness reluctantly answered, "Yes!"

David turned back to look at the witness, "Now I am going to ask you what I suggest were your true dealings with my client Rachel Wilson. Would you like me to ask that your wife leave the public gallery whilst I do so?"

The witness gave David a look of pure hatred, "No, I've got nothing to hide."

"Very well. Firstly, my client accepts that you first met her about two years ago, and it was in the Bull's Head pub. However, she was not drunk, nor was she singing. She was perfectly sober and going to the bar where you were standing with some of your male friends?"

"I don't remember."

"When you go to the pub do you take your wife."

"Sometimes."

"Not on Fridays though, that's a 'lad's night out' isn't it?"

Thomas hesitated before answering, "Sometimes."

"When you first met Rachel Wilson, she made her way to the bar and you moved aside for her and then put your arm round her and asked her name?"

The witness was really squirming now.

"No, I never, I'm not like that."

"How did you learn her name?"

"I don't know, someone must have told me."

"Well I suggest Rachel did, when you had your arm round her trying to fondle her breast?"

"No, that's not true."

"Thereafter, almost every Friday night that Rachel went into the pub, you waited until she was alone and you made your way towards her, and you always spoke to her?"

"No, I never said more than, 'Hello' to her."

"There came a time when her partner Bob was away for a few weeks. You heard, he was serving time for assaulting Rachel?"

"I heard something like that, but I can't remember when."

"Well this was in early 2015 when Rachel was pregnant. She was in the pub with some girlfriends. You went over to Rachel and told her that her partner, 'Bob' was, and I quote your words, 'a 'wrong 'un' and that if she wanted a real man, you would be there for her?"

Thomas was really squirming now and had broken out into a sweat. "That's a lie, nothing like that ever happened."

"You carried on making such approaches until Bob was released from prison after about six weeks and he had a 'word' with you, encouraging you to desist?"

"That's not true."

Thomas turned to the judge, "Is he allowed to make up these lies about me?"

Tanner looked at him sternly, "Just answer the questions Mr Adams."

David continued, "You did desist, you stopped approaching Rachel in the pub, indeed you stopped going to the Bull's Head pub?"

"I might have stopped going to the pub for a few weeks but it's not because of what you say."

"So why do you say you stopped going to the pub?"

"I can't remember, I probably wanted a change of scenery."

"Surely one pub is just like another?"

"I don't know why I stopped going."

"Did you even go to the Bull's Head pub on the night of 19th February?"

"I did."

"You certainly never saw Rachel Wilson there?"

"I did."

"It was months later, after her baby's death that you bumped into her in a shop?"

"No, it was the week after."

"I suggest it was not until mid-July that you approached her, no doubt once you had heard that her boyfriend Bob was no longer around?"

"No, that's not true."

David paused and took Thomas' witness statement from his papers, "I note that you never made a witness statement in this case until 25th July of this year."

Thomas paused before replying, "Yeah, so what?"

"Why did it take so long before you approached the police?"

"I don't know. I didn't think I had anything important to say."

"Really, you gave a version of events that a mother and father, instead of looking after their baby, had left the baby alone at home, where the baby had died. That was quite important information, wasn't it?

"I don't know why I waited until July."

"Let me help you. The meeting you had with Rachel that I have described, took place in July, didn't it?"

"I've told you, it was a week after the baby died."

"And Rachel told you she had been charged with causing the death of the baby?"

"Yes."

"She was not arrested or charged with that offence until 4th March 2016. She could not have told you she had been charged with this offence in the week after 19th February, that is yet another lie on your part?"

Thomas looked confused now. He squirmed for a few more moments looking towards the judge and prosecutor, both of whom ignored him and finally said, "I might have got the date wrong."

"So, the meeting might have occurred in July?"

"No, it was much earlier than that."

"I suggest this meeting took place mid-July, on a Saturday. You work during the week so it would have been a Saturday that you saw her?"

"It may have been, I don't remember, but it wasn't in July."

"I suggest it was. You went up to her and told her you had heard that her baby had died?"

"No, I never, she told me."

"She did become tearful, she told you it was worse than that, not only had she lost her baby, she had been charged by the police with causing her death?"

"She did say that, but it wasn't in July."

"After she had told you, you put your arm round her and tried to kiss her, telling her she needed a real man to look after her?"

"No, I did not."

There was a loud noise as the woman in the public gallery got up and quickly made her way to the door. David looked up at her and waited until the door had closed before he continued.

"Rachel was annoyed with you and pushed you away and told you to, 'Fuck off'?"

"That never happened."

"You responded by telling her to 'Fuck off', and you then added, 'You've had your chance'."

"No, I never."

The witness was looking very uncomfortable now.

"It was just a week or so after that, that you went to the police and made up this pack of lies saying Rachel was in the pub the night her baby died?"

"No, it's the truth."

"You did it simply because, this grieving mother, had once again rejected your unwelcome harassment."

"That's not true."

David looked up to the public gallery where the witnesses' wife had been a few minutes earlier. Some members of the jury followed his gaze.

After a few seconds, he added as he sat down, "I have no further questions, but there may be some more when you get home!"

CHAPTER 32

BOB'S MOTHER

It had been close to 1pm when Thomas Adams finished his evidence so the judge adjourned the case for lunch. Just over an hour later, after David had the Bailey canteen's usual Friday fish and chip meal, the court sat again. Owen waited until everyone was seated before he announced that he had one more witness for the day and that the court would probably end early as the lawyers would work on a list of 'agreed facts' to present on Monday.

He explained to the jury that this was a document that both the prosecution and defence prepared and which would include uncontentious facts. He told them that it was designed to save time as the alternative would be to call a large number of witnesses to court to deal with matters that no one challenged.

David nodded in agreement to the jury as Owen addressed them. In fact Owen had not produced even a draft copy of any agreed facts he wanted but David was happy with the offer of an early Friday.

Owen then announced that his last witness for the day was Joan Harwood, the mother of Rachel's partner Bob. Almost all the members of the jury sat up when they heard that news, clearly wondering what she would have to say.

It took a few minutes to locate Joan as she had decided at this time, rather than during the luncheon adjournment, to visit the lavatory, but at 2:10pm she entered the court room. As she did, she immediately looked towards the dock and gave Rachel a sneer before she made her way to the witness box.

David had noticed through her poorly applied makeup, that she had a ruddy complexion and a barely disguised set of broken veins on her nose giving it a purplish colour. He had also noticed her walk very carefully to the witness box as if she was worried that she might fall. He remembered what an actor friend had once said to him. If you want to play a drunk on stage, act sober because that's how drunks act, always exaggerating their movements in an effort to look as if they had not had a drink. He had no doubt where Joan had spent her lunch time and why she needed a toilet break at this time!

Joan took the oath and gave her name when she was asked to. She slightly slurred her words but it was barely noticeable and David doubted that the jurors realised it. Just as Owen was about to ask his first question, she turned to the judge and asked in a wheezy voice, "Can I sit down your worship, my ephysema is playing up?"

Tanner looked at her sternly, "You have emphysema?"

"Yes, your worship."

He gave her permission without any comment about her addressing him by the wrong title. He only reserved such sternness for counsel and police officers. After she was seated and had been given a glass of water by the usher, Owen asked his first question, "You are the mother of Robert 'Harwood, the former partner of the defendant in this case, Rachel Wilson?"

Joan glared at Rachel in the dock before answering with a simple, "Yeah, I'm Bob's mother."

"Now I suspect the jury will want to know the answer to this question, so I will ask it now. We know that your son skipped bail and has not been seen since March of this year. Do you know where he is?"

She reddened slightly as she answered, "No, not a clue."

She then turned to look at Rachel again, "He wouldn't have gone anywhere if it wasn't for that bitch!"

Tanner reddened as he shouted at her, "Mrs 'Harwood, I will not have that language in my court unless you are quoting a relevant

275

conversation. Please remember where you are and just answer counsel's questions!"

It seemed to have the desired effect as she seemed to visibly shrink in her seat as she replied meekly, "'Sorry, sir."

Owen quickly intervened, "I am sure we all understand how difficult this must be for you, but you will not be here for long. I want to ask you a few questions about the defendant, Rachel Wilson. Please just answer the questions without making any comments."

She looked at him, "Sorry sir, it's just so difficult for me. I've lost my son over this as well as my granddaughter. I'll never see her again and I don't know if I'll ever see him again either."

Owen nodded sympathetically, "I'm sure we all understand. Now can I ask you, when did you first meet the defendant?"

"It was in our local, the Bulls Head. I was having a drink with both my sons as it was my birthday. I remember she was in the pub with a few friends. They were making quite a racket and Bob went over to ask if they would quieten down. They did but he stayed over there chatting with her. The next I knew they were living together!"

"When did this first meeting occur?"

"On my birthday, 21st January 2014."

"How often did you see the two of them after that?"

"Probably every week. He moved into her house which was just a few streets away from me."

"Did you get on with the defendant?"

"At first, but after a few months I didn't."

"Why?"

"I thought she was a bad influence on my Bob. They were always drinking heavily when I saw them. He never drank that much when he lived with me."

"We know that Rachel became pregnant, when did you become aware of that?"

"A few days after she told Bob."

"Was he happy?"

"Not at the time, he was unemployed and enjoyed his socialising. He didn't know if he would be able to do that once the baby was born."

"We know that there came a time when Bob was sent to prison for hitting the defendant when she was pregnant. Do you recall that?"

She looked at Rachel with a bitter expression, "I do, it was all her fault, Bob told me ..."

Owen quickly intervened, "Don't tell us what Bob has told you unless the defendant was present when he said it. We have rules about that. You weren't there when the incident between Bob and the defendant occurred so you cannot tell us what happened."

She appeared to acknowledge the direction, but then blurred out, "Alright, but it wasn't Bob's fault, she hit him first and he was just defending himself."

Tanner intervened now, "Please just confine yourself to giving evidence of what you have witnessed and do not tell us what your son has told you!"

"Sorry sir."

Owen quickly took over the questioning again, "We have heard that they got back together after he was released from prison and they continued to live together until Annie was born."

Joan suddenly looked down and reached into her handbag and pulled an off-white, stained handkerchief from it and blew her nose. She then had a sip of water before replying, "Yes that's true, the poor little mite."

"Did you see them after the birth of Annie?"

"Yes, I did."

"How often?"

"Every week or so. They asked me to babysit a few times whilst they went out."

She looked over to David as she heard him noisily scribbling a note.

Owen ignored him and continued, "When was the last time you babysat for little Annie?"

"Probably a week before she died."

"So, you weren't babysitting the night she died?"

She blew into the stained handkerchief again before replying with sobs, "No, if I was babysitting, this would never have happened!"

Owen paused for a few seconds letting the last answer sink in with the jury.

"To your knowledge, from what you saw, did your son, Bob, ever look after Annie?"

"Yes, he doted on that little girl. He changed nappies and fed her. He was a good dad."

"Did you ever see the defendant looking after Annie?"

She frowned, "Yes, I did."

"Did you notice anything in particular when she was caring for Annie?"

"Yes, she didn't seem to have a clue. She never seemed to change her nappies. She never had any spare nappies with her. She never seemed to dress her properly in warm clothing. She never had anything for Annie to drink, never seemed to carry any milk around with her. She was always unwilling to feed poor little Annie."

"Did you ever see her feed Annie?"

"I did once at my house. Annie was crying and I told her she needed a feed. Rachel said she'd feed her later but I told her she should feed her now. I told her to boil the kettle to make up the feed.

Eventually she went into the kitchen but I couldn't hear the kettle boiling so I went to see what was happening. I was horrified to see her filling up the bottle with hot water from the tap!"

"When was this?"

"It was in January this year, just after my birthday…"

She sobbed as she added, "… just a couple of weeks before poor little Annie died."

CHAPTER 33

UNRAVELLING FAMILY ISSUES

Owen sat down with a. "Thank you", leaving Joan sobbing in the witness box. David waited until the sobs had ceased before he asked his first question.

"Ms Harwood, are you sure you don't know where Bob is now?"

She transferred her look of hatred from Rachel to him, "No, I don't."

"I understand that you've had four children?"

"Yes."

"And Bob was the youngest ..." he paused before adding, "... and your favourite?"

She stiffened as she responded, "He's my youngest but I love all my children the same."

"Did you once tell Rachel that Bob was your favourite?"

"I don't remember."

"It's right, isn't it, that Bob stayed with you at your home until he moved in with Rachel?"

"Yes."

"And whenever he and Rachel had a serious argument, he would come back to stay with you."

"Yes."

"When he assaulted Rachel…" He paused before adding slowly, "… causing her to have a nasty scar above her left eye, he was bailed to live at your address, wasn't he?"

"Yes."

"And I suggest that when he left this last time, to avoid a police prosecution in this case, he went to live with you?"

She looked uncomfortable now, "He might have stayed with me for a few days but then he just left and didn't tell me where he was going."

"Your favourite son, who has always lived with you apart from when he was with Rachel, would have told you where he went. You are lying about that, aren't you?"

"No, I'm not, I don't know where he is."

"You know the police were investigating him about this matter, don't you?"

"I know he got arrested and bailed, though he had nothing to do with it."

"You can't know that, you weren't there."

"Bob told me he had nothing to do with Annie's death!"

"When did he say that, when he had absconded on bail?

Joan looked at him through squinted eyes, "No."

"Well when then?"

"I don't know now."

"You dislike Rachel Wilson, don't you?"

She looked at the dock, "Yes, I do."

"She took your favourite son away from you?"

"I've told you, I treat all my children the same way."

"She complained to the police when he assaulted her?"

"She complained to the police, I don't know what happened ..."

She paused before adding smugly, "... I wasn't there."

"As you've told us, you thought they drank too much and you blamed her for that even though Bob was a grown man and you knew he had abused alcohol many times before he met Rachel?"

"She was a bad influence on him."

283

"You no doubt feel that the reason that Bob has had to leave the area, is because of Rachel?"

"Yes, I do."

"And that is why you do not like her and would do anything you can to harm her, even lying in court."

"I'm not lying."

"When Annie was discharged from hospital, Rachel brought her to see you didn't she?"

"Yes, she did."

"You told her that because you had four children, you were very experienced as a mother and you would give her advice?"

"I did, I was trying to be helpful."

"And she thanked you and welcomed the advice?"

"She said, 'thank you', I don't know if she 'welcomed' the advice."

"Do you recall that about a week after Annie was discharged from hospital, you were ill and Rachel brought Annie round to see you because you had some clothes for Annie and also Rachel wanted to see if there was anything she could do for you?"

"I remember getting some clothes for her, I don't remember if I was ill, I can't recall now."

"You never complained once about Annie not wearing enough warm clothes, did you?

"I did."

"Apart from the one time Rachel brought Annie round, when you were ill, Annie always had a coat on when Rachel brought her to you?"

"No, she never had a coat."

"Never?"

She replied smugly, "No, never."

"Really, let me show you this."

David produced a photograph which he showed to the witness. He waited for her to look at it for a few seconds before asking, "That was taken in your home around December 2015. It shows you holding a smiling Annie, who is wearing a coat, doesn't it?"

Joan paused, "She may have worn a coat once."

"Really. The one time a photograph was taken! She wore that coat frequently didn't she?"

"I don't remember now."

"Was Annie ever cold when you saw her?"

"Yes, she always looked a bit bluish to me."

"Her skin was bluish?"

"Yes."

"Did you notice that she had breathing problems?"

"She always seemed to have a cold and she wheezed a lot."

David nodded, the witness was being helpful despite herself.

"As you have told us, you would willingly babysit for Bob and Rachel when they went out?"

"Of course, Annie was my granddaughter."

"And they never asked you to babysit the night she died?"

"No, I wish they had!"

"So presumably they never said anything about the two of them going out that night?"

"No, they never."

"If they had wanted to go out together that night, you would have babysat for them, wouldn't you?"

"Yes, of course."

"After Annie was born, to your knowledge, did Bob ever go out at night on his own, leaving Rachel with Annie?"

"He was a good dad, but he needed his space now and then. He needed to relax with his mates. It's not easy being a dad, ask his father …"

She paused before adding bitterly, "… he found it so difficult he did a runner when Bob was born!"

David looked at the faces of the jurors, hoping they had understood the point. He turned back to the witness, "Let's deal with the incident with the bottle that you have told us about. Rachel only lived a five-minute walk away from your address, didn't she?"

"Yes."

"Annie was crying and you did say she should feed her. However, Rachel told you that although she had the Pepti junior powdered milk with her, she didn't have a clean bottle to make it in?"

"I don't remember that."

"You quite forcefully told her she should go and boil a kettle and make a feed."

"That's because she wasn't feeding Annie."

"She went into the kitchen and you came in a few seconds later?"

"That was because she wasn't boiling the kettle."

"You saw her putting hot tap water in the baby's bottle?"

"Yes."

"You never saw any milk powder in the bottle?"

She hesitated before replying, "I don't remember now."

"I suggest you didn't because what you saw was Rachel washing the bottle out with boiling hot tap water, not using the tap water to make the feed."

She hesitated again before answering, "I'm sure that's what she was doing."

"Did she feed Annie at your house that day?"

"I don't remember now."

"I suggest she didn't. She decided to take Annie home and feed her there using a properly sterilised bottle!"

"I can't remember now, it's a long time ago."

"You have come here to court to lie and try and suggest that Rachel was not a good mother, simply because you cannot stand her and have never forgiven her for being responsible for sending Bob to prison?"

"That's not true."

David paused and looked at his notes, there was one further area he wanted to cover with this witness.

"You saw Annie probably twice a week after she came home from hospital."

"Something like that."

"You have told us you recall that Rachel brought Annie round to you just after she came home from hospital?"

"She brought her round a few days after Annie came home."

"Try to think back, do you remember now that you were ill around that time?"

"I don't remember, I might have been. My emphysema does play up now and again."

She coughed as if to emphasise the point.

"Rachel brought Annie over to see you every couple of days in January and early February of this year, didn't she?"

"Yes."

"Do you remember Rachel saying that Annie was vomiting a lot during this period?"

"I remember her saying something about that."

"She also told you that Annie had a lot of diarrhoea around that time. Indeed, you would have seen it because you changed her nappy occasionally?"

"I did change her nappies whenever she came. That's because I never thought Rachel changed them enough!"

"You couldn't know that, but let's move on, did you see that she had a lot of diarrhoea around this time?"

"She did, but I thought that was normal. All babies are like that."

"And that is what you told Rachel isn't it?"

She did not answer.

"Do you recall that she told you she was worried about Annie because of the vomiting and diarrhoea and was thinking of taking her to the doctors' surgery. You responded by saying there was no need, it was normal in babies of that age?"

Joan looked very uncomfortable and hesitated before answering, "I don't remember now."

CHAPTER 34

MORE TRAGEDY

David looked forward to this weekend. The first week of the Rachel Wilson trial had been an exhausting affair with the difficult subject matter and professional witnesses to deal with as well as the high emotions that the case aroused.

He had planned to take Wendy away for one night. He knew she would not stay away any longer than that because she did not want to be away from Rose, but he also knew she needed a rest and a change of surroundings as much as he did. He had suggested the 5-star countryside hotel, 'The Highwayman' which had a fantastic spa and was renowned for its fantastic menu and wine cellar. It was also just ten miles north of Wembley and therefore easily accessible and they could be back at Rose's side within a very short time should anything happen.

As he arrived in the Special Care Unit on Friday night, the first sight that he saw was a crying Wendy. He stopped immediately and looked at her, thinking the worse and he then quickly went up to her to put his arm round her.

"What's wrong?" He asked fearing the answer.

Wendy sobbed a reply, "It's poor little Robin, he died in his sleep this morning."

David's immediate reaction was one of relief that Wendy's crying was not about Rose and the thought, 'Thank God', sprang to his mind. However, he instantaneously realised he was being remarkably callous and he was glad he did not express his thoughts verbally. Instead he managed, "That's terrible news, his poor parents. How are they taking it?"

Wendy looked at his expression knowing he was thinking something else, but she ignored her own thoughts and replied, "Badly, poor Angela was screaming when she first heard. Robin seemed to be doing so well. He had recovered from his operations, he was digesting more food, and they had even been allowed to wheel him around the hospital grounds with an oxygen tank. They really thought they would be taking him home soon!"

"How did it happen, surely he was being monitored?"

"He was, but apparently, he stopped breathing during the night. They tried to resuscitate him but they couldn't and he died before they could contact his parents. It's just so awful. You think that your child is doing better, is out of harm's way, all will be fine, and then this."

She looked into David's eyes, "What's worse is the hospital have suggested that they have some photographs taken with Robin. How awful is that, a photograph with your deceased child. How are they going to be able to look at that in the future? The doctors claim it may be therapeutic, I think it's just bizarre!"

She paused as a thought struck her, "God, what if that happens to us?"

David was speechless, by the nature of his job he was rarely lost for words, but he was now. It was a few seconds before he responded, "I'm sure..." God how he wished he could stop using that expression! "...that won't happen to Rose."

Of course, in reality, he was no longer sure of anything!

He thought for a few moments about his weekend plans and he asked hopefully, "Do you still want to go to the hotel tonight or would you ..."

Wendy responded quickly with a dismissive expression, "What do you think!"

"It might take your mind off things."

"Do you think I could possibly go away and leave Rose today, of all days. I would never forgive myself if something happened to her!"

"But ..."

Wendy's look guaranteed that he never finished the sentence.

David quickly resigned himself to a weekend at the hospital and put out of his mind, the fine wines, the great food, the luxurious surroundings and a relaxing massage that he had planned for them both. Instead he could look forward to Spartan accommodation with an overly hard bed and hospital canteen food!

On Saturday morning, he rose early to go to the communal kitchen to make Wendy a tea and some toast. As he went through the cupboard marked 'Brant', he noted that cupboard marked, 'Whitgift' was already empty. Angela and Richard Whitgift, Robin's parents, had already left the hospital and their cupboard, that they had been using was for months was bare. It was strange to David that he found the sight of that empty cupboard to be the most poignant reminder of the tragedy that had befallen them. For a moment, he wondered how many other parents had stayed in this property and suffered the same loss. The whistle if the boiling kettle brought him back to reality and he wiped away a tear as he made his way back to Wendy's room.

It was something of a relief when Monday morning arrived and he made his way to the Old Bailey to appear in front of his least favourite judge, HHJ Tanner QC. Appearing in front of Tanner was nothing in comparison to staying in the charity house with tragedy etched into its walls.

CHAPTER 35

THE OFFICER IN THE CASE

The eleven jurors took their seats as Owen announced that he was calling his last witness, the officer in charge of the case, Detective Sergeant Caroline Leadbetter.

She was sitting behind him as he made the announcement. She got up and walked to the witness box. She looked briefly in David's direction. She already had an idea what he was going to ask her about as a result of his requesting that she be excluded from court. It did not concern her. As a murder squad detective, she had been cross examined by some of the best barristers there were. She knew the basic rules on how to deal with cross-examination. 'Always be polite, admit mistakes and never lie unless it is absolutely necessary.' They were rules that she knew many of her colleagues did not abide by and were often professionally embarrassed in the witness box as a result!

Owen took her through her involvement in the case, getting her to deal with a brief chronology of what had happened and asking her to confirm that Bob had been arrested and would have been charged if he had not skipped bail. She confirmed she did not know where he was although there were warrants out for his arrest and the police had taken active steps to execute those warrants and apprehend him.

Owen then asked her to produce an agreed transcript of Rachel's interview which was read out to the jury. As was customary, Caroline read out the questions that she asked and Owen read out the answers that were given by Rachel.

The jury had a copy of the transcripts and followed it closely, except for the male in the front row who David noted, never seemed to listen to anything that was said in the case, whether the evidence was favourable or not to the defendant.

After the reading of the interview was completed, Owen asked her to stay there as there may be some questions from the defence.

David stood and looked at her sternly, she responded by smiling at him. He ignored the smile and asked, "Officer, can you confirm that you have checked Ms Wilson's antecedents and she has no criminal convictions, cautions or warnings recorded against her?"

"That's right, sir."

David nodded, then asked, "How long have you been in the police force officer?"

"Twelve years, sir."

"In that time, you must have seen a great number of changes?"

She wanted to reply, 'Not as many as you have in your career', but replied, "I have seen a few, sir."

"But one thing that never changes officer, is that you and no part of the prosecution team, are allowed to coach witnesses in the evidence that they give."

She was prepared for this, "Yes, sir, and we never do."

"But that is what you did in this case, isn't it officer?

"No, sir."

"You were in court when I asked the paramedic, Andrew Briggs, who had called the young police constable, 'a paki cunt'. He could not recall who it was, but he said, 'Caroline told me the Asian officer said it was the female.' Did you tell him that?"

Caroline did not hesitate, "I did, sir, and I regret it. It was a mistake on my part which I made when I was taking his statement. He said, he thought it was the female who said it but he could not be sure. I remembered that Police Constable Tanvir Sidhu, was adamant that it was your client who called him' 'a Paki cunt'. I thought as the words were directed to him, he should know who said them, and I inadvertently said this to Mr Biggs. I regret it now but at the time I was concentrating on other more important matters in this investigation and I made an error of judgment that I assure you I will not repeat."

David was impressed. Most police officers he dealt with would not admit they had told a witness what to say. The fact this one did and then apologized for the 'error' meant that the jury would believe everything she said. It was a classic case of 'confess and avoid' and what was worse, she had emphasised why the police officer at the scene should know who used the abusive language and there was little he could do about it.

"Ms Leadbetter, as a senior police officer with twelve year's experience, you must have been aware that this was improper behaviour on your part and that potentially, you changed a witness' statement. Why didn't you make some comment on his statement or in one of the many statements you have produced in this case, referring to this serious mistake? Unless of course, it wasn't a mistake?"

Caroline sighed before replying, "As I have stated on oath sir, it was a mistake and one I regret. However, I did have other things on my mind, and I failed to notice the mistake I had made. I accept I should have done and I apologise."

David sat down, he had been hopeful that he could at least make a point out of the officer which might make the jury question whether the prosecution had been deliberately oppressive against Rachel. Regrettably, he was convinced that his cross-examination of the officer had been almost wholly ineffective. She was the last prosecution witness and he felt that he had barely dented the prosecution case. Now he had to rely on Rachel and the defence expert and looking at the faces of the jurors, he was not convinced that would be enough to secure an acquittal in this case.

CHAPTER 36

A MOTHER'S EVIDENCE

The moment David dreaded in every trial had arrived. It was time to call his client to give evidence. He had had several conferences with Rachel now and he was not convinced that she would make a good witness. Ideally, he would not call her to give evidence and rely on the defence expert. However, the problem in a case like this, was that the jury would want to hear from her and HHJ Tanner would direct them that they could hold it against her if she did not give evidence and he had no doubt that they would. He asked the judge if he might have a short adjournment in order to take final instructions from his client.

HHJ Tanner looked at him as if he was wasting time, but surprisingly agreed to the suggestion and told the jury to take twenty minutes and go for a coffee. David could only assume, that this unusual act of generosity, was because the judge desperately wanted a break for some reason of his own. Probably the need for a toilet break or to phone his bookmakers! David mused for a moment. He recalled that when he was Tanner's pupil, Tanner frequently had him go to the local bookmakers and put a bet on a horse. David had dawdled once and not been in time to put the bet on and Tanner had been furious when the horse won and he had nothing to show for it. It was probably why they never got on!

Outside court seven, David put his memories of pupillage behind him and he and Sara sat down next to Rachel.

"Rachel, I asked for a short adjournment just to make sure that you are ready to give evidence. I know you have already said that you would but obviously, we have reached that moment and I wanted to be sure that you are prepared."

She looked at him on an oddly cold way, "I am Mr Brant. As ready as I'll ever be. I am a bit nervous, but I want to tell everyone I did not kill my Annie, and I didn't neglect her. The prosecution witnesses are a bunch of lying b...". She did not finish the word and adopted a scowl before continuing, "... just like that dishonest police officer who just gave evidence."

David ignored the comment, he was sure the officer had not lied about anything, in fact she was disarmingly honest!

"OK, well if you a bit nervous, why not take the opportunity to have a coffee or tea to calm yourself down?"

"No thank you Mr Brant. I've had enough coffee and tea throughout this trial!"

301

David nodded and left her and went for his coffee. He needed the caffeine intake before he called Rachel as a witness. He really did not know how she would react to giving evidence and deal with what he expected would be a skilled cross examination by Owen, and he feared the worse.

Twenty minutes later, in his most confident tone, he announced to the packed court, that he was calling Rachel Wilson to give evidence.

Everyone in court looked towards her as she made the relatively long walk from the dock to the witness box, clutching at a handkerchief, dabbing her eyes and whimpering as she made her way slowly, flanked by two, rather burly, female prison officers.

Once she was in the witness box, she took the oath, gave her name, dabbed at her eyes again, and then waited for David to ask her a question.

"Ms Wilson, please tell us a little about your background and your relationship with your own mother."

She now clutched at the handkerchief as she began, "My mum and me got on until my dad died in a factory accident. Then she just ignored me and started to drink heavily. She used to tell me how she wished it was me who had died and not him."

The handkerchief was now rag-like in its appearance as she continued, "She brought a lot of men home and slept with them. None of them seemed to care for her, including Peter, the man she eventually lived with when I was twelve."

"What was your relationship with Peter like?"

"At first he seemed nice. He always gave me a cuddle and sweets and I liked him, but then after a few months, he started to touch me and make comments."

"I know this must be distressing and we don't need to go into great detail, but what did he say or do?"

"He used to call me his 'little girlfriend' and tell me secrets. He would say my mum drank too much and he was worried about her, but that I mustn't say anything, it must be our secret.

Then as time went on, he started to tell me other 'secrets', ones I didn't want to hear."

"What sort of secrets?"

"He told me he preferred me to my mum. He said I was prettier and he wanted me to be his girlfriend."

"How did you feel?"

"I was young, I was alone, I couldn't speak to my mum as she would never listen to me. A first I felt flattered, but then the touching started."

"What do you mean?"

"He touched my breasts and used to put his hand in between my legs when no one was looking."

"Did you complain to anyone?"

"There was no one to complain to. My mum never listened to anything I said."

"How did this touching come to an end?"

"On my fourteenth birthday, he told me he had a special present for me. He forced my mum to have a party for me and some friends from school were invited. He bought plenty of booze for my mum and she got drunk and fell asleep. Then when my friends had gone he told me he had a special present for me in his bedroom. I went with him…"

Rachel stopped for a minute as she started crying and screwed up her ragged handkerchief. David, fearful she might be overdoing it, immediately asked, "Would you like a short break, I am sure his lordship would agree to one if you are finding this particularly distressing?"

David ignored Tanner's contemptuous look as Rachel replied, "No, I'm alright. I want to get this over with."

"Very well, what happened when you went with Peter to his bedroom?"

"He stripped off and told me his special present was to make me a woman!"

"Did you know what he meant?"

"I had an idea, we had sex education classes at school."

"What did you say?"

"I told him I didn't want to be a woman."

"What did he do?"

"He forced me onto the bed and raped me."

"Did you tell anyone?"

"Yes, after he let me leave, I rushed downstairs and woke my mother up. I was in tears. I told her that Peter had raped me."

"What did she do?"

"She hit me across the face and called me, 'a filthy slut'. She said I was always leading him on."

"What did you do?"

"I went to my room and pushed a chest of drawers in front of the door. I didn't come out until I was hungry a day later."

"Did you tell anyone else?"

"Yes. My birthday party was on the Saturday. On the Monday I went to school and told my best friend, Trudy Richards."

"Did you tell anyone else?"

"I hadn't intended to, but Trudy told Ms Chambers, our English teacher and she took me to the Headmaster's office. I then told the Headmaster what had happened. He called the police and they came to the school. I wasn't allowed home that night, I was taken into care."

Rachel looked hurt relating this difficult memory and there were more tears.

"Did you speak to your mother again?"

"She wouldn't have anything to do with me. Peter was arrested and I had to give evidence against him."

"What happened?"

"He was convicted and sentenced to twelve years inside. My mum never spoke to me again."

"We heard from an x-social worker, or whatever title she holds, Ms Head, that you told her on two occasions that she could not see Annie because you were going to see your mother. Did you ever tell her that?"

"No, I haven't seen my mother since I was fourteen. I would never say I was going to see her.

I told the social worker I was going to see Bob's mother."

"Were you going to see Bob's mother on those occasions?"

"Yes, I was."

"The prosecution might suggest you were just making up a story, to avoid the social worker seeing Annie. Is there any truth in that?"

"No, I had no reason to avoid her. Annie was fine."

"Very well, let us move on. Tell us a little about your relationship with Robert Harwood, the father of Annie."

She dabbed at her eyes once more.

"I met Bob in the pub as his mother said, though I wasn't with a rowdy crowd. He just came across to chat to me. We got on straight away and went to bed together the first night we met. He was really nice at first but he had a terrible temper when he was drunk. I never found that out though, till we moved in together!"

"What happened?"

"One night I asked him if he was going to marry me. He said we had a good thing together, why spoil it by getting married. I pushed him a bit and he lost his temper. He slapped me hard across the face giving me a nasty bruise on my cheek."

She involuntarily felt her right cheek as David asked, "Was that the only time he hit you?"

"No, after that it was almost every time he got drunk and he got drunk every week."

"His mother blames you for his drinking, did you encourage him to drink?"

"No. He was a heavy drinker before I met him. He told me he had become involved in a lot of scrapes because of his drinking."

"We have heard that you became pregnant with Annie. How did he react to that?"

"At first it seemed to make things better. He calmed down and he didn't hit me for a few weeks. Then one day I had a go at him for being messy. He really was a messy person. His mum doted on him and never seemed to tell him off for anything. As a result, he never seemed to wash or clean up after himself. He would just leave things all over the place. I tried to tell him to clear up but he would just get angry.

This happened when I was pregnant. He'd left a mess all over the place. I told him I was six months pregnant and I wanted him to tidy up as I could fall over and hurt myself and the baby. He was drunk and he just attacked me, saying he would kill me and the baby! He hit me hard across the face and I fell into the wall and cut my head open."

"What did you do?"

"I tried to stop the bleeding but couldn't. He just left and went to his mum's. I went to the Accident and Emergency department of the local hospital and told a young doctor what had happened. He put some stitches in my head and then, unbeknown to me, called the police. I wasn't allowed to leave the hospital until the police arrived. When they did, I told them what he had done."

"What happened?"

"Bob got arrested and charged. He was bailed to stay at his mum's home and not to come to my house, but he did."

"What did you do?"

"He seemed really sorry for what he'd done. He begged me not to proceed with the prosecution and so I let him stay with me and then the next day I went to the police station and tried to withdraw my complaint."

"Did they allow you?"

"No! They told me that if I said he hadn't hit me, they would charge me with wasting police time. I had to go ahead or I would go to prison and I was heavily pregnant at the time."

"We heard that he pleaded guilty to injuring you and was sentenced to three months' imprisonment. Did you go to court when he was sentenced?"

"Yes, his solicitor asked me to give evidence for him, which I did. I said he was drunk when he hit me and I didn't think he would hit me ever again. I asked them to give him a suspended sentence, but the Magistrates wouldn't."

David noticed a contemptuous tone creep into her voice when she said 'Magistrates'. He hoped the jury did not notice. He quickly asked, "We also heard that he served six weeks of that sentence. What happened to you during that period?"

"Well, firstly, Bob's mum wouldn't talk to me at all when he was in prison. She never forgave me for telling the police what happened, she thought I'd lied which is why I think she lied in this court."

"Did anything else happen during that period?"

"Yes, I met Thomas Adams a few times in the pub and in the street. I knew him from our local pub. He came up to me in the street during that time and put his arm round me and told me Bob was a 'wrong un'. He offered to take me out. I told him I wasn't interested. I knew he was married."

"We have heard that Annie was born prematurely at thirty weeks. Do you know why that was?"

"No, but it could be the stress I was going through, what with Thomas Adams pestering me, Bob's mother ignoring me and Bob in prison."

"Was Bob still in prison when you gave birth to Annie?"

"Yes."

"Bob came out of prison after six weeks. Did he come back to live with you?"

"Yes, as soon as he was released from prison. I think that annoyed his mother even more. She hoped he would go back and live with her."

"Was he ever violent towards you again?"

"A few times when he was drunk, but they were mainly slaps. It was never as bad as the time I had to go to hospital."

"Did you stay at home all the time when Annie was in hospital?"

"No. I stayed in the hospital as often as I could, but they had problems finding me a bed and I had to go home quite a lot."

"Whilst Annie was in hospital, what did you do for her?"

"I did everything I could for her. I would try to help with feeds, I would cuddle her when they let me and I'd clean her when I could."

Rachel looked like she was going to cry again, but she stopped herself. David waited a few seconds for her to become composed and then asked, "We heard from the health visitor that she contacted you in the hospital and asked you to contact her when Annie was discharged from the hospital. You didn't and she had to contact you, why was that?"

"I was really busy when I came out of hospital with Annie. I just forgot."

"Were you trying to avoid her?"

"No, not at all, I could do with all the help I could get."

"We also heard that the health visitor arranged to meet you on 16th November, but when she arrived you were on the way out. Is that true?"

"Yes, she arranged to see me at 10:00am, she hadn't arrived by 10:15am and I had to go and see Bob's mother who was ill. Bob had insisted I visit her with Annie. I was a bit afraid that if I didn't go, he'd hit me again. It was as I was leaving the door, that the health visitor arrived."

"As you've told us, she made an error, believing you said you were off to see your mother when in fact you said you were off to see Bob's mother?"

"That's right."

"Another visit was arranged?"

"Yes, and she had no problem with that. She never complained about me going out."

David looked at his notes before asking, "The health visitor also told us that she was concerned that Annie did not have enough warm clothes on when she first saw her. Did she say that to you?"

"She did comment on what Annie was wearing but it was a warm day and I thought she had enough clothes on. Also, Bob's mum had said she had bought some clothes for Annie and I thought I could go and get those and dress her in them if she needed anything else to wear."

"What was your relationship like with Bob's mum at this stage?"

"It was the same as before. I think she only talked to me because she wanted to see Annie."

David asked her to look in the jury bundle at some of the photographs of the house.

"These photographs do show a cluttered house. Why was it so cluttered?"

"It's all Bob's things. The weights were his, I couldn't even lift them. They were his F1 racing magazines. The beer bottles were his, I only drink vodka, not beer.

I was always tidying up after him and I was always asking him to tidy up. However, he either ignored me or threw more rubbish on the floor or occasionally he'd give me a slap."

"We can see photographs of a full ashtray in the living room, did you smoke round Annie?"

"I never did. Bob did sometimes and I would ask him not to but he kept on doing it. If I told him off it would put him in one of his dark moods and I knew too well not to push him when he was like that."

David nodded at her and then asked sympathetically, "Now I know this is difficult, but we need to deal with the days and weeks leading up to Annie's death. What condition was she in during that period?"

"Annie was always a difficult eater. She would never want much and she would vomit up most of the contents of a bottle of milk. I used to prepare two bottles in the hope I could get one down her."

"How did you prepare those bottles?"

"I used a sterilised bottle at home. I had a steriliser that I put in the microwave. It was easy to use and took no time to set up."

David made a mental note, that could be useful for Rose!

"Bob's mother told us that there was a time when she saw you preparing a bottle using tap water, did that happen?"

"No! There was a time when I said I was going to take Annie home for a feed and she insisted I make up a feed there. She has very hot water in her house, she's always complaining about the heating bills. I decided to wash the bottle out with the boiling tap water whilst I waited for the kettle to boil. She came into the kitchen and saw me and must have assumed I was making Annie's feed up with tap water. I was annoyed at her reaction and so I took Annie home, we only lived five minutes away. There I used a sterilised bottle and made her a feed using boiled water.

"How was Annie during those last weeks?"

"She was always bluish in colour. I thought it was cold so I rapped her up more. She also was wheezing and a lot, did not feed well and vomited a lot. She also seemed to have constant diarrhoea."

"Did you think about taking her to the doctors?"

"I did think about it, but I spoke to Bob's mum and she said there was nothing wrong with her and it was normal for babies to be like this and Annie would get better."

"Why did you take her advice and not go to the doctors yourself?"

"I don't really like doctors. It's like the time I had stitches above my eye and the doctor called the police and that led to Bob being imprisoned.

Anyway, Joan had brought up Bob so I presumed she knew what she was talking about."

"I want to ask you about the day Annie died. Did you go out that night and leave her alone?"

"No! Bob went out. He needed his time away from us otherwise he would get moody and angry and hit me. I stayed in and he said he would be home at about 9pm."

"I kept Annie up with me that night until about 8:30pm. I remember taking her to the living room window and looking out and telling her, her dad should be home soon. I put her to bed. She didn't seem well and wouldn't take a feed so I hoped with a little sleep she would be better in the morning..."

Suddenly Rachel broke down and started sobbing frantically. David asked her if she was alright but she did not answer and collapsed in the witness box. He looked up towards the judge who looked at Rachel without the slightest hint of sympathy. Tanner did look towards the jury some of whom were showing sympathy for Rachel. He turned to meet David's gaze and asked, "It is approaching lunchtime Mr Brant, would that be a convenient moment to stop for lunch. We can carry on with your examination in chief this afternoon when the witness has composed herself!"

David watched as the jury left court followed by the judge. Rachel was then led to some seats by the side of the court. For a split second, he thought he saw a smile on her face, but he assumed he was mistaken, her tears and sobbing looked genuine to him.

CHAPTER 37

RACHEL CONTINUES

After lunch, the court hearing recommenced and Rachel was again led back to the witness box by the burly female prison guards. She confirmed to David, that she was fit to continue giving evidence and he then reminded her of the last topic they were dealing with.

"Ms Wilson, we were dealing with the day that Annie died. You told us before lunch that you had put Annie to bed at 8:30pm and were expecting Bob to be home around 9:00pm. Did he come home at that time?"

"No, he was late."

"Did you try to contact him?"

"I couldn't contact him because he'd lost his mobile phone when he was drunk and we couldn't afford a new one for him."

"Did you check on Annie again?"

"I did. I went up at about 9pm and she was sleeping."

"When did Bob finally come home?"

"It was about 9:45pm."

"Had you seen Annie since 9pm?"

"No, but I went up to see her when Bob came home."

"What happened?"

"She wasn't making a sound and I couldn't hear her breathe. I picked her up and she was cold. I just panicked, I didn't know what to do. I took her downstairs to the living room and as we were both so stressed, Bob poured us large glasses of vodka. We drank those wondering what to do. Then he said I should phone for an ambulance, so I did."

"We have heard evidence that call was made at 10:04pm. We have also heard that call played in court. In it your speech is slurred and you were swearing."

Rachel looked down at her feet, "I am ashamed of that. I just can't believe it's me, even though I know it is. I was just in a state of shock."

"Were you drunk?"

"I was a bit tipsy, I opened the vodka once Annie had gone to sleep at 8:30pm and I had a couple of small glasses waiting for Bob."

"Did you continue to drink waiting for the ambulance?"

"Yes, and when they arrived. I thought it would help me ..." she paused before adding, "... but it didn't."

"Did you smoke?"

"Yes, but only after I put Annie in bed."

"We have been told that an Asian policeman arrived and someone was abusive to him, was that you?"

"No, that was Bob. I don't use that sort of language."

"We know you were arrested and interviewed and eventually charged with the offences you face now. Did you tell the truth in your interview with the police?"

"Yes, I did."

"We know that Thomas Adams has given evidence that he saw you in the pub with Bob the night that Annie died. Is that true?"

"No, not at all, I was with Annie at home."

"Do you know why he would lie about this?"

"No. I can only think it's because I rejected him. He's constantly pestered me since we first met in the pub. I remember him coming up to me and putting his arm around me, I shrugged him off. I wasn't too upset at the time as it happened a lot when I went to pubs. But he continued. He pestered me when Bob was in prison. He kept coming up to me and touching me and asking me out. He only stopped when Bob was released from prison and thumped him outside the pub. He avoided us after that!"

"When did you next see Mr Adams?"

"I saw him in the shops and some pubs but he avoided us until Bob disappeared. Then in July this year, just after I was charged, he came up to me in the shops. He was really friendly and I was feeling down. I let him put his arm around me, but then he tried to kiss me on the mouth. I didn't want anything to do with him so I pushed him away and told him to fuck off. He told me to fuck off and that I'd had my chance. The next I heard was that he had gone to the police and made up a pack of lies about me."

David nodded and then asked her to face the jury, "Ms Wilson, you have been charged with wilfully neglecting your daughter Annie and with causing or allowing her death. Did you wilfully neglect her?"

"No, I loved her, I did everything I could for her."

"Did you cause or allow her death, did you starve her to death or ignore the obvious signs that she was ill?"

"No, not at all, I never knew she was that ill. I fed her every day. I knew she wasn't well, but I thought she'd get better. God knows I've thought about it over and over since then, but I don't believe there is anything more I could have done!"

CHAPTER 38

A DIFFICULT TIME

Owen turned around and whispered something to his junior. This case on the face of it should be a simple one to prosecute, however, he was impressed with the way Rachel gave evidence and he knew he had to make some headway in cross examination to put the case back on track.

His junior nodded at his whispered suggestion.

"Ms Wilson, you portray yourself as an innocent victim in this case. A mother who tragically lost her child…" he paused before adding, "… but that is not the truth, is it?"

Rachel looked at him coldly wondering what was coming next, "I am a mother and I lost my child who I deeply loved!"

"From the moment, your daughter was born, she was an inconvenience to you, wasn't she?"

"No."

"You couldn't even provide a safe environment for her. Please look at the photographs, showing the cluttered state of your house."

Owen directed her to the jury bundle that contained photographs of her home.

"Was that a safe environment to bring a young baby into?"

"No, but it was Bob's mess. I tried to clean up but he just kept on making a mess."

"Annie was your baby, your responsibility, if your partner is not willing to provide a safe environment for his baby, you should have insisted or thrown him out!"

"You don't know Bob."

"You even smoked in front of Annie, a premature baby born with chronic lung disease!"

"I didn't smoke in front of her."

"We have heard evidence from Ms Head, the safeguarding nurse that the living room smelt of smoke when she arrived and she saw ashtrays with cigarettes in them."

"But we weren't smoking when she arrived."

Owen looked at her with a bemused expression, "If the living room smelt of smoke, you were either just smoking before she arrived or the room had been used for such heavy smoking that the smoke lingered for hours. In either event, it was not a safe environment for a child with chronic lung disease!"

She whimpered a response, "I never smoked in front of her."

"You never stopped Bob smoking in front of her?"

"I couldn't, he would have hit me!"

"The truth is, this child was an inconvenience to you. You resented having to do such menial tasks as changing her nappies?"

"No, I didn't."

"That is what Joan Harwood has told us."

"She's lying."

"She told us you couldn't even be bothered to feed Annie properly?"

"She lied."

"She told us she had to insist that you make up a feed for Annie and that you couldn't be bothered to boil any water, you simply put hot tap water into the bottle."

"I was washing it out."

"Why couldn't you use boiling water from the kettle to wash it out."

"The tap water was very hot."

"But it's not recommended by paediatricians is it. You would know that if you had any interest in the welfare of your baby."

Rachel began sobbing. Owen showed no sympathy as he told her, "Ms Wilson, you have broken down a few times whilst giving evidence. Your ordeal will end much sooner if you can control your emotions and just answer the questions!"

David looked at him with surprise, he was about to object to this style of cross examination which in his opinion amounted to bullying, but he noticed Rachel stop sobbing, tucked her handkerchief into the sleeve of her jumper and face Owen fully composed.

Owen smiled at her, "There that's better. Did they advise you in hospital, not to use tap water alone, however hot, to sterilise a bottle?"

"Yes, but Joan was insisting that I feed Annie there and then."

"You were her mother. She was your responsibility, not Ms Harwood's. You should have insisted on going home and using a properly sterilised bottle?"

"I know that now."

"You knew that then."

"Yes."

Owen looked down at his notes again, "How often did you feed Annie?"

"She slept through the night so I didn't feed her then…"

"You mean you didn't wake her up to give her a feed?"

"Sometimes I did, but most of the time I thought she needed her sleep."

"How often would you wake her during the night to give her a feed?"

"Probably once or twice a week."

"Or less?"

"Possibly."

"How often did you feed her during the day then?"

"Every two to three hours."

"And when was the first feed of the day?"

"About 8am."

"Ms Head told us that she visited you on 23rd November 2015 at 10:05am and you were feeding Annie. Is that true?"

"Yes."

"She also told us that you said that was Annie's first feed of the day. I notice your counsel did not challenge that assertion so presumably that's true?"

Rachel looked a little panicked, "I don't know, I can't remember now."

"What time would you put Annie to bed?"

"About 8:30pm every night."

"So, over the night of 22nd to 23rd November, she slept from 8:30pm until 10:00am, thirteen and a half hours without a feed!"

"No, I probably woke her up at midnight and fed her."

"You have just told us you tended to let her sleep because she needed her sleep. Or is it she was an inconvenience and you could not be bothered to feed her properly."

She gave an emphatic, "No." in reply.

"Let us move on to clothing young Annie. You didn't even dress her in proper clothing, did you?"

"Yes, I did."

Owen picked up his notes of the evidence again, "Ms Harwood also told us, and this was confirmed by Ms Head on one occasion, that you did not dress Annie warmly enough?"

"That's not true, I always put a coat on her or a jumper or something."

"Except the time when Ms Head saw you?"

"That was just once."

"In winter when it was cold out."

"It was quite mild."

"In November!"

"Yes."

"You have told us that your boyfriend's mother has lied on oath in this court, what about the health visitor or safeguarding nurse, Ms Head. Did she lie when she said you had told her at the first arranged visit that you could not see her because you were visiting your mother?"

David rose to his feet, "I do object to the way that question is phrased. My learned friend knows that the purpose of cross examination is not to elicit argument about whether one witness is lying or mistaken, but to put a case to a witness and elicit facts."

Owen immediately responded, "The defendant was the one to start calling witnesses liars, I just wanted to see whether it is her case that every prosecution witness who gave evidence lied in this court, or whether some told the truth!"

Tanner was unimpressed with both arguments. "Just continue Mr Jenkins, but try to ask admissible questions!"

Owen turned to face Rachel who was looking at him coldly.

"Ms Wilson, did you tell Ms Head you could not see her because you were going to see your mother?"

"No, I told her on both occasions, I was going to see Bob's mother."

"So, she has either lied or made the same mistake twice, when she recorded that you said you were going to see your own mother?"

"Yes."

"Or is it you were just making up an excuse not to see a health visitor and the first thing you thought of as an excuse, was the invention of an infirm mother?"

"No."

"You had so little interest in your own child's welfare that you couldn't even spare the safeguarding nurse a few minutes of your time to give you much needed advice, could you?"

"That's not true."

"On the first visit that was arranged Ms Head said she arrived five minutes late and you were already leaving when she arrived."

"She was fifteen minutes late."

"Even if it was fifteen minutes, and I suggest it was only five minutes, why, in the interests of your child could you not keep Bob's mother waiting a few minutes and let the safeguarding nurse in to see your baby?"

"Bob insisted I go and see his mother."

"But he wasn't going to do anything whilst Ms Head was in your home?"

"But he might have when she left."

"What about the second occasion she states you told her you had gone to see your ill mother again. Did she get that wrong?"

"Yes, I told her it was Bob's mother who was ill."

"Why couldn't Bob go and see his own ill mother and you stay and show Annie to the safeguarding nurse?"

She hesitated before replying, "Bob wanted me to go."

"But you didn't even get on with his mother. According to the questions put on your behalf, she blamed you for taking Bob from her and for having Bob imprisoned."

Rachel didn't answer.

"Very well, let's move on and see what other witnesses have told lies or got it wrong.

You accept that you were drunk and swearing when you made the emergency call?"

"Yes."

"Of course, you have to, as we have heard the tape of the call?"

"I have admitted that and I am sorry for that call."

"You were still drinking when the ambulance men and the police arrived?"

"Yes."

"So, if anything you were getting more and more drunk?"

"I'd just lost my child."

"When you were drunk did you call the Asian police officer, 'A Paki cunt'?"

"No, that was Bob."

"The officer was adamant that was you. He's not likely to have made a mistake about that, is he?"

David turned towards Owen and stared at him. Owen returned the stare and smiled, "I can see that my Learned Friend is making a silent objection to that comment. He is right, so I will withdraw it.

So, if I can sum up the position. Bob's mother, Ms Harwood is lying about her evidence, Ms Head is mistaken in her evidence, PC Sidhu is presumably mistaken in his recollection and then we have Mr Adams who must be lying when he said he saw you in the pub, the night Annie died..." he stopped and looked at the jury for a few seconds before continuing, "...of course the alternative is that these witnesses are all telling the truth and it is you who are lying!

I suggest that is the reality here isn't it, you are lying?"

"I'm telling the truth."

"I suggest that this poor child was an inconvenience to you and you never even wanted her?"

"That's not true."

"You did not want assistance from social services, you could not be bothered feeding your child properly, you could not be bothered clothing your child properly or even providing a safe environment for her to live in?"

"That's not true. I loved Annie."

"On the last day of her life you barely fed her and then you left her alone in your house whilst you went out getting drunk in the pub?"

Rachel burst out an answer, "That's not fucking true, I loved her and I didn't want her to fucking die."

Owen looked at Rachel's angered look of hatred directed at him and paused so the jury could absorb the image of angry hateful look before he turned to HHJ Tanner and said he had no further questions.

Just as he was sitting down, he turned to his junior and whispered more audibly this time so that David could hear, "I told you she was the type who would show her true colours if you probe enough!"

CHAPTER 39

THE DEFENCE EXPERT

Rachel's ordeal was over. She had been a better witness than David feared but he still could not tell whether any of the jury had warmed to her, or, more importantly, believed anything she had said.

Owen had finished his cross examination by lunchtime so it meant that Rachel could speak to her lawyers again. David took the opportunity to congratulate her, that her part in the case was over, trying not to comment on the quality of her evidence.

"Well that's it Rachel, there is nothing more that you have to do, nothing more you can say. You just have to sit back now and listen to your expert and us lawyers droning on!"

"How was I Mr Brant? I didn't let you down, did I?"

David hesitated slightly before answering, "I know how difficult it is for anyone giving evidence, particularly someone who walks from the dock to the witness box, wondering if they will be believed. I will be honest with you. I was worried that you would find the strain was too much and you might make some basic mistake, but you didn't appear to. The prosecutor, despite his strenuous efforts, and his deliberate efforts to wind you up, did not catch you out in an obvious lie, so well done."

She beamed at him not realising that he had deliberately not made any reference to her losing her temper. Although she was smiling, David could see that she clearly had something on her mind.

"Is there something wrong Rachel?"

"No, there's nothing wrong."

She looked at him with seeming embarrassment.

"It's just I was approached last night by a neighbour, Philip Price. I wanted to tell you this morning but the judge said I couldn't speak to anyone when I was giving evidence.

Philip has been very friendly recently. He stopped me in the street on my way home from court and wished me good luck. I was feeling a bit down so I started talking to him. He said he remembered the night Annie died. He told me he remembered seeing me looking out of the curtain a few times until Bob came home."

She paused before adding, "I don't know if that might be any use to you?"

David had been about to go for lunch but the news stopped him in his tracks. He gave Sara a quick look, trying not to convey in front of the client what he thought about such information at this stage of the trial.

"Do you know if he available to take a statement from and, will he come to court?"

She grinned at him, "Oh yes, he said he was willing to come to court if you want him. He said he'd do anything he can to help me."

"Have you told your solicitor about this?"

"No, I thought I'd tell you first."

David turned to Sara, "Sara, can you take details of this Mr Price from Rachel. The usual things, address and telephone number, if known, and give them to the solicitors immediately. Tell them to get a statement from him today and get him to come to court first thing tomorrow."

David thanked Rachel for the information and made his way to the advocates' dining room. He had to catch Owen and have a quick word with him.

At 2:05pm the court was sitting again when David announced that he was calling his next witness, the defence expert, Malcolm Williamson.

After a few minutes the witness made his way into the court room and strolled confidently into the witness box. After he had taken the oath and given his name, David took him through a few background matters, including his impressive list of qualifications, before asking him his opinion on the case.

"Mr Williamson, you have had an opportunity of reading all the relevant papers in this case, the pathologist's report, the prosecution expert's report and the transcript of Ms Wilson's interview?"

"Yes, I have."

"Essentially you agree with much of what the prosecution's experts say?"

"Yes, I do. I agree that the cause of death is unascertained, although I do consider that dehydration undoubtedly contributed to the child's death."

"Where do you differ?"

"With two aspects of Mr Roberts' report. Firstly, the reason for the dehydration in my opinion cannot be determined. It could be starvation but equally it could have been as a result of some other condition, such as malabsorption or even a chronic infection that was not diagnosed during life and could not be diagnosed after death. Secondly, in my opinion the gradual reduction in the rate of the child's weight gain is not something that should have necessarily alerted the parents that there was a serious medical concern. If there had been dramatic weight loss, then the parents should have been aware there was a problem. Here though, there was a steady weight gain, albeit an inadequate one."

David asked him to take the jury bundle and turn to page 25 where Annie's WHO chart was located.

David waited until he had located it and asked, "Have you seen this chart before?"

Mr Williamson looked at the chart closely and nodded, "Yes, I've seen this chart before."

"You will be aware that it plots the child's weight a number of times including her weight at the time of the post mortem?"

"Yes, I see that."

"It does not refer to her weight on the day she died because she was never weighed that day. Can you assist as to whether that is an important fact in this case?"

Mr Williamson again nodded, "It depends upon the use that you are trying to make of the information. Normally, I would not expect a child's body to be weighed at the time of death. There is usually little relevance in the weight at that stage. However, bodies are usually weighed by pathologists during post mortem so there is some relevance to weighing a body then.

However, in this case Mr Roberts took the weight at the time of the post mortem and in his report, he appears to have assumed that was the weight at the time of death."

"In your opinion was that a correct approach?"

"No, I consider it wholly unsafe to do so. There are no known studies out there of how much weight or more correctly, mass, a body can lose after death, but it can clearly lose some."

"Dr Numan, the pathologist stated it might be up to 100gms."

"In a baby, when you are calculating growth centiles, 100gm might be significant, but in any event, there are no studies out there so we cannot know whether it was 50 gms, 100gms, 200 gms, or even more!"

"Thank you, I would now like to turn to the question of oxygen. We know that the baby originally was given oxygen at the hospital, but that was discontinued before she was discharged."

"Yes, that's correct."

"Are you aware that there is a note in the medical records that shows that one hospital doctor was concerned that they may have discontinued the use of oxygen too early?"

"I am now. I confess I did not see the note when I first looked through the hospital papers, but once my attention was drawn to it, I did read it."

"Mr Peters told us that he thought it unlikely that the doctors would have discontinued giving oxygen at too early a stage. Do you have an opinion on that?"

"Sadly, mistakes like that can be made. A baby may seem to be responding well but then have a relapse and need oxygen again."

"Mr Peters explained the consequences to a baby if oxygen was discontinued too early. He explained that there would be obvious signs of breathing problems, flaring nostrils, rapid shallow breathing, wheezing, susceptibility to respiratory illnesses, a blueness to the skin. Do you agree that those conditions would appear?"

"Yes, but there is a question who would notice this. A doctor would, but a lay person might think the baby simply has a cold."

David looked towards the jury as he asked, "A lay person, such as a mother?"

"Yes."

"Mr Peters concluded that a baby suffering from an inadequate oxygen intake, may have difficulty eating, which in itself may result in inadequate weight being gained and a failure to thrive."

"Very possible."

"And eventually, this could lead to death?"

"Yes."

"Which could have been the case here?"

"Yes. I'm afraid so."

CHAPTER 40

THE WEIGHT OF THE SOUL

Owen rose slowly from his seat and turned to speak to his junior before commencing his questioning of Mr Williamson. David now assumed this was his normal style, keeping a witness waiting and anticipating before he asked any questions. He very much doubted it would have any effect on an expert witness and noted that Mr Williamson simply looked bemused by the wait.

Owen turned back and beamed at the witness, "Mr Williamson, what is the duty of an expert witness?"

Mr Williamson hesitated before answering, he assumed he was going to be asked about his findings, not basic matters, but he answered, "An expert witness' duty is to give his professional opinion to assist the court. He is to ensure that his opinion is impartial and based on the facts, and he must not be influenced in that opinion by the fact that he is called by one party or other to the proceedings."

"Precisely, and do you think you have acted in accordance with those principals?"

The witness started to look uncomfortable, "I believe so."

"Believe so, you should know so!"

"I believe I have given an impartial opinion based upon the facts that were presented to me."

"How often do you hear one expert make a statement that he is 'surprised' that another expert in the case has given a certain opinion."

Mr Williamson was uncomfortable now, "Experts differ in many cases, otherwise only one would be called in a trial."

"Of course, experts differ, but I asked you how often an expert states that he is 'surprised' by an opinion given by another expert?"

"It happens frequently."

"In cases you are involved in?"

"Yes!"

"Let me ask you about weight loss after death. Is it right that there are no studies out there concerning weight loss in a body after death?"

"There are no reliable ones that I am aware of."

"By 'reliable ones' do you mean to say that you are aware of 'unreliable ones'?"

"Well I am aware of the work of Dr Duncan MacDougall, an American doctor from Massachusetts, which he carried out in 1901."

343

"And perhaps you can tell us what those experiments were about?"

"As I understand it he postulated that a human soul must have some mass and when a person dies they immediately lose that mass. He did a number of experiments and concluded that the loss was ¾ ounce or approximately 21 gms. However, he only experimented on six bodies and his weighing equipment was not that accurate so no one relies on the experiment."

Owen stared at him with a look bordering on contempt, "Mr Williamson we are not dealing with fanciful notions, but science. Is it right there are no studies out there that can assist with whether a body loses weight or mass after death?"

"As I said, none that I am aware of."

"Obviously over time a body will lose weight or mass as it decomposes?"

"Obviously."

"But if a body is immediately refrigerated, you would not expect it to lose weight or mass?"

"Well that's the problem, there are no studies one way or the other."

"So, you cannot say that the child's body lost any weight between the time of death and the time of the post mortem?"

"No, I cannot."

"If there was no loss of weight, it would mean that the child had lost weight in life. In other words, there was not an inadequate weight gain, there was in fact a weight loss?"

"Yes, it would."

"Would you agree that a parent should certainly notice a weight loss in a baby and should take that baby to a general practitioner or to an Accident and Emergency department of a hospital?"

"It would depend on the amount of weight lost, but broadly I agree with the proposition."

"In this case, we know at the post mortem that the child had sunken eyes. Do you agree that she was likely to have sunken eyes in the last few days of her life?"

"Generally, yes, although it might depend if there was a significant weight loss after death which could have given the appearance of sunken eyes after death."

"Would you agree that a caring parent would be likely to notice if their child had sunken eyes?"

"I would have thought so."

"And again, that should alert them that there was a condition that needed medical treatment."

"It probably would, depending how long they noticed this condition."

"In relation to the hospital note relating to oxygen. If a hospital doctor concluded that a baby may have been taken off oxygen too early, he would surely insist that she was put back on it?"

"In an ideal world, but mistakes are unfortunately made."

"Finally, Mr Peters concluded that the baby died from dehydration caused by starvation. Were you surprised by Mr Peter's opinion in this case?"

"No, it is a perfectly legitimate opinion based on the facts."

"Similarly, for Dr Numan's opinion as to the cause of death?"

"Yes."

"So, in your opinion they both could be right in their findings?"

"Yes, I accept that they both have given honest opinions, based upon the facts presented to them. They could be right but I consider that my opinion is the correct one."

"You accept that this baby could have died from dehydration?"

"Yes."

"And that dehydration could have been as a result of the mother and/or the father starving the baby?"

"Yes, but I consider it equally possible that the cause of death was as a result of some undiagnosed condition such as malabsorption."

"But, even on your conclusions, death could have been as a result of starvation?"

"Yes, as I've said."

"It is your conclusion, that this poor baby could have died as a result of being starved by this defendant ..." He pointed to Rachel, "... her own mother?"

"Yes."

CHAPTER 41

FURTHER PROBLEMS

Mr Williamson finished his evidence at 4:20pm. As soon as he was released the judge addressed David in the presence of the jury, "I presume that is your final witness Mr Brant and you will be closing your case now?"

David paused and looked towards the jury before turning back to face the judge.

"My Lord, I would like to reserve my position until tomorrow morning. I was made aware at lunchtime today, that there is a potential witness who may have some relevant evidence to give."

Tanner assumed his usual red shade, "How has a potential defence witness suddenly appeared at this late stage of the case?"

He picked up two documents he had in front of him and after a cursory read, he added, "There is no reference to a further witness in the Defence statement or the PTPH form!"

"That is because, as I just stated, we have only just become aware of this witness today! No time is being wasted. I suspect Your Lordship would rise for the day at this time in any event."

The judge assumed his usual colour changing trick and now turned his brightest shade of red. He turned to Owen, "I suppose you know nothing about this supposed witness Mr Jenkins, and object to an adjournment."

Owen tried to assume a respectful expression, "My Lord, Mr Brant was kind enough to inform me about this potential witness at lunchtime today, as soon as he became aware of his existence. In the circumstances, I have no objection to an adjournment overnight. Of course, the situation may change if a further application to adjourn is made again tomorrow."

Tanner looked at him as if he had no idea what he was doing, shook his head and turned to David, "Very well Mr Brant, I shall grant you an adjournment until 10:00am tomorrow. If your witness is not available, I will be unlikely to grant you any further time!"

A few minutes later, after releasing the jurors for the day, Tanner left the court without a further word to any of the advocates.

Owen waited until he had left, smiled and looked at David, "Its looks like HHJ Tanner thinks I am too lenient with you."

David laughed, "Don't ask him for a reference, he might give you one!"

Owen chuckled, David had already explained his own personal history with this judge.

David went home to his flat to prepare for the following day and put the finishing touches to his speech, which in reality would probably mean he would rewrite it for the fourth time.

He phoned Wendy at 6pm just to check on Rose's progress. Wendy sounded down when she took his call.

"What's wrong love?"

"They are a worried about Rose. She has diarrhoea and they are worried that she might have picked up the Rotavirus."

David closed his eyes for a few seconds before replying wondering why Rose seemed to have everything thrown at her.

"What's the Rotavirus?"

"They told me it's a virus that can cause gastroenteritis. The symptoms include diarrhoea, vomiting, fever and pains in the stomach. They are worried that she has a fever and has been crying and so may have stomach pain. They told me that if it's not treated properly, babies can become severely dehydrated and can even die!"

David wondered for a second whether he should have investigated this condition with the experts in Rachel's case but then put the thought out of his mind as it was too late now. He immediately began to be fearful for Rose.

"What are they doing about it?"

"Well apparently, it's very contagious. They've moved her into her own room in case she passes it on to any other babies and they've started her on a course of antibiotics. They are going to keep a close eye on her."

"When will they know?"

"They can't say. Oh, David I wish you could be here!"

"I do as well, but you know I've got my final witness tomorrow followed by my final speech. I'll probably be working all night."

Wendy said she understood and shortly afterwards they finished the call. David slung a supermarket pizza into the microwave, opened a bottle of claret and poured himself a glass. It was going to be a long night.

CHAPTER 42

THE NEIGHBOUR

At 10:00am the following morning, HHJ Tanner invited the jurors to take their seats before he asked David, "Well Mr Brant, has your mysterious witness attended?"

David beamed at him, "My witness has arrived My Lord, and with Your Lordship's permission, I shall call him to give evidence. I understand the prosecution have no objection!"

Tanner did not even look at Owen, "That does not surprise me! Very well, call the witness."

Five minutes later Philip Price had entered the witness box, taken the oath and given his name. David rose from his seat to ask his first question,

"Mr Price, do you know the defendant in this case, Rachel Wilson?"

Price looked towards the dock and saw Rachel who smiled at him, "Yes, I know her."

"How do you know her?"

"She lives in the same street as me. She has done for a few years now."

"Are you close friends?"

He looked slightly uncomfortable, "I wouldn't say that. We have become friends, I suppose. I know her to say hello to and to have the occasional chat in the street, or when I see her in the shops…"

He reddened slightly as he added, "… but nothing more than that."

"Did you know Ms Wilson's x-boyfriend, Bob Harwood?"

"I saw him around. I don't think we ever said more than 'hello' to each other though."

"Did you know that they had a child together?"

Mr Price looked embarrassed for a moment, "Yes, I did. I used to see her with the little baby in the street."

"Did you notice anything about the way she treated her child."

He looked towards the dock again at Rachel, "It seemed to me she was like any mother, she always seemed to dote on the child."

"In what way?"

"She always seemed to be fussing over the baby when I saw her."

"You are aware that Ms Wilson's baby, Annie, died, aren't you?"

Mr Price looked at his feet, "Yes I am aware of that. It was very sad. The baby was so small. So young."

"How did you become aware that the baby died?"

"I live across the road from Ra.., sorry, Ms Wilson. I saw the ambulance and the police arrive and I heard the next day that the baby had died."

"Did you see Ms Wilson earlier that day, before the ambulance and the police arrived?"

"Yes, I saw her a few times that night, looking out of her window."

"Do you know what time this was?"

"It was probably just over an hour before the ambulance arrived."

"Can you be more precise on the timing?"

"I think the first time I saw her was 8:30pm, then it was every ten or fifteen minutes until her partner came home, about ten minutes to ten."

"How do you know what the time was?"

Mr Price nodded, "I remember looking at my clock when she was first looking out and I glanced at it again when her boyfriend came home."

David paused and watched the eyes of the jurors intently staring at Mr Price, before asking, "Where was Ms Wilson when you saw her?"

"She was constantly looking out of her front room window."

"She was in her house then?"

"Yes."

"Could you tell what she was looking for?"

"Not at first. She kept going to the window, looking out, then going back into the room. She did this several times until her boyfriend appeared. Then she went to the door and let him in."

"Did you ever see her baby that day?"

"Yes, on one of her early visits to the window, she was carrying the baby."

"How did the baby look?"

"Normal, like any baby. She did look like she was crying."

"Did you see Ms Wilson leave the house that day?"

"Yes."

David looked surprised, he was not expecting that answer. He immediately asked, "When was that?"

"I saw her leave the house when she got into the ambulance after the police had visited.

David tried not to show his relief, "Did she leave at any other time?"

"Not that I saw."

David paused before asking his final question of the witness, "Mr Price, some people may be wondering why you have only just come forward now to give this evidence. Is there any reason why you have left it so late?"

Mr Price turned to look at the jurors' faces, "I didn't think I had anything important to say."

"What changed your mind?"

"It was only two days ago, when I saw Rachel in the street. She looked sad, so I asked her how she was. She told me she had to give evidence in court and the prosecution were alleging that she left her baby all alone the night she died. That's when I said that I knew that wasn't right because I had seen her constantly going up to her window that night and looking out. She then asked if I would be willing to come to court to say this. I said I would and the next day her solicitor contacted me and asked me to come here today."

David thanked him and sat down.

Owen rose slowly from his seat and looked towards the dock at Rachel. Without looking at Mr Price he asked, "Do you find the defendant attractive?"

Mr Price was clearly embarrassed by the question, "I've never really thought about it." He looked closely at Rachel, "Yes, I suppose she is."

"Her boyfriend has disappeared, she is now single again. Have you replaced him or are you planning to?"

"No I have not and no, I'm not!"

"Your evidence is very conveniently timed. This case has been reported in the national and local press. You must have seen reports on the trial?"

"I don't really follow things like that."

"Oh, come now Mr Price. Your attractive neighbour is on trial for causing the death of her child, you were bound to read the newspaper reports?"

"Well I didn't."

"I suggest you would have known last week, at the latest, that the prosecution were alleging that the defendant had left this baby all alone on the night that she died and the defendant had gone to a local pub?"

"I didn't know that until I saw Rachel, two days ago and she told me."

"Have you come here to help an attractive friend, and to lie on her behalf if necessary?"

"No!"

"I suggest that is exactly what you have done. You

did not see her at home that night. She was not constantly looking out of the curtains because she was in the local pub getting drunk with her then boyfriend..." he again looked towards the jury. "... whilst her tiny baby died all alone at home!"

He sat down before Philip had a chance to answer.

CHAPTER 43

THE PROSECUTION FINAL SPEECH

David closed his case at 11:30am. HHJ Tanner sent the jury away until after lunch so that he could discuss the law and the contents of his summing up with counsel, just in case there was anything they objected to or wanted to correct. It was not something he enjoyed doing but the Court of Appeal had quashed a conviction in a case he had presided over in the past and been highly critical that he had not discussed such matters with the advocates in the case. He had no intention of receiving such a public dressing down again.

At 2:05pm Owen rose to address the jury for the final time. He picked up the large jury bundle of documents and put it on the lectern in front of him. He gave a quick flick through the papers before looking at the jury for a few seconds until he had got the attention of most of them.

"Ladies and gentlemen, I am conscious that having had a sight of those documents you are thinking one thing, 'help'."

There were a few smiles from the jurors save for one man on the front row who seemed to be avoiding Owen's look and was satisfying himself with stacking and unstacking the plastic cups

359

that were in front of him. They were there to provide all the jurors with water but he had taken control of them and was making a tower. It was the man David had noticed in the past who had not seemed to listen to a single word of evidence. David wondered for a moment if he had taken against the prosecution case and was an ally of the defence? He soon ignored the thought. He remembered the way this juror had looked at Rachel when she gave evidence. There was certainly not going to be any support from this quarter. He looked away from the man who he had now branded, 'Cupman' and looked at Owen, who had either not noticed Cupman's antics or had wisely chosen to ignore them.

"This case is in a sense about keeping your eye on the ball over what happened over the last few weeks of little Annie's life.

Let me say this to begin with. We appreciate that you are dealing with a difficult and highly emotional case. It is never easy to deal with allegations like this, involving, as they do, the death of a young child. However, we ask you to put emotion aside and look at this case coldly and impartially. The defendant is entitled to your verdict based entirely on the evidence and not on prejudice or emotion.

You have heard a great deal put to witnesses, quite properly by the defence. They had to investigate possibilities. However, please do not be sidetracked by irrelevant considerations. One such issue is motive. The defence might state in this case, what is the motive here? What possible motive could a mother have for starving her child? Well, as His Lordship will direct you, the prosecution does not have to establish what the motive was. We do not know what the motive was. We would only be speculating if we did. Was it laziness, a lack of care, apathy, or was it deliberate, truly wilful and intentional? We do not know what the motive was, nor is it relevant. If a mother starves a baby to death, it does not matter what her motive was, she has still starved the baby and caused its death.

Another matter that has been raised in this case relates to the care exercised by the health professionals. You may think there was more that could have been done by some of the health professionals in this case. You heard Mr Peters criticise a number of them. There may be something in those criticisms, he is after all an expert in these matters, but such considerations are irrelevant to your deliberations. No one is really suggesting that the potential lack of care by a health professional had anything to do with the death of little Annie.

Whether there were such failings is for others to determine, it is not for you. You are here to determine whether this mother wilfully neglected her child by starving her or by failing to obtain medical assistance when required to do so and then whether by that neglect she caused or allowed the child's death.

We, the prosecution, say there was deliberate and wilful conduct on the part of Rachel Wilson not to feed this baby properly. This wasn't an accident. This wasn't because of personal inadequacies. This was criminal behaviour towards a baby who could not defend herself.

The evidence is clear we suggest. Rachel Wilson could not be bothered to look after this baby, the poor child was an inconvenience to her. An inconvenience that no doubt interfered with her social life in the local pubs. The defendant ignored the advice of professionals, doctors, nurses, a health visitor and she ignored poor Annie when she started her inevitable decline and lost weight instead of gaining it, or at least had a wholly inadequate weight gain. Something that would have been noticeable to any caring mother.

You have heard all the evidence now, there will not be any more. We suggest the evidence is clear. Towards the end of her life Annie was suffering from dehydration. The signs would have been obvious, the reduced crying, the difficulty breathing and most dramatic of all, her eyes were sinking slowly into her skull. What mother would not notice that? What mother would not, at the very least, seek help from a doctor or other health professional? Help that would have undoubtedly saved Annie's life.

We say on the evidence, you can be sure that is what happened here. You may find it useful as a starting point to consider the medical evidence first.

Noticeably the prosecution and the defence experts agree on important facts. Both agree that dehydration played an important part in the death of this baby. Yes, the pathologist listed the cause of death as 'unascertained', but as he told us that is mainly for statistical reasons and in his opinion dehydration played an important role. That is enough for our purposes. If dehydration played a more than minimal part in Annie's death, then as His Lordship will direct you, that is enough to find that it was the 'cause' of death in law.

What caused the dehydration? There were only two real possibilities given in court, malabsorption and starvation. Mr Williamson, the defence expert said it could be either, Mr Peters the prosecution expert stated he believed it was starvation. Malabsorption is a rare condition and there were no other signs here to suggest that was the case. Annie thrived in hospital, she put on weight at an adequate rate so there was no problem with malabsorption there. Once she left hospital she failed to put on sufficient weight and fell through the centile charts. That wasn't malabsorption, that was inadequate feeding.

What about the issue raised by the defence about whether she had been taken off oxygen, too soon? There was one reference in the hospital papers to one doctor wondering about that, but he did not insist that Annie be put back on oxygen and no other expert thought it was necessary. I suggest the oxygen like the Meckel's diverticulum we heard so much about, are red herrings in this case and wholly irrelevant.

You heard the defendant give evidence and of course you will want to consider that evidence carefully. Did she come across as someone who was trying her best to tell the truth, or did you get the impression that she was trying to fool you with the false tears. Did you get a true glimpse of her character at the end of my cross examination? A character that was clearly on display in that 999 call you heard and in what she said to the young Asian policeman who had gone to her assistance.

Was she a caring mother or an indifferent one? You have important evidence that answers that question. Firstly, we have the evidence of the health visitor, Ms Head. The defendant did not contact her to tell her that Annie had been discharged from hospital. Apparently, that happens a great deal but what was the reason in this case? Was it that the defendant was busy or just that she didn't want social services breathing down her neck? Ms Head also gave other important evidence. She arranged a meeting with the defendant and when she arrived, five minutes late, the defendant was on her way out. What was so important that she could not wait a few minutes for the health visitor to check up on her baby? Ms Head is adamant that she was told that the defendant's mother was ill. She was told this on two separate occasions. Of course, we know now that the defendant has not had any contact with her mother for years so that cannot be the truth. The defendant says that it was her boyfriend's mother who was ill and that is what she said, but did she?

Her relationship with her boyfriend's mother was not a good one, and there was no suggestion the mother was dying so what was the hurry.

I suggest that it's just another lie. She just did not want to the health visitor to see Annie and so she invented a story about her mother being ill. She has had to change that story since because she told the health visitor on another occasion that she had not seen her mother for years.

The health visitor also allowed us to glean some other important information. The standard of care by the defendant of her child. On a cold November morning, she had not adequately dressed Annie saying she was picking up some clothes when she saw her mother. Another lie, she just couldn't be bothered dressing this child properly.

Ms Head also told us about the presence of smoke in the house and the clutter which we can see ourselves in the police photographs. Hardly the environment a caring mother would bring a baby into.

We then have the evidence of her boyfriend's mother, Ms Harwood. She confirmed what the health visitor said, that the defendant did not adequately clothe Annie. She also gave evidence of how the Defendant was reluctant to feed Annie. Now she might not like the defendant, but that doesn't mean she's lying. Didn't her story about Rachel trying to make up feed using a hot tap, actually ring true?

We also have the evidence of what happened the last night of Annie's life. It is obvious that the defendant was drunk when she made the 999 call. She was undoubtedly drinking between the time she discovered Annie was dead and the time the paramedics arrived, but she must have started drinking heavily much earlier in the evening. It is unlikely she got drunk in the few minutes between discovering that Annie was dead and making the 999 call.

You may be sure she was drinking all night, just as the witness Thomas Adams told you. Did he lie to you about seeing the defendant that night, drunk in the local pub? Is he yet another witness who apparently dislikes the defendant so much that he lied to you on oath? Did he really harbour such resentment because of some rejection, that he would perjure himself? I suggest not. He told the truth.

Of course, you will want to consider the evidence of Mr Price, the defendant's neighbour, who came so late in the day. Is it feasible that he did not know what the prosecution were alleging against his attractive friend until she told him during the trial? This case has been reported in both the national and the local press, he would surely have followed the case of a close attractive friend, a neighbour who lived just across the road and known what was being alleged?

Does he have a reason to support her? What impression did you get when I asked him how close his relationship with the defendant is and what are his intentions towards her?

No, we suggest that all the evidence points one way. This child died from dehydration. That dehydration was not caused by some undiagnosed condition but by the simple fact that the child was starved of food by a mother who did not care.

However, if what she says is or maybe true and Annie was ill and not feeding properly, why didn't she take her to her general practitioner or the Accident and Emergency department of a local hospital? Annie was clearly not putting on adequate weight. Her eyes were sunken. How many mothers think their child is not putting on adequate weight even when they are. It is usually one of the major concerns of a mother even when a child is gaining weight at an acceptable rate. However, here Annie was either not gaining weight at an adequate rate or she was actually losing weight at the end. This would surely have been noticed by a caring mother who, if she truly cared, would have taken her child to the doctors.

No, the sad truth is this mother simply did not care. She criminally neglected the wellbeing of her own child so she could pursue her own drinking habit in the pub. The result was that her child died and she was the cause of that."

Owen looked at the jurors one by one, only Cupman ignored him. He concluded with a degree of irony, "Thank you for your attention," and sat down.

CHAPTER 44

THE DEFENCE FINAL SPEECH

His Honour Judge Tanner did not offer David the opportunity of having an adjournment before making his speech and simply announced, "Mr Brant", as Owen sat down.

David took one long look at 'Cupman' before looking at each of the other jurors in turn and began.

"I'm conscious that when I stand up to address you on behalf of Rachel Wilson, that some, if not all of you are wondering, what has he got to say, surely we've heard it all by now?'"

A few of the jurors smiled acknowledging that he was right.

"Well the good news is that the case is almost over now. It's now almost two weeks since it began and you have heard; a lengthy opening, a great deal of evidence and a relatively lengthy final speech from my learned friend. You've no doubt discussed the case amongst yourselves. Some of you, may have formed opinions, even strong opinions in this case and no doubt you will express them in the jury room, as you should.

However, can I ask for one last indulgence. That you try to keep an open mind until then. A trial continues until your foreman, whether male or female, delivers your verdicts. Until then it consists of hearing evidence, hearing counsel's speeches to you and the summing up from His Lordship and only then, is it the time to make a decision.

Counsel's speeches are not evidence but they are our attempts to draw the threads of the case together to demonstrate arguments why, in the case of the prosecution, they say you can be sure of guilt, and why, in the case of Rachel Wilson, we say for the defence, that you cannot be sure of guilt.

You are free to reject any arguments any of us makes, but it's impossible to reject an argument unless you've heard it, which is why I ask you bear with me over the next hour or so."

There were a few nods from some of the jurors but Cupman contented himself with building yet another tower from the plastic cups, interspersed with regular looks at his watch. David knew he was a hopeless cause, so he ignored him and concentrated on the remaining jurors.

"Let's begin by dealing with what this case is not. It's not a family case, it's not a case as to who bears the moral responsibility for Annie's death. It is not an investigation into the conduct of the professionals involved in the case.

It is a case of criminal responsibility with criminal penalties in the case of a conviction. Put simply it's a criminal trial, and the sole test is, have the prosecution proved the particular charges they have brought, so that you are sure of guilt.

There are some important words I must mention at this stage; emotions, sympathy and prejudice.

This is a tragic case involving as it does the death of a young child, in fact a young baby, barely six months old. A young child who never had the opportunity to grow up. Who never had the chance to make the mistakes we all make and to ultimately learn from them.

It's terribly sad when you think of that poor baby dying in that cluttered house. When you think of her very short life. It is inevitable that you will feel a great deal of sympathy for little Annie and it's right that anyone who calls themselves human, should do so. Indeed, let's be honest, it's absolutely natural in a situation like this to want to blame someone for her death whatever the evidence might actually be. It is almost natural to think that someone should pay!

However, that is not the purpose of this trial. You will recall your juror's oaths, to try this case on the evidence, not on feelings of sympathy for Annie, not on feelings of prejudice against Rachel Wilson and her lifestyle and poor choice in men. It is so important in a case like this that this young woman has a fair trial and you put aside emotion, sympathy and prejudice and concentrate solely on the evidence.

What is this case all about? Perhaps one phrase sums it all up. An American author, Patrick Jake 'P. J.' O'Rourke once wrote, 'Everybody knows how to raise children, except the people who have them.'

How true those words are. How true they are in this case. Everyone has an idea on how children should be brought up, until they have children themselves. It is only then everyone finds out how inadequate they are as parents. Indeed, isn't that the moment we start to have more respect for our own parents and what they had to deal with!

Those of you who are parents have no doubt thought many times like all parents; I wish I had done something differently. I should have pushed my children a little harder or I should have pushed them a little less hard. I should not have let them watch so much TV or I should not have let them play so many computer games, or I should have let them have more playtime than force them to study.

Of course though, this case is not about whether Rachel Wilson was an adequate mother. You may have little difficulty with that question!

The question is not whether she was inadequate, it is whether she is guilty of these serious charges that the prosecution has brought against her. She is not charged with inadequacy, incompetence, stupidity, or foolishly smoking in the presence of a baby. A significant percentage of parents and grandparents in the world, may be guilty of those allegations!

She is charged with wilful acts and omissions, wilful neglect in the case of count one, deliberate, intentional neglect or simply not caring what happened to Annie. In count two she is charged with causing or allowing Annie's death.

At this stage let me deal with another important concept, 'hindsight'.

You may think the whole of this case is based upon hindsight. Looking at it not as things were at the time Annie was alive, but looking at it after the event. Thinking about what might have been if everyone's approach had been different.

The experts in this case make their careers out of hindsight. After all the pathologist, Dr Numan, only deals with the dead. The doctors and nurses in this case no doubt applied a lot of hindsight about the decisions they took, especially when they were informed of the criticisms of their care by Mr Peters.

The health visitor certainly used hindsight, she has looked at her own role in this case and decided not to take on the professional responsibility for children again.

Mr Peters, the clinician, whose expertise is with the living, not the dead, gave evidence based entirely upon hindsight as did the defence expert, Mr Williamson.

Please be careful, hindsight is a wonderful thing, it might prevent us making the same mistake twice. However, it does not really help when you are trying a serious issue like this. It's why we have the phrase, with the 'benefit of hindsight'. In reality it is no benefit at all in a case like this. We are looking at something long after the event with the benefit of knowledge that Rachel Wilson did not possess at the time.

Let me move on to deal with the evidence in this case. You have heard a great deal of evidence from both prosecution witnesses and defence witnesses, including Rachel Wilson.

Please bear in mind, as His Lordship will direct you, it does not matter whether a witness is called by the prosecution or the defence. You should apply the same standards to them all. However, please remember when you are considering the evidence of Rachel Wilson, she does not have to prove anything. She does not have to prove that she wasn't wilfully neglectful, she doesn't have to prove she did not cause or allow Annie's death. It is always for the prosecution to prove those allegations and to prove them to a very high standard.

Please also bear in mind when you consider Rachel's evidence, she is what is called in law, a person of good character, a person with no criminal convictions cautions or warnings. She is not someone with a string of previous convictions for dishonesty which might make you doubt the evidence she gave. She is not someone with a string of convictions for child neglect which might make you question her conduct in this case. She is someone who has led an honest life. There is therefore nothing from her past to suggest she lied to you when she gave that evidence or that she is a person who would neglect or cause the death of her own child.

That leads me to another topic.

Expert evidence.

You heard from three expert witnesses in this case. No doubt you will want to consider their evidence carefully. Expert evidence can often be very useful in a case like this but there is a danger of relying on it too heavily. Expert evidence should assist you, but I suggest you should view it carefully. There is a great danger that we all have of putting experts on a pedestal, particularly medical experts, and accepting what they say at face value, particularly when an expert is so adamant that he is right, like Mr Peters was in this case. The problem is they can be wrong like any other witness and sadly, in practice, it can take years before it is discovered they are wrong.

Let me give you a couple of examples of where experts got it wrong. They are well documented cases. From the United States of America, we have the case of Patricia Stallings. Her child became ill and was taken to the local hospital. There he died. The hospital believed he had been poisoned with antifreeze. The only possible candidate for the poisoning was his mother. Doctors gave expert evidence that they believed he had been poisoned, they knew of no other possible cause of death. As no one else could have poisoned the child, the mother was convicted and sent to prison.

Mrs Stallings was pregnant at the time she was incarcerated and she gave birth to another child who was, almost immediately, taken away from her. Later, it was discovered that the child had the same symptoms as her first child. Of course though, the mother could not have poisoned this child. A new expert was instructed and he discovered that the child had a rare genetic condition that produced symptoms similar to antifreeze poisoning. Mrs Stallings was eventually released from prison, but by then she had spent many years in custody.

In this country, we had the tragic case of Sally Clark. She was charged with murdering her two infant sons. One had died in 1996, aged 11 weeks. The second had died in 1998, aged 8 weeks. The prosecution, 'pointed to a number of similarities in the detailed history of the death of each child which they suggested went far beyond coincidence.' In other words, the jury could safely infer guilt. An expert was called by the Crown who gave statistical evidence about the chances of two cot deaths occurring naturally in one family. The odds he said were so low it just wasn't feasible and therefore it was argued that the only realistic cause of the babies' death was that the mother had murdered them. The jury agreed and she was convicted in November 1999.

It was years later that it was discovered that the expert had got his basic maths wrong. He wasn't a statistical expert. The chances of two babies dying in one family were nowhere near as low as he suggested, indeed the chances of having a cot death in the family increase if you already have had one. In January 2003 Sally Clark's convictions were quashed and she was released from prison. Unfortunately, it was too late for Sally Clark, who suffered serious psychiatric problems on her release a result of her incarceration and a few short years later, she died from alcoholic poisoning.

Please be careful about the expert evidence. They are no doubt honest witnesses and no doubt trying to help. Also, they can be very convincing, adamant they are right. Particularly those who have given evidence in court on a large number of number of previous occasions like Mr Peters and the pathologist in this case, Dr Numan. However, that does not mean that they are right. Their evidence can be of great assistance, but experts are human, and they can get it wrong, particularly when they are speculating on the cause of a baby's death.

They may be able to give you the most common cause of death in a case like this but that does not mean they give you the right one, which could be because of a rare condition. As Mr Peters accepted, common things happen commonly, rare things happen rarely, nevertheless they do occur. The question is can you exclude them in this case?

Little Annie died from an 'unascertained cause'. However, according to all the experts, dehydration was a contributory cause. It is a long way from accepting that proposition to then come to the conclusion that Rachel Wilson starved her own daughter to death, but that was the effect of Mr Peters' evidence.

Alternatively, the prosecution case is that it was clear to Rachel Wilson that Annie was not thriving, that she was losing weight and even though that was clear, Rachel deliberately ignored her own daughter's health, failed to feed her properly, failed to obtain medical help and left her home alone on the very night she died.

Let's look at the evidence for each one of those propositions:

Let's take the first, the suggestion that the cause of the dehydration was starvation. The prosecution are saying, you can be sure that she starved her child to death. That proposition is in reality speculation, because no witness says they saw her starve her child. The highest the evidence goes, is that of Rachel's boyfriend's mother, Ms Harwood, who has every reason to lie. She hates Rachel because Rachel caused her son, the pregnant-woman-beater, to go to prison. What did she say, she claimed that Rachel, 'never had anything for Annie to drink, never seemed to carry any milk around with her. She was always unwilling to feed poor little Annie.'

Of course though, when I asked for specifics of this sweeping statement, she only came up with one tale of seeing Rachel supposedly making up a bottle from hot tap water. When asked about that incident she accepted that it might have been Rachel washing the bottle out in hot tap water, not using it for a feed. Further, she accepted that Rachel only lived five minutes away from her address, so when Rachel did visit her, she was only five minutes away from home where she could feed Annie properly.

The prosecution case is not based on evidence, it is based entirely on speculation. The only witness who can really help you about whether Rachel starved her child is Rachel. You heard her give evidence. She is adamant that she gave Annie proper and frequent feeds. Annie was a difficult feeder she told us, but nevertheless she constantly tried to feed her. There is no evidence that contradicts her in this regard.

Can you be sure Annie was starved, or may the dehydration have been as a result of malabsorption or some other, currently unknown condition as in the case of Patricia Stallings? Mr Peters says it was starvation but the defence expert, Mr Williamson stated, "The reason for the dehydration in my opinion cannot be determined. It could be starvation but equally it could have been as a result of some other condition, such as malabsorption or even a chronic infection that was not diagnosed during life and could not be diagnosed after death."

Can you really dismiss that opinion? We suggest not, it is as valid an opinion as Mr Peters. Mr Williamson could be wrong, but you cannot be sure he is any more than you can be sure that Mr Peters is right.

Let's move on to the next proposition. The prosecution say that it was clear to Rachel that Annie was not thriving. Again, they rely entirely on the evidence of Mr Peters. An expert witness certainly, but a man who never saw Annie alive, a man who never examined her dead body and a man who has relied entirely on the reports of others. He can only speculate on what Annie looked like in life and what signs would be present.

That leads to another point, if it was obvious to Rachel that Annie was failing to thrive, it would have been obvious to others as well. If Annie fell through the centiles in hospital, as seems to be the case, the doctors and nurses should have seen this, but there is no reference to them being unduly concerned in the hospital medical reports.

She fell through the centile points when she left hospital but was this obvious to anyone? She was still putting on weight and noticeably neither the health visitor, nor the local general practitioner or indeed, anyone else, including Ms Harwood ever commented upon it.

Indeed, in relation to Ms Harwood it appears that she did not notice anything wrong with Annie. You will recall that Rachel gave evidence that towards the end, Annie was bluish in colour, wheezing and vomiting a lot with constant diarrhoea. She asked Ms Harwood if she thought she should take Annie to the doctors and Ms Harwood replied that there was nothing wrong with her and it was normal for babies to be like this and Annie would get better.

You may recall that when I asked Ms Harwood about this incident she looked distinctly uncomfortable and said, she couldn't remember!" She would surely remember if Annie was looking as though she was being starved and she would have said so.

Please bear in mind these people saw Annie whilst she was alive. Mr Peters never did. Maybe, just maybe, he is speculating a little as to what Annie would have looked like. Maybe, just maybe Annie's condition was not so pronounced as Mr Peters has suggested it may have been.

Maybe Mr Williamson was right when he said, "In my opinion the gradual reduction in the rate of the child's weight gain is not something that should have necessarily alerted the parents that there was a serious medical concern."

There is also the issue relating to Annie's weight at the time of her death. You heard Mr Peters give evidence that there was a difference in Annie's weight of 50gm between the time she was last weighed by Ms Head and when her weight was taken at the post mortem eighteen days later. He states that this demonstrates that she was losing weight due to starvation.

However, yet again there is a direct disagreement between the experts. Mr Williamson stated that he considered it 'wholly unsafe' to use the post mortem weight after death when trying to calculate weight loss, as he put it, "There are no known studies out there of how much weight or more correctly, mass, a body can lose after death, but it can clearly lose some."

Even the prosecution pathologist estimated that it might be a hundred gms even though he accepted there were no studies out there. If it was only one hundred gms, it would still mean that Annie weighed more at the time of her death than she did when Ms Head, the health visitor weighed her. It could have been even more than one hundred gms. In other words, she was still putting on weight and was obviously being fed.

So, what else do the prosecution rely upon in this case. They point to the clutter in the house and allege that Rachel smoked around her baby. Neither of these will help you in determining whether Rachel is guilty as charged. Firstly, there is no evidence that she did smoke around the baby. Yes, there was the smell of smoke but that could have been Bob, and Rachel may have been too afraid to tell him what to do for fear of receiving another injury at his hands. In any event, no one suggests that Annie died of smoke inhalation so there is nothing in this point.

As for the clutter, there is no dispute the house was cluttered, you can see it from the photographs produced by the prosecution and taken after Annie's death. However, just because it was a cluttered house, does not mean that the house was dirty. Ms Head, the health visitor, recorded that the house was clean despite the clutter.

Was the clutter even the responsibility of Rachel? It appears not as the material causing the clutter, the weights and the magazines belonged to Bob.

In any event, there is no correlation between the clutter and Annie's death.

That leads me to the final point, the final act of desperation by the prosecution to establish a case. The allegation that Rachel left Annie alone on the last night of her life. What an absurd suggestion this is when you think about it. Why would she have left Annie alone? As we heard Ms Harwood lived just five minutes away and would have been willing to babysit that night. It would have been so easy to ask her and it would have taken no more than five minutes for her to walk to the address.

Where does this suggestion come from? It comes from one witness, Thomas Adams. You were able to see Mr Adams for yourselves. You had a perfect view of him coming into court with a swagger and contempt for Rachel. Did he come here to give honest evidence or to exact revenge because his constant unwelcome advances had been rejected?

You will recall that my learned friend Mr Jenkins spent some time cross examining Mr Price on how late he was in coming forward as a witness in this case, but in reality, the earliest he was likely to have discovered that it was alleged that Annie was alone when she died was day two of this trial, when the papers reported on the prosecution speech. Mr Adams waited months, not days, before he came forward to give evidence. If he had seen Rachel and Bob in the pub together on the night Annie died, he would have realised the significance of that evidence within days when he discovered that Annie had died. He would have come forward then. But he didn't, he only came forward months later when Bob was no longer on the scene. There is only one possible reason for that, he had made a last final effort to prey on Rachel in July and had been rejected for the final time and he now sought his revenge.

Was his account compelling? I suggest not. Was it supported by anyone else? Surely there were plenty of witnesses in the pub who could and would have come forward, if Rachel was in the pub Annie died. The fact no one else has speaks volumes.

Thomas Adams' evidence was a last desperate attempt by the prosecution to sure up a leaking prosecution case and I suggest they failed miserably by calling such an obviously dishonest witness before the court.

His evidence is not only contradicted by Rachel Wilson, it is flatly contradicted by her neighbour, Mr Price. His evidence was challenged by the prosecution, but no credible reason was put forward for why he would lie, simply some vague suggestion that he might be attracted to Rachel! I suggest he told the truth as did she. She was home that night with Annie who died in tragic circumstances from an unknown and undiscovered illness, probably malabsorption.

That's it, there is no other relevant evidence. You are not going to determine this case on the comments Rachel made in the 999 call or the comment she made to the paramedics or may or may not have made to a policeman when she was suffering shock and grief, and had just had a few drinks to try and dull the pain.

It's not an easy case by any means, but we suggest when you consider the evidence carefully, putting aside speculation, there is only one proper verdict, not guilty to both the counts that Rachel faces."

David looked at all the faces of the jurors in turn finishing with Cupman's face. Cupman had not looked at him once throughout his entire speech and it was clear from the towers of cups that he had made he had not listened to a single word. Now as David was silent, Cupman looked towards him as David said, "Thank you for patiently listening to my address."

Cupman nodded and smiled in response.

CHAPTER 45

THE JURY DELIBERATIONS

On Thursday afternoon at 12:48pm, after listening to the judge's summing up for close to three hours, the eleven jurors walked into the jury room and took their seats. There was no argument over who was to be the foreman, Harry Brook, a manager of a Superstore in North London announced to the other ten jurors, "I've chaired a few meetings in my life, unless anyone has any objections I'll act as foreman and chair our deliberations."

He looked around the room and saw that everyone was stunned into silence. Before anyone had recovered and said anything he added, "No, good, then I'll take the chair at the head of the table."

Danielle Ettrick was already seated at the head of the table but at Harry's announcement, she looked around the room to see if she could see any discernible support, seeing that there was none, she got up and took a vacant seat, three chairs away.

Harry waited until they were all quiet and looking at him before he announced, "OK, I think this case rests entirely on the medical evidence, so shall we discuss that first?"

Terry Knapkin, the man who David had nicknamed 'Cupman', now intervened, "What's to discuss, she's obviously guilty! Her baby died, she obviously starved it and if she didn't, she must have known the baby was ill and should have sought medical help. Let's not waste any more time. Let's find her guilty and move on."

Susan Hennessy had taken a dislike to Terry early on in the trial for the simple reason that he had completely ignored her when she spoke to him. She quickly spoke out, "You don't know what you are talking about! Babies can die suddenly without being ill and after the mother has done everything she can for them."

She did not add that only four years previously, she had given birth to a seemingly healthy child who had died a 'cot death' at the young age of just eight months. She had found the trial particularly difficult but had persevered with the evidence because she believed Rachel may have been the victim here and not the villain.

Terry looked at her as if she had announced the moon was made of green cheese. "Are you mad? The evidence is overwhelming! She starved her baby! If a baby dies suddenly, it's always the parents' fault!"

Susan burst into tears and got up quickly and ran to the toilet. A number of jurors looked harshly at Terry and it looked to Harry as if they might start on Terry. He could see that he was in danger of losing control of these deliberations and quickly intervened. "Terry, there is no need for that tone of voice and rudeness. We all have our opinions in this case and I won't allow you to bully any of the ladies here. We will discuss it calmly and politely without insulting each other. Now I think we should break off here deliberations until Susan is feeling better and can join in with them."

Danielle Ettrick and another female juror, Daphne Alcock showed their complete agreement with him and their support for Susan. She had discussed with them how difficult the case was because of the death of her own child. They were not going to inform the other jurors of something said in confidence, but they wanted to show their support for her and their contempt for Terry. Other jurors showed their agreement as well and soon Terry saw he was outnumbered and became quietly resigned to the fact that his fellow jurors were all idiots!

In ten minutes Susan reappeared and apologised, "I'm so sorry I've kept you all waiting, it has been a very difficult trial and I was overcome with emotion. I'm much better now."

Harry saw the look of sympathy from most of the women jurors and replied for them all, "You have nothing to apologise for. Please take your seat and if you feel up to it, we'll resume our discussions."

Terry made an audible groan but quickly fell silent when he saw the looks he received from the other jurors.

Harry continued, "Let's get back to our discussions."

It was Terry who immediately butted in, "She's scum. Did you see the utter contempt she showed when she was talking about 'Magistrates'? She almost spat the word out. That should tell you the sort of person you are dealing with!"

Susan had gained her composure now and saw this as an opportunity to challenge Terry, "I do think you are being a little unfair on her. She did not want her boyfriend prosecuted for assault, however, she was forced to give evidence against him. Then she begged the Magistrates to give him a suspended sentence but they imprisoned him. It's not surprising that she resents the court system and the people in it. Look at her situation now!"

Danielle and Daphne both nodded in agreement and pointedly looked at Terry as they did so. All he could think of as a reply, was to let off one of his audible groans. He desperately looked around the room for some empty paper cups to find so that he could occupy himself, but disappointedly noted that they were all being used.

Harry decided to move on the discussion, "I think we should discuss the medical evidence. It did seem compelling to me that the baby had died of dehydration. Even the defence expert seemed to agree with that!"

Susan looked at him quizzically, "Yes, but the issue is what caused the dehydration. I'm not convinced it was starvation as opposed to malabsorption or some other condition that wasn't diagnosed."

She paused as she had another thought, looking down at notes she had taken during the trial, "And what about that point the defence made about the baby being taken off the oxygen too soon at the hospital. That could have caused her difficulty in breathing, difficulty feeding, failing to thrive and inevitably death!"

She was proud of herself that she had made an accurate note of the prosecution expert's evidence.

Terry let out another groan. Again, he was looked at with contempt by most of the other jurors. So, he tried to interrupt more politely, "Doctors are not going to make mistakes like that, my dear."

All the females gave him a frosty look now and even Harry was avoiding eye contact.

Susan gave him a cold smile, "My dear, hospitals do make mistakes and can miss things that can lead to the death of a baby."

Terry looked at the nods from around the room and made no reply but let out one of his grunts.

An hour later, Terry's contribution to the discussion continued in a similar vein, with him groaning each time someone else raised a point to discuss in favour of Rachel. He simply could not understand this. Everything was so blindingly obvious to him!

Terry turned to face Geraldine Skinner, a thirty-four-year-old, married music teacher at a North London Comprehensive school. She had said nothing so far but when Susan raised the issue of Thomas Adam's evidence she felt the need to say something and Terry listened intently in the hope there would be someone else here who might support his point of view.

Geraldine was quietly spoken and he strained to hear her voice across the room, "Did you see how that Thomas Adams strode into the courtroom. He took one look in the direction of the dock and saw the defendant. She looked like she was pleading with him to tell the truth. He just smirked at her, then looked away and made his way to the witness box! I don't doubt for a second her barrister was right. I know his type. He had tried it on with her and when he was rejected, he sought revenge!"

She ignored yet another audible groan from Terry. To be fair, all the other jurors were ignoring them as well now.

Daphne looked at her surprised, "I never noticed that. I thought he was telling the truth. I thought he just wanted to help the court out, not lie because he wanted some petty revenge!"

Danielle felt she should add, "I saw the look he gave her, I felt there was something between them, though I didn't think he was lying. It might have been that he was telling us she had left the baby alone the night she died because he wanted revenge, but he may have been telling the truth."

Geraldine reacted quickly to this comment, "But what about that neighbour, Philip Price, he was adamant that he had seen her looking out of the window several times that night and he saw her boyfriend come home alone. She must have been in the house looking after the baby."

"I didn't like the look of him," was all that Danielle could think to say in reply, "If you ask me, he could have been lying because he likes Rachel Wilson and fancies his chances now her boyfriend's not around."

Terry could not control himself any longer, "What rubbish! What does it matter whether she was in the pub or in the house. The baby died when she should have been caring for it. Rigor mortis had set in by the time she phoned the ambulance. Obviously, she wasn't caring for it whether she was in the house or not!"

He noticed the frosty looks he received from Susan and two of the other female jurors and stopped talking. There seemed no point any more, he could not get through to any of them. Even Harry, the only other male in the room was ignoring him! He made his mind up, he would not take any further part in these discussions. Whatever they all discussed was not going to change his opinion. He was going to vote guilty to all the charges and nothing was going to stop that!

CHAPTER 46

A NEW ARRIVAL?

At 12:39pm on Friday afternoon the jury filed back into court. The clerk of the court, Janice, announced solemnly that the jury had been in retirement for a total period of five hours and seven minutes. The jury had been sent home overnight and had been given a majority direction (telling them they could now bring in a majority verdict of ten to one rather than being unanimous) at their request at 12:05pm. She then asked the foreman, Harry Brook to stand and asked him a series of questions.

"Have you reached a verdict upon which at least ten of you agree?"

"Yes, we have."

"On count one of the indictment alleging wilful neglect, do you find the defendant guilty or not guilty?"

Harry looked towards Rachel as did most of the jurors. Noticeably Terry Knapkin looked away from her with a bitter expression on his face.

"Not guilty."

"And is that verdict unanimous or by a majority?"

"By a majority."

As it was a not guilty verdict, she knew not to ask what the majority was even though it was obvious and she went on to ask the next question, "On count two, on a charge of causing or allowing the death of a child, do you find the defendant guilty or not guilty?"

Everyone who had listened to the judge's summing up knew the answer to this question. He had directed the jury that if they found Rachel not guilty of count one, they should also find her, not guilty on count two.

"Not guilty."

"And is that verdict unanimous or by a majority?"

"By a majority."

Janice looked surprised, it should be unanimous and she turned to look at the judge, he just shook his head at her. As the verdict was an acquittal it was going to stand.

There was immediately uncontrolled crying from the back of the court as Rachel burst into tears interspersed with her mumbling the words, "Thank you," every few seconds.

Tanner thanked the jurors and dismissed them. He merely scowled at the advocates and left the court without a word.

Owen walked across to David, "Well done David, I thought we would have you on that one. I suspect the judge thinks I did not do my duty to the prosecution case!"

David thanked him and then left the court with Sara. Rachel was already outside the court laughing and smiling with her solicitor.

They had a brief conversation where she thanked David and Sara for their efforts. They did not spend long with her and after a few minutes they went upstairs to the robing room to get changed.

Fifteen minutes later David and Sara left the building and bumped into Rachel who was just outside, alone and smoking a cigarette. There were no reporters around as there had been on other days, they were only interested in convictions, not acquittals.

David smiled at her and said, "Goodbye," and was just walking off when Rachel caught him by the arm.

"Mr Brant, I just wanted to say thank you to you both again. I also thought I might let you in on the good news, I'm pregnant again!"

David tried to smile at her but his eyes were fixed on the cigarette. She did not seem to notice his gaze and carried on, "If it's a boy, I'm going to call him David!"

She turned to Sara, "If it's a girl, I'll call her Sara."

Sara nodded sweetly at her.

David could not help himself ask, "I thought Bob was no longer around?"

"No, it's not his. I have a new man in my life now. We only started a relationship a few weeks ago and almost immediately I became pregnant. It's funny, Bob and I were trying for another kiddy for ages but we got nowhere and here I am, getting pregnant almost the moment another man looks at me!"

David looked at her with barely disguised contempt but with just enough disguise that she did not notice. He remembered her saying in interview she would never have another child. Was that another lie?

He hesitated for a few seconds, before asking, "Did you think it wise to get pregnant during a trial? After all the verdict could have gone against you and there would have been an immediate sentence of imprisonment."

She opened her mouth widely in a smile showing the gaps amongst her browning dentures where there were a few missing teeth. "That's why I did it silly. I thought I would be found guilty but I didn't think the judge would imprison a pregnant woman. I have been thinking about having an abortion now, but I've decided against it. My new boyfriend wants the kid and anyway the child benefit and the extra income benefits will come in useful. I missed them when Annie died."

David nodded, at least she had some sense of loss!

"Thanks Mr Brant for what you done. I'm happy this is over. I'm going to go out tonight and celebrate and get thoroughly trashed."

David was unable to disguise his contempt now. "Do you think that's wise? You are pregnant and as you know, alcohol and smoking can harm a foetus."

She looked at him as if he was mad, and suddenly assumed a cold and indifferent look that had been missing during the trial, "No fucking baby is coming between me and my enjoying myself. The last one didn't and neither will this fucking one!"

As she left the entrance of the Old Bailey, she waved to a man across the street. "There's my new boyfriend now, waiting for me. Do you know any decent pubs around here, I'm parched?"

David looked across the road at the tall thin man who was staying on the other side of the road and trying to avoid David's gaze. It was Philip Price!

"Do you want to meet him?" Rachel asked innocently.

"No thank you." David quickly replied before adding, "We barristers have strange rules about meeting witnesses, so it's better we don't."

Sara looked at him with a quizzical expression. There were rules about meeting and talking to witnesses before and during a trial but not usually afterwards. One look at David and she realised that he was imposing his own rules in this case, probably because he had concluded like she just had, that Philip Price had committed perjury on the witness stand, and the reason why was now obvious. It was in order to try and save his new girlfriend, the mother to be of his child.

David shook Rachel's hand and added, "All the pubs and bars around here are terribly expensive. You might want to wait until you get home before celebrating."

With that he turned and nodded to Sara who said her goodbyes to Rachel and then joined him on his journey back to the Temple. He seemed remarkably down for someone who had just achieved a victory in the Bailey in a challenging case. She had to ask, though she suspected that she knew the answer.

"Are you ok, David?"

He stopped his musings and smiled at her. "Yes thanks. I was just thinking about all the potential loving parents out there who cannot have children; or who have children still born or born prematurely and/or with some terrible debilitating disease that will greatly affect the quality of their life. Then there are the Rachel Wilsons of the world. People who have no problem conceiving a child, but have no concept or even a desire to look after their children properly. I just tried to give her poor foetus an extra hour's respite before Rachel poisons it with a cocktail of booze and tobacco. God alone knows what will happen to the child."

He paused before continuing, "Anyway, I shouldn't have to remind myself, it's just a case and like all cases, it's not for me to judge. That's the function of the judges like Tanner and juries like the one we just had. They did their job based on the evidence they heard."

"But you think they got it wrong?"

He began to nod but stopped before replying, "No, it's no part of my job to make that judgment!"

CHAPTER 47

HOMECOMING

David arrived at St Basil's hospital with Wendy on a bright November morning at just after 10am. They had spent their last night together at their flat as a couple, before they became a family of three. Today Rose was coming home with them.

Rose was still in her own room, the fears about the rotavirus had proven groundless but the hospital had not moved Rose back into the Special Care Unit. Wendy began to posit that it was her who had been moved into a separate room away from other mothers because she asked too many questions of the hospital staff in front of the other mothers. She was probably thought of as a bad influence and her presence might encourage the other mothers to question their own babies' treatment. She became convinced this was the reason when Rose was given the all clear and not moved back onto the ward.

David merely put it down to administration. He assumed that once a baby was moved into a private room it would take a great deal of time before the slow wheels of the NHS started up and moved her back.

As they arrived they saw that Rose was awake and staring at a device that the nurses had brought into her room. It was a tube with flashing lights and polystyrene balls that floated on air to the top of the tube before falling down again and then recommencing their journey. Apparently, it had been purloined from an older children's ward as the nurses felt sorry for Rose being in this room on her own with nothing to look at but bare walls and oxygen pipes.

David was fascinated with the device and watched it in a childlike way determined that he should get one for Rose.

It took forty minutes for them to complete the necessary paperwork and for Rose to have a feed before starting her journey to their home. Wendy had brought a large car seat into the hospital which doubled as a carrying chair for babies, but which to David was impracticably heavy. His arm ached from just taking the empty seat from the carpark to Rose's room.

Once Rose was placed into the seat, David took a last look around to make sure that they had not left anything. The only remaining item in the room was a card which had been sent from his chambers. It was signed by most of the members and the clerks room with various comments made, some of which were even polite. The one he particularly liked was written by Sara and read, 'To Rose, get ready for the adventure of life with your great mummy and daddy, who will always be there to guide, the Silk's Child."

Books by John M. Burton

THE SILK BRIEF

The first book in the series, "The Silk Trials." David Brant QC is a Criminal Barrister, a "Silk", struggling against a lack of work and problems in his own chambers. He is briefed to act on behalf of a cocaine addict charged with murder. The case appears overwhelming and David has to use all his ability to deal with the wealth of forensic evidence presented against his client.

US LINK
http://amzn.to/1bz221C

UK LINK
http://amzn.to/16QwwZo

THE SILK HEAD

The second book in the series "The Silk Tales". David Brant QC receives a phone call from his wife asking him to represent a fireman charged with the murder of his lover. As the trial progresses, developments in David's Chambers bring unexpected romance and a significant shift in politics and power when the Head of Chambers falls seriously ill. Members of his chambers feel that only David is capable of leading them out of rough waters ahead, but with a full professional and personal life, David is not so sure whether he wants to take on the role of *The Silk Head*.

US LINK
http://amzn.to/1iTPQZn

UK LINK
http://amzn.to/1ilOOYn

THE SILK RETURNS

The Silk Tales volume 3

David Brant QC is now Head of Chambers at Temple Lane Chambers, Temple, London. Life is great for David, his practice is busy with good quality work and his love life exciting. He has a beautiful partner in Wendy Pritchard, a member of his chambers and that relationship, like his association with members of his chambers, appears to be strengthening day by day.

However, overnight, things change dramatically for him and his world is turned upside down. At least he can bury himself in his work when a new brief is returned to him from another silk. The case is from his least favourite solicitor but at least it appears to be relatively straight-forward, with little evidence against his client, and an acquittal almost inevitable.

As the months pass, further evidence is served in the case and begins to mount up against his client. As the trial commences David has to deal with a prosecutor from his own chambers who is determined to score points against him personally and a co-defending counsel who likewise seems hell-bent on causing as many problems as he can for David's client. Will David's skill and wit be enough this time?

UK LINK
http://amzn.to/1Qj911Q

US LINK
http://amzn.to/1OteiV7

THE SILK RIBBON

The Silk Tales volume 4

David Brant QC is a barrister who practices as a Queen's Counsel at Temple Lane Chambers, Temple, London. He is in love with a bright and talented barrister from his chambers, Wendy, whose true feelings about him have been difficult to pin down. Just when he thinks he has the answer, a seductive Russian woman seeks to attract his attention, for reasons he can only guess at.

His case load has been declining since the return of his Head of Chambers, who is now taking all the quality silk work that David had formerly enjoyed. As a result, David is delighted when he is instructed in an interesting murder case. A middle class man has shot and killed his wife's lover. The prosecution say it was murder, frustration caused by his own impotency, but the defence claim it was all a tragic accident. The case appears to David to be straight-forward, but, as the trial date approaches, the prosecution evidence mounts up and David finds himself against a highly competent prosecution silk, with a trick or two up his sleeve.

Will David be able to save his well-to-do client from the almost inevitable conviction for murder and a life sentence in prison? And what path will his personal life take when the beautiful Russian asks him out for a drink?

UK LINK
http://amzn.to/22ExByC

USA LINK
http://amzn.to/1TTWQMY

THE SILKS CHILD

The Silk Tales volume 5

This is the fifth volume in the series, the Silk Tales, dealing with the continuing story of Queen's Counsel (the Silk), David Brant QC.

Their romantic Valentine's weekend away in a five-star hotel, is interrupted by an unexpected and life-changing announcement by David's fiancé, Wendy. David has to look at his life afresh and seek further casework to pay for the expected increase in his family's costs.

The first case that comes along is on one of the most difficult and emotionally charged cases of his career. Rachel Wilson is charged with child cruelty and causing the death of her own baby by starvation.

The evidence against Rachel, particularly the expert evidence appears overwhelming and once the case starts, David quickly notices how the jurors react to his client, with ill-disguised loathing. It does not help that the trial is being presided over by his least favourite judge, HHJ Tanner QC, his former pupil-master.

David will need all his skill to conduct the trial and fight through the emotion and prejudice at a time when his own life is turned upside down by a frightening development.

Will he be able to turn the case around and secure an acquittal for an unsympathetic and abusive client who seems to deliberately demonstrate a lack of redeeming qualities?
UK
https://goo.gl/YmQZ4p
USA
https://goo.gl/Ek30mx

PARRICIDE

VOLUME 1 OF THE MURDER TRIALS OF CICERO

A courtroom drama set in Ancient Rome and based on the first murder trial conducted by the famous Roman Advocate, Marcus Tullius Cicero. He is instructed to represent a man charged with killing his own father. Cicero soon discovers that the case is not a simple one and closely involves an important associate of the murderous Roman dictator, Sulla.

UK LINK
http://amzn.to/14vAYvY

US LINK
http://amzn.to/1fprzul

POISON

VOLUME 2 OF THE MURDER TRIALS OF CICERO

It is six years since Cicero's forensic success in the Sextus Roscius case and his life has been good. He has married and progressed through the Roman ranks and is well on the way to taking on the most coveted role of senator of Rome. Meanwhile his career in the law courts has been booming with success after success. However, one day he is approached by men from a town close to his hometown who beg him to represent a former slave on a charge of attempted poisoning. The case seems straight forward but little can he know that this case will lead him on to represent a Roman knight in a notorious case where he is charged with poisoning and with bribing judges to convict an innocent man. Cicero's skills will be tried to the utmost and he will face the most difficult and challenging case of his career where it appears that the verdict has already been rendered against his client in the court of public opinion.

UK LINK
https://goo.gl/VgpU9S
US LINK
https://goo.gl/TjhYA6

THE MYTH OF SPARTA

A novel telling the story of the Spartans from the battle of the 300 at Thermopylae against the might of the Persian Empire, to the battle of Sphacteria against the Athenians and their allies. As one reviewer stated, the book is, "a highly enjoyable way to revisit one of the most significant periods of western history"

UK LINK
http://amzn.to/1gO3MSI

US LINK
http://amzn.to/1bz2pcw

THE RETURN OF THE SPARTANS

Continuing the tale of the Spartans from Sphacteria, dealing with their wars and the political machinations of their enemies, breathing life into a fascinating period of history.

UK LINK
http://amzn.to/1aVDYmS

US LINK
http://amzn.to/18iQCfr

THE TRIAL OF ADMIRAL BYNG
Pour Encourager Les Autres

BOOK ONE OF THE HISTORICAL TRIALS SERIES

"The Trial of Admiral Byng" is a fictionalised retelling of the true story of the famous British Admiral Byng, who fought at the battle of Minorca in 1756 and was later court-martialled for his role in that battle. The book takes us through the siege of Minorca as well as the battle and then to the trial where Byng has to defend himself against serious allegations of cowardice, knowing that if he is found guilty there is only one penalty available to the court, his death.

UK LINK
http://goo.gl/cMMXFY

US LINK
http://goo.gl/AaVNOZ

TREACHERY – THE PRINCES IN THE TOWER

'Treachery - the Princes in the Tower' tells the story of a knight, Sir Thomas Clark who is instructed by King Henry VII to discover what happened to the Princes in the Tower. His quest takes him upon many journeys meeting many of the important personages of the day who give him conflicting accounts of what happened. However, through his perseverance he gets ever closer to discovering what really happened to the Princes, with startling consequences.

UK LINK
http://amzn.to/1VPW0kC

US LINK
http://amzn.to/1VUyUJf

Printed in Great Britain
by Amazon

38849520R00235